A Tale of Courage and Triumph of

Science....

To Grietje and Simone

Science knows no country, because knowledge belongs
to humanity, and is the torch which illuminates the
world…

—*Louis Pasteur*

PARALLEL LIVES

A NOVEL

INDER VERMA

Published By: Inder Verma

ISBN 978-1-964452-55-5 (HardCover)
ISBN 978-1-964452-54-8 (SoftCover)
ISBN 978-1-964452-56-2 (Digital)

2025906887 (Library of Congress Control Number)

Printed in the United States of America

Table Of Contents

Chapter 1

GRAHAM BUNKER'S 50TH BIRTHDAY

THE PHONE RANG AT 8 A.M. on May 6, 2004, and after three rings, Graham Bunker picked it up and heard on the other end, "Happy birthday, dear Daddy, happy birthday, dear Daddy, happy birthday to you." It was Cynthia and Graham's twin daughters, now living in San Francisco.

Graham's wife, Cynthia, with her hair casually rolled into a circular bun and her long legs tucked under her nightgown, sat next to him, drinking coffee and browsing through the local newspaper. She had been the first person to give Graham a big kiss and a tight hug on his fiftieth birthday that morning.

Almost three decades ago, they had met in the lunchroom of a small private high school in Princeton, New Jersey. Being undecided about his future plans after graduating from Princeton University and wanting to gain experience that would help him decide if he'd like teaching, he had volunteered to be a substitute teacher at the high school.

Cynthia Barlow, having completed her undergraduate degree in Psychology at Rutgers University's Piscataway campus just a year earlier, already knew she wanted to be a special education teacher.

She spent her summers helping camp organizers by engaging with children who needed extra help, many of them with physical and mental issues. She worked at the same high school as Graham, volunteering to fill in for a teacher on maternity leave as a favor to the principal, a family friend. In a nice arrangement, she had agreed to stay at her parents' house, only a few miles away from the school, until it was sold. Afterwards she would join them on the west coast where they had moved after retiring from their dental practices in Newark.

Cynthia's mother, part Japanese, grew up in Santa Clara, cherishing many fond memories from her childhood. Her father was a multi-generation American with ancestral roots in England. Cynthia resembled both of her parents. A genetic admixture with light blue eyes and skin with a light shade of white that appeared translucent. She had a Caucasian nose with a higher bridge, uncommon among Japanese, long dark hair, and very shapely legs that complemented her five-feet-seven-inches stature.

As their love blossomed, Graham repeatedly extended his voluntary teaching position until it was time for Cynthia to move to the west coast. When she left, he decided to move back to Palo Alto to become a teacher so he could be closer to her. They were married in 1980 in a beautiful ceremony in Redwoods. Their twins, Jessica and Amber, were born in 1981, and their son, Nigel, arrived in 1983.

Graham always reveled in telling his children that he had instantly fallen for their mom because of her very calm demeanor, even-pitched, and a mesmerizing smile. Their children would often remark how embarrassing it was that Mom and Dad were always hugging and kissing, even in front of their friends.

Two giant Mylar balloons with "Happy 50th Birthday" printed on them were soaring in the living room, anchored to the ground with heavy plastic weights. They had been happily married for twenty-six years. Soon, their son Nigel, in his final year at Pomona College, also phoned to sing "Happy Birthday" to his father.

Graham did not know that there would be a surprise birthday bash for him at an old colleague's house on Saturday, but he suspected that something was in the offing. A day before, when he passed by Cynthia in the kitchen, she stopped her phone conversation mid-sentence. Additionally, there was the message on the answering machine from Gayle's Bakery regarding the delivery of a cake on Saturday, May 8th.

Before biking to Menlo-Atherton High School in Menlo Park, where he taught world history, he received two more congratulatory calls. First, there was a message from his mother, who was now living outside London in the countryside with her second husband, Scott Jepsen, her former boss at British Pharma who later became its CEO. Next, his father and his father's girlfriend, Linda, who were now living on Vancouver Island, His sister, Adelaide, who was in the process of moving with her husband, Roger, from Botswana to Singapore, left a congratulatory message.

Graham, however, was not enjoying all the birthday-related festivities. For the last two weeks, he had been experiencing persistent dull headaches and had not been sleeping well. He became increasingly irritable and sensitive to noise. He nearly snapped at Cynthia, who was humming his favorite theme song from the movie *A Beautiful Mind*, while cooking dinner.

The end of the school year was always very busy, especially this year because he had to write an unusually large number of letters of recommendation for students applying to various colleges and universities. He was a diligent letter writer, so he worked late into the night, woke up early, and felt that this was the culprit causing his lack of good sleep. He tried different sleep aids, felt better for a day or so, but then again had recurring headaches and irritable moods. Worst of all, a keen long-distance runner, he recently became tired and exhausted after running just a couple of miles. This bothered him a lot because he prided himself on his fit physique. Not wanting to alarm his wife, he quietly made an appointment with his physician, Dr. Gordon, at his Palo Alto clinic.

The day of the surprise party, Graham, upon waking up and going to the toilet, realized that he was unsteady. By holding on to the bathroom counter, he stabilized himself and again attributed this episode and accompanying dizziness to be the consequence of diminished sleep.

At his birthday party, the normally gregarious Graham was uncharacteristically subdued and at times, quite irritated and querulous. As a marathon runner, he had been unusually critical of the performance of the Kenyan Marathon runner Timothy Cherigot, who'd won the men's 108th Boston Marathon a few days prior with a timing of 2:10:37 on a day when temperatures had soared to 87°F.

His friends had been aghast when he declared, "The Boston Marathon has become a joke," and walked away.

Half an hour later, while cutting the birthday cake, he was his usual jovial and jocular self. Soon, however, he again felt dizzy and asked his daughter Amber to take him home, to which she complied, despite the protests of the hosts' that the party had just started.

Cynthia knew something was wrong but saved the situation by saying, "I'll stay and help to clean up."

When she arrived home, Graham was very agitated, pacing the kitchen. He yelled at her, "Why did you stay behind? And why did you come home so late?" Even though it was only 9 p.m.

To placate him, she put her arms around him and asked, "Darling, what is wrong? You seem so upset."

Graham burst into tears and said, "I haven't been feeling well for some time, and I'm really worried, really worried that something is wrong with me."

She tried to calm him down by suggesting, "Perhaps you're tired with all the extra work at the end of the school year. Honey, let's take a week off and go up north to Napa and Sonoma, taste some wines, and have some gourmet meals." Giving him another big hug, she said, "We'll be fine."

Graham agreed, "A vacation would be great. Let's go after my checkup on Friday morning with Dr. Gordon."

Taken aback that he had set up an appointment with the doctor, she maintained her normal composure and instead talked about the party and the great birthday cake. Not wanting to seem anxious, she went to bed early and was asleep when Graham slipped under the flannel bed sheets.

Unable to sleep, he tossed and turned till midnight, got up, took 400 mg of ibuprofen to lessen the severity of his headache. However, he woke up again around 4 a.m. and banged the bathroom door with his unsteady gait. He would have hit his head on the sink if Cynthia, woken up by the noise, had not gone to the bathroom and put her arms around him. In the morning, she left a message on Dr. Gordon's answering machine, urging him to see Graham sooner than his scheduled visit.

Sunday, May 9th, was Mother's Day. Graham called his mother in England but had to leave his greeting on the answering machine. Jessica and Amber brought a big bouquet of yellow roses for their mom, and they all went for a late lunch at their favorite Mexican restaurant, where they had celebrated many Mother's Days.

At lunch, Cynthia bravely kept the conversations going as if everything were normal while their dad mostly stared at the menu and complained about the shoddy service.

He did, however, evince interest when Jessica mentioned a new guy in her life and asked, "Who is this Prince Charming?" "All in good time, Dad. I don't want to jinx it," she replied coyly.

"I'm usually the last one to know," Graham lamented, and then continued to berate the poor quality of the beef burrito lying half-eaten in front of him.

Cynthia felt their dad was behaving strangely, and in an effort to restore calm without upsetting the girls, she added, "You're right. The food is not as good as it used to be. Maybe they are now too popular and are worried about numbers rather than quality."

The rest of the lunch conversation centered around the war in Iraq, the twins supporting the candidacy of John Kerry as the Democratic presidential candidate, and the fuss on the new social media site Facebook. Of course, no family conversation was complete without the sisters analyzing their brother Nigel's many girlfriends.

Around 2:00 p.m., Amber said that they had better be going soon because loads of laundry had piled up and she had an early morning conference call. They hugged their mother, said again, "Happy Mom's Day," and then kissed their dad.

As the girls were leaving, Cynthia playfully said, "Don't keep us guessing too long about your new mystery man." Bemused, Graham put his arm around his wife and admonished her to stop being so nosy.

Chapter 2

FIRST CHECKUP

CANCELLATION OF A PATIENT'S APPOINTMENT to see Dr. Gordon made it possible for Graham to visit him late afternoon on Monday, rather than waiting until Friday morning. Cynthia dropped him at the clinic and asked if he would like her to come along.

Hearing no positive response, she said, "OK, I will wait in the lobby," and parked in the empty slot designated for patients.

Thanking Dr. Gordon for accommodating him earlier than his scheduled appointment, Graham went on to describe his symptoms: "Over the last few weeks, I've experienced persistent headaches, dizziness, uncoordinated movement, slurred speech, and uncontrolled emotions."

"Some days are better," he added, "but they're becoming less frequent." Dr. Gordon listened carefully, asked a few more questions, and then said, "We will need to conduct brain imaging to check for abnormalities." Ordinarily, I would recommend doing a CT scan, which is fast and relatively cheap, but it is less sensitive in detecting issues related to soft tissues. Therefore, I suggest an MRI, where the resolution is much better. My office will arrange for you to have an MRI, hopefully on Wednesday or Thursday afternoon, at the Moore Imaging Center across the street."

"How long does it take to get the results?"

"Depending on when the MRI is done, let us tentatively plan to meet on Monday to go over the results. Meanwhile, reduce your workload, relax over the weekend, and try to rest so you can get some good sleep."

After a thirty-minute visit, Graham went out to the lobby, walked up to Cynthia, who was reading the local paper, and said, "Dr. Gordon isn't too worried, but to be sure, he has scheduled me for an MRI."

On the drive back home, they talked about mundane things, like the neighbor's new fence, the upcoming retirement of the school's long- time athletics coach, and the possibility of installing a hot tub in their backyard, carefully avoiding any discussion of Graham's health or the upcoming MRI.

When they arrived home, the red light on the message machine next to the phone in the kitchen was flashing—a message from Dr. Gordon's assistant confirming Wednesday at 2 p.m. for the MRI.

That evening Graham spent quite a bit of time browsing the internet to learn about Magnetic Resonance Imaging (MRI) and its applications to human disease.

Tuesday was almost a normal day. Graham went to school, taught his class, and collected the assignments, but he was quite tired and irritable, and he skipped the staff meeting in the afternoon.

The silence during dinner was pregnant with gloom. Graham was undecided whether to take the next day off or just the afternoon for the MRI. They both went to bed early, pretending to be asleep but worried about what the future might hold if the MRI revealed something dreadful. At some point during the night, Cynthia turned towards her husband, put her arm around him, squeezed close to his body, and silently muttered, "It will all be okay soon," and attempted to sleep.

During the drive to the Moore Imaging Center for his 2 p.m. appointment on Wednesday, Graham, ever the teacher, tried to explain to Cynthia how MRI uses powerful magnets, radio waves, and computers to make detailed pictures that can identify any abnormal structures in the brain. She put her hand on his arm and gently admonished, "No weird structures are going to be found in your brain." After dropping him off in front of the imaging center, she parked the car in the new six-story parking lot and hoped she would remember the floor where she had left it.

When she arrived in the lobby of the imaging center, her husband was finishing signing some papers before being taken to a room with a brand-new cream-colored MRI machine, emblazoned with GE in big red letters.

A burly technician, dressed in a light green uniform with a name badge dangling from the breast pocket, took some vital signs, handed him a hospital gown and pointed to a small room where he could change.

When he emerged from the changing room, the technician beckoned him to lie on his back on the stretcher extending from the tubular MRI machine studded with big magnets. He made sure that Graham had no metal objects on him and then covered him with a warm blanket.

The technician inserted an IV needle into Graham's

left arm to introduce the contrast dye and said, "As the magnetic field is altered, you will hear loud banging noises, which are perfectly normal." He then began the process of slowly sliding the stretcher into the MRI machine, and once Graham was fully inside the tube, he turned on the machine.

The technician had warned Graham that he had to undergo three stints of fifteen, five, and ten minutes of imaging, during which time he had to remain as still as possible. Lying motionless on the stretcher, Graham began to wonder if there was something really wrong with him and what if the MRI revealed that he had an incurable disease? Normally a man of great strength and courage, he was suddenly scared of dying. How much time would he have left to spend with his family? What would Cynthia do if he died? He was taking a mental note of his life, starting with his happy childhood in England, his move to California, his life alone with his father, hiking trips in the Sierras, medals at swim meets, his many travels, the thrill of meeting Cynthia, falling in love, and the birth of his twin daughters, when suddenly the stretcher he was lying on was withdrawn from the MRI machine. This oddly reminded him of a plane being pushed back from its parked position.

As Graham was alighting from the stretcher, the technician gave a thumbs-up sign. After changing out of his hospital gown into his own clothes, Graham left to join Cynthia.

Upon seeing him walk toward her, she quickly put down the magazine, got up, and asked, "How did it go?"

"Fine, I think. The technician seemed satisfied," Graham replied, adding, "Now we wait until Monday afternoon for the results."

To cheer him up, she had arranged an early dinner with their twin daughters in a Japanese restaurant in

San Mateo. This was a great success because they all loved sushi, and it helped divert Graham's mind from his health concerns.

On the drive back, despite Cynthia's efforts to engage him, Graham was subdued, quiet, and barely responded to any of her queries. He had not shaken loose the possibility of a fatal anomaly or some tangled web in his brain, and alternated between hope and despair.

He went straight to bed, woke up a few hours later, felt dizzy, and slowly got out of bed, making sure to not wake Cynthia. With an unsteady gait, he walked to the guest bathroom, closed the door, and vomited. He sat for a long time on the toilet seat, dazed and disoriented.

After a while, he cleaned the sink of any residual vomit and lay on the sofa in the living room.

He must have fallen asleep because when he woke up, Cynthia was sitting next to him with a cup of coffee. For a while, both looked at each other without saying a word and silently wondered about their future.

The weekend was going to be tense, and Cynthia wanted to make it as nice as possible without adding any additional stress on Graham, who had not said much since their return from the imaging center. Although Saturday turned out to be a beautiful day, she was reluctant to ask him to go for a walk on the beach because he tired easily and had an unsteady gait.

She prepared his favorite lunch of spinach salad with tangerines, walnuts, crisp apple slices, and raisins with poppyseed dressing, which he seemed to enjoy.

He rested in the afternoon, and around 5 p.m., suddenly announced, "I have been neglecting my work at school and have not yet graded the papers that the eleventh graders submitted nearly two weeks ago. I know that some of them must be very anxious to know their grades as they start applying for college. Can we drive down to the school so I can retrieve the papers from my office and grade them later tonight and tomorrow?"

At first Cynthia thought that reading and grading might be stressful, but then she considered that this would keep him occupied and not thinking about the outcome of the MRI. She drove him to the school, a mere five-minute ride on weekends.

He was visibly pleased to be back at the school and looked forward to reading and grading the assignments.

That night Graham had another vomiting episode, and for a moment, panicked that he might be having a seizure. He steadied himself and sat on the kitchen chair, cradling his head in his hands until he felt safe to get up and go back to bed.

He tried to grade the papers all day Sunday, taking multiple naps and having occasional outbursts of anger at the quality of the writing. After dinner, they watched TV, but he had a very hard time concentrating, often missed the plot, and became cantankerous.

She took another day off on Monday from her part-time work as a substitute teacher and drove him to his 11 A.M. appointment with Dr. Gordon. During the short drive, Cynthia, a very careful driver, twice ran a red light, and Graham, normally alert to any traffic infraction, was too lost in his thoughts to notice, much less make any comment.

Her insistence that she should accompany him to see Dr. Gordon came as a relief to Graham because he did not want to face the doctor and the diagnosis alone. Unlike other times, when one waited for quite some time before being ushered into the doctor's office, today Dr. Gordon was waiting for him, and he was glad that Cynthia had come along.

Graham's heightened sensory antennae took this gesture as a bad omen. "Why would he be waiting if the news was good?" he thought.

After formal greetings and a bit of chit-chat, Dr. Gordon projected the results of the MRI onto his computer screen and began to explain, "Graham, the MRI shows that you have a growth in your brain," and pointed to the irregular white area in the MRI scan on the computer.

"Wow, that is big," said Graham, surprised and shocked.

"Yes, it appears to be the size of a golf ball," said Dr. Gordon with professional confidence. He quickly clarified, "Many of these growths in the brain turn out to be benign, and many of the symptoms you described to me last week can be due to pressure of the extra mass on your brain, which can be excised by surgery. In fact, a few months ago, one of my female patients, a bit older than you, had a large mass in her brain that turned out to be a benign meningioma, a type of non-cancerous growth from the membranes surrounding the brain and the spinal cord. She's on an excellent path to recovery and prognosis of long-term survival is good."

He then paused, first looked at Cynthia, then turned to Graham, and said, "To be circumspect, I'm going to refer you to a neuro-oncologist so they can weigh in with their expert opinion. Someone from my staff will call you with the details, and I will forward the results of the MRI to the neuro-oncologist."

Graham couldn't believe that he had been carrying a golf ball-size lump in his brain. How long had it been there? "He had only noticed symptoms a few weeks ago. Had it grown this big in just a few days?" Is it still growing? He needed the surgeons to excise it as soon as possible. How did it get into my brain in the first place? Was It something I ate, or was I infected with some bug? How can someone like me, who is in such good shape, get such a massive growth in my brain? He was totally in a state of shock, fear, and uncertainty, especially of what the future held for him.

Cynthia was just as shaken as Graham when she saw the big white shadow on his brain and was still processing how a golf ball-size growth is and how it can just be sitting in his brain. She didn't want to think about this growth being anything but benign and instead focused on Dr. Gordon's comments that many of such growths turn out to be harmless. Still, it needed to be removed, and the sooner the better.

Exiting Dr. Gordon's office, they locked hands and walked to the parking lot, and sat in the car for a few minutes without saying much, just staring into space.

Before turning the ignition key, Cynthia said, "I'm sure it is not something serious. You're in such good physical condition, careful with your diet, exercise routinely, not to mention your preparation for the marathons." She didn't sound too convincing to either one of them.

Graham was listlessly looking out of the car window and said, "Let's not yet alarm the children."

During the drive, they talked about their children and how their daughter Jessica was planning to go to Europe with her new boyfriend. They also talked about his father's upcoming trip with his girlfriend, Linda, and whether they should stay with them now that there was all that space since the children had moved out.

Cynthia wasn't in denial but saw no reason to dwell on the worst outcome. She was holding onto hope and wanted to maintain the outward comportment of a normal life. They stopped at a grocery store and bought the usual items to give the appearance of everything being normal…and yet there was nothing normal.

The MRI picture of a fuzzy white irregular growth on Graham's brain was now haunting the entire house.

Chapter 3

THE NEURO-ONCOLOGIST

THREE DAYS LATER, CYNTHIA DROVE Graham to the brand-new Morgan Hospital in Redwood City, where the lobby displayed beautiful multicolored chandeliers designed by the renowned glass artist Dale Chihuly. After dispensing with appropriate insurance information, Graham was called by the nurse and taken to the examining room. There, she measured his height, weight, blood pressure, and temperature—the basic vitals. She asked about any medication he took, noted it on a pad, and said that the doctor would soon see him.

Dr. Rakesh Mehra, a handsome, trim, and well-trained neuro-oncologist who looked even younger than his thirty-two years of age, extended his hand to Graham with an apology for being a few minutes late.

Graham asked if his wife, Cynthia, could also join him during their conversation, to which Dr. Mehra immediately concurred and asked the nurse to bring in Mrs.

Bunker, who had been waiting in the lobby.

Cynthia thanked Dr. Mehra, and he introduced himself as a neuro-oncologist, born in India, where he had his early education. He completed his residency in Neurology at Boston University School of Medicine and received neuro-oncology training at Mass General Hospital in Boston, which also included research on brain tumors at Stanford University School of Medicine.

"Early this year, I joined the Brain Tumor Group at the Morgan Hospital as one of the three neuro-oncologists," he said. "That is quite a journey. What made you wish to become a doctor?" asked Graham.

"Oh, it's a long story. Like all upper-middle-class Indian boys, I wanted to be a cricket player, but of course, all Indian parents want their children to be either engineers or doctors or to become civil servants. My fate was sealed early to become an engineer, but then when I was seventeen years old and in the last year of my high school, my Babba ji, my paternal grandfather, had a heart attack right in front of my mother and me, and we could do nothing for him. By the time the ambulance came and took him to the hospital, it was too late, and he was pronounced dead. I was very close to my Babba ji and decided then and there to become a doctor because I wanted to save lives. So here I am, some fifteen years later, some 10,000 miles from where I resolved to be a doctor," narrated Dr. Mehra. Cynthia asked, "Is your family still in India?"

"Most of them, except my wife, Lakshmi, who is taking courses at Stanford in Microeconomics," replied Dr. Mehra. "Enough talking about me. I see, Graham, you're a highschool teacher in Menlo Park. What made you go into the teaching profession?" "First of all, Dr. Mehra, I love cricket and played it when I was in my school in England. But they don't play cricket here, so I played a lot of baseball instead, which is a bit like cricket. I did my undergraduate at Princeton and wanted to pursue a doctoral degree in International Relations and Global History. But I had grown up in the turbulent years in California, watching nightly on the TV the carnage, mayhem, and increasing casualties of the Vietnam War. There were daily demonstrations against war, poverty, and social injustice when I was a high school student in Palo Alto. Some students from my school were drafted, and two who I knew died in Vietnam. I just missed the draft and, like you, resolved to do something socially relevant. I felt that as a teacher, I could influence hundreds of young minds, mold the lives of many that could have a lasting effect on future generations."

Graham continued, "Right after graduating from Princeton, I took up a part-time teaching assignment and, as luck would have it, met Cynthia, another part-time teacher in the same school, and the rest, as they say, is history."

Cynthia held Graham's hand in hers and added, "We both grew up in California in the Bay Area, so we decided to come back and settle in Palo Alto." After bestowing several kisses on Graham's knuckles, she slowly let his hand go.

After a pause, Graham looked at Dr. Mehra, swallowed, cleared his throat, and wistfully said, "Life was going well until a few weeks ago when I started to have these persistent headaches, dizziness, and uncoordinated movements." He repeated the detailed description of his symptoms that he had shared with Dr. Gordon before the MRI scan of his brain and added that the frequency and severity had been increasing.

Dr. Mehra listened carefully and then undertook an

examination of Graham's reflexes, muscle strength, eye and mouth movement, coordination, and alertness. Dr. Mehra then projected the MRI scan of Graham's brain onto the large screen of his computer, took out a clay model of a human brain from the cabinet, and asked them to sit around the table so he could explain the results of the MRI to them.

"Graham, the MRI shows that you have a growth, which could be a tumor of about three to four centimeters in the frontal lobe of your brain." He then showed them where the frontal lobe was located by showing them the two halves of the brain, the two cerebral hemispheres. He then pointed to the thin outer layer of the cerebral hemispheres, the cortex, folded into peaks and grooves, responsible for much of the planning and execution of actions in everyday life. He added, "Brain is about three pounds, roughly equal to the size of two fists. These folds and crevices of the cortex make up nearly 40% of the brain mass and can be divided into four major lobes. The one in front is the frontal lobe, involved in higher functions of thought, memory, judgement, reasoning, planning, emotional problem-solving, parts of the speech, and also movement."

"When there is an extra mass, as in your case, these important functions get out of balance, leading to increased agitation, incoherent thinking, lack of coordinated movements, and an inability to organize or plan."

Graham countered, "Dr. Gordon told us that these symptoms can also be due to a benign growth in the brain. How does one know that this is not benign growth?" He consciously avoided the use of the word cancer.

Cynthia locked her hand in Graham's again, in a panicked voice, pleading, "Is it curable?

Dr. Mehra was circumspect in his response. "The MRI results show an irregular pattern of growth without any clear margins, and if it's cancer, it will grow very fast. From my experience, this growth appears to be malignant, but to understand the nature of the tumor, we'll need to do a pathology analysis of the tumor tissue by cutting it into small slices and then looking at it under the microscope to see if it has hallmarks of brain cancer." Then Dr. Mehra gently added, "Whether it is benign or malignant, we'll need to remove the mass from your brain by surgery. The neurosurgeon will take small bits of the excised mass and give it to a pathologist to confirm the identity of this growth on your brain. If needed, the results from the biopsy can also help us to tailor a specific treatment for you."

Shocked and stunned that he may actually have cancer, the first thing Graham asked was, "Are you sure it is cancer?"

"No. I am relying on my experience. That is why it is important to perform a pathology on the excised mass to know whether it is benign, malignant, or another type of cancer that has lodged in the brain but is not a brain cancer," explained Dr. Mehra with considerable empathy.

Concerned by what she just heard, Cynthia asked with great urgency in her voice, "When'll you do the surgery." "Is it safe?"

"The surgery will be done by one of our very experienced neurosurgeons, and the procedure is very safe. Besides, Graham appears to be in excellent health, which should improve the chances of a rapid recovery post-surgery. If the operating rooms and neurosurgeons are available and your circumstances allow it, I'd recommend surgery as early as next week."

Alarmed by what he just heard, Graham recoiled and incoherently mumbled, "That soon? Is it that bad?"

"Surgery will remove the pressure caused by this extra mass on your brain and will also give us a chance to analyze the biopsy material. Of course, we can wait, but I'm afraid the mass may continue to expand," responded Dr. Mehra. He then put his hand on Graham's shoulder and said, "You'll feel a whole lot better after the surgery. In the meantime, I'll prescribe Decadron, a steroid, which will reduce the brain swelling caused by inflammation and also edema, an accumulation of fluids caused by leakage into the growing mass. In fact, you may feel recovered just by taking steroids, but that is temporary, and I don't recommend long-term use of steroids because they've terrible side effects."

After a pause, he continued, "When your family and you have decided on the timeline for surgery, I'll set up a meeting with the neurosurgeon so they can describe the procedure, any risks, postoperative recovery, and additional therapy that could include radiation and chemotherapy." Dr. Mehra then asked Graham the name of the pharmacy where his nurse could phone in the prescription for Decadron pills (4 mg/every six hours for a period of one week). Cynthia bent down to open her large shoulder bag, took out her pen, and neatly wrote down the name of the pharmacy near their house.

Dr. Mehra picked it up, pushed his chair back, stood up, and warmly shook hands with both of them, adding, "Here is my mobile number, and please call me if you have any questions or concerns. Let's hope for the best," and exited the examining room.

Graham and Cynthia were slowly coming to terms with the idea that there was a serious issue with his health but were not prepared for the possibility of a malignant tumor. They sat quietly in the room for a while, held hands again, and then slowly walked out of the office towards the parking garage to retrieve their car.

Cynthia unlocked the car doors, sat in the driver seat, and started to cry. Graham put his arms around her and said without conviction, "It will be okay. If it turns out to be a tumor, the sooner it's removed, the more likely I'll get back to normal life. I feel that we're in good hands and hope for the best." Still sobbing, Cynthia slowly drove out of the parking garage.

During the drive home, Cynthia was still clinging to the hope that the abnormal growth would be benign and the nightmare would soon be over, but Graham was already beginning to think about what life with cancer might look like: chemotherapy, radiation, hospital visits, and increasing dependence on others, especially Cynthia. Externally, he appeared calm, but inside he was scared and afraid of the future.

To change the subject, Graham said, "I liked Dr. Mehra, a very decent chap."

"Great," said Cynthia. "Good rapport with your doctor is important."

She added, "We should also call Dr. Gordon to tell him about our conversation with Dr. Mehra and see what he says. After all, we have known Dr. Gordon for over a decade."

Upon reaching home, Graham immediately called Dr. Gordon's office and left a message with the assistant to return his call at the earliest convenience. Still shaken by the possibility of harboring a golf ball-size tumor in his brain, he aimlessly sat on a chair in the kitchen and was on the verge of tears when Dr. Gordon called back. Graham haltingly narrated his conversation with Dr. Mehra, emphasizing the part that called for surgery as soon as possible.

Dr. Gordon opined, "I agree with your neuro-oncologist that the abnormal mass should be removed immediately to relieve the pressure on your brain and ameliorate some of the symptoms you've been experiencing. Of course, it'll also give us a chance to examine the biopsied tissue to determine if there are any malignant cells in the unruly mass growing in your brain. Let me talk to Dr. Mehra and see if we can get Dr. Sherry Jabbar, perhaps one of the best neurosurgeons around, to do the surgery.

"Sherry Jabbar. The name sounds familiar. Wasn't there recently an article on her in the Chronicle? She had operated on and saved one of those pop singers who had fallen from the staircase in his house and had suffered brain injury."

Right, same Dr. Jabbar. I know her because she operated on two of my patients, and they were happy with the outcome and commented on her warm and friendly bedside manner. Graham, I know brain surgery instantly evokes fear, danger, a sense of doom, but it's quite safe, and the results are often transformative."

"Thanks, Dr. Gordon, there's so much information to absorb, and it all comes so suddenly. I'll call Dr. Mehra tomorrow with our decision." "Don't hesitate to call me if you've any questions or queries," urged Dr. Gordon before putting the receiver down.

* * *

Sitting in his comfortable swiveling chair, Rakesh Mehra started to think about Graham, and based on the irregular shape of the growth, was leaning towards the possibility of Glioblastoma Multiforme (GBM), the most malignant form of brain cancer.

For the last many years, the standard regimen to treating brain tumors has not changed, and there has been little or no improvement in the life span of patients with certain types of brain tumors. On the other hand, we are witnessing a revolution in understanding and deciphering our genome, the role of stem cells in cancer, and tailoring medicine specific for an individual. Why are we not taking advantage of these new technologies in treating these very aggressive brain tumors?

Dr. Mehra placed a call to Dr. Gordon, whose admin said that he was with a patient and would call him back as soon as he was free.

Dr. Mehra saw two other patients, one of whom was recovering from glioma surgery, and the other had had a benign tumor excised and came for a post-op checkup.

Back in his office, he was thinking of his friend Yacov Kaufman, whom he had first met at a seminar at Stanford and who had been urging him to start integrating genomic technologies in the treatment of brain tumors. Yacov had immigrated to America from Israel and was already a bit of a legend in the biotech industry because he was credited with introducing two oncology drugs in the clinic. He was also a pioneer in introducing the concept that every cancer cell in malignant brain tumors was a stem cell, meaning that if the surgeon removed 99.99% of the tumor, the remaining few cells could regrow to become a tumor. This was an astounding insight in the field of cancer biology and offered the opportunity to cure brain tumors by blocking the growth of stem cells.

Dr. Mehra was speculating about the types of drugs that might be able to stop the growth of tumor-initiating stem cells when the phone rang, and he answered,

"Thanks, Dr. Gordon, for calling back. Early today, I met Graham Bunker and his wife, a delightful couple, and going through his MRI scans, I'm leaning towards a diagnosis of GBM." Pausing to give Dr. Gordon to absorb the information, he continued," As you know, the current treatments will at best extend his life by twelve to fourteen months after surgery. The patient just turned fifty just a few days ago, is in good health, and I was wondering if he would be willing to explore novel experimental therapies based on genomic technologies for possible new treatments."

Dr. Gordon replied, "Before calling you back, I'd talked to Graham, who, not surprisingly is still in shock from the idea of surgery and the possibility that the unruly growth lodged in his brain may be cancerous. They are a very educated and well-informed couple. He's an outstanding teacher, communicator, and community activist. Please explain to them how newer technologies can be helpful in his treatment, and I'm sure he'll embrace the opportunity to participate."

"That's great. I'll speak to them."

"If you need my help, I'll be happy to talk to them. Incidentally, if Graham goes in for surgery, I wonder if Dr. Sherry Jabbar would be available to do the surgery. My last two patients spoke volumes of her competency and comportment."

Dr. Mehra agreed enthusiastically, "I was also thinking of Sherry and will call her office to see her availability."

Afterwards, Rakesh Mehra called his friend Yacov Kaufman at CancerTech and reminded him of their previous conversations about how clinicians should start integrating genomic technologies into their repertoire of treatments.

"Yes, I remember well and still believe in it, even more now that technologies are advancing so fast."

"Yacov, I have a fifty-year-old patient who likely has a glioma and will shortly be undergoing surgery to remove the golf ball-sized growth on his frontal lobe. He has no prior history of disease, has been in excellent health, runs long distances, and I was wondering if scientists at CancerTech would be willing to process the tumor tissue to make immortal cell lines, if it turns out to be a GBM," asked Rakesh.

"Thanks for thinking of us at CancerTech. I think it would be a great idea. If we succeed in making the immortal cell lines from the patient's tumor tissue, we can use them to test a plethora of drugs to see if we can block their proliferation," replied Yacov with great excitement. "But make sure that after the pathologist confirms the preliminary diagnosis, we get the excised tissue as soon as possible. We need a bit of coordination with the neurosurgeon," cautioned Yacov.

"Thanks. I will first raise the issue with the patient so he can sign a consent form in advance of the surgery," said Rakesh.

"Yoffi (good in Hebrew). Keep us informed," Yacov said before putting the phone down.

* * *

It was now Thursday evening, and Cynthia, after canceling her monthly book club gathering, sat across from Graham at the dining table and solemnly said, "We'd tell the girls if you decide to undergo surgery next week. Nigel has his finals, so we can spare him the news."

"No, no. If we tell the girls, we must also tell Nigel. Otherwise, he'll feel left out from such an important family matter," Graham replied with some apprehension.

"Okay, let's tell them tomorrow," said Cynthia, walking towards the fridge to take out some food for dinner, even though neither of them had any appetite. It was too late to go to the pharmacy to get the steroid prescription. It would have to wait until tomorrow.

After a light supper, Graham decided to read more about brain tumors on the internet and learned that the survival rate depended on the type of tumor identified by pathology and the number of cancer cells in the mass growing in the brain. He went to sleep hoping that if the growth in his brain was malignant, it would be the type with a better prognosis of long-term survival.

Cynthia was trying to read but was stuck on the same page because all she was thinking of was how to break the news to the children and then to his parents and his sister.

After another restless night with fitful sleep, the couple was up early, and while she was brewing coffee, Graham, whose head was throbbing with pain, with a touch of resignation in his otherwise firm voice, said, "I agree with Dr. Mehra that I should have surgery soon to remove the mass and find out if it is benign or malignant. Dr. Gordon also supports this course of action."

She nodded and, ever practical, said, "Soon the school will have summer vacations, so you won't have to take much time off during the recovery. We can cancel our upcoming trip to Italy in mid-July without paying any major penalties."

"Next week there are no major school functions that I'm required to attend, and Barry can cover for me. I'll call Dr. Mehra to see if Dr. Jabbar, the neurosurgeon recommended by Dr. Gordon, is available," Graham added with conviction of someone who has firmly made up their mind.

Around 9 a.m., he called Dr. Mehra on his mobile number and caught him just as he arrived in his office.

After a few pleasantries, Graham conveyed, "Cynthia and I have been thinking about our conversation yesterday and agree with your recommendation to have surgery as soon as possible. My physician, Dr. Gordon, suggested that we check with you to see if Dr. Jabbar is available to do the surgery."

"I am glad that you've elected to undergo surgery. I'll check if Dr. Jabbar is available and ask her office to get in touch with you for scheduling a pre-conference meeting," responded Dr. Mehra.

"Shall I start the medication you recommended yesterday? "inquired Graham".

"Oh, yes, please go ahead and take your first pill as soon as you can. It'll, in short order, relieve some of the symptoms, especially those throbbing headaches," reinforced Dr. Mehra.

Just before noon, Dr. Mehra's admin assistant called Graham's residence and left a note to call back. A few minutes later, he connected with Dr. Mehra, who said, "I'm happy to let you know that Dr. Sherri Jabbar will be available next week, and her office will call you with the scheduling details."

"Many thanks," said Graham, feeling relieved.

Before ending the conversation, Dr. Mehra asked, "Graham, I wanted to mention some potential novel treatments you may want to consider if your tumor is malignant."

Startled to hear the word malignant, Graham asked, "What kind of novel treatments?" Would they involve the use of genomic technologies?"

Dr. Mehra enthusiastically explained, "Each of us has trillions of cells in our body, and the DNA of every cell contains three billion nucleotides. A nucleotide is the smallest building block of the gene, and there are probably over 30,000 genes in each human genome. The entire genome, what some people also call our DNA, is composed of four nucleotides arranged in a random order, which is faithfully maintained during our entire life. Unfortunately, in a cancer cell, sometimes this pristine order is not maintained and undergoes changes, which wreak havoc on the affected individual. If we can find out the altered (mutated) change in the order of the nucleotides in a cancer cell, we can then design drugs to overcome the unwanted consequences of the mutation and stop the cancer in its tracks. The technologies to determine the order of the nucleotides in the genome of a cell are making great strides." Graham chuckled, "If you live in the Menlo Park/Palo Alto area, you read almost on a daily basis the great strides being made in genomic technologies and the miracle drugs based on this knowledge of the human genome."

"Would you be willing to allow some of the biopsy material from the mass growing in your brain to be sent to a small Biotech company to analyze its genome and grow the tumor cells in a petri dish to learn about the nature of the tumor cells?" asked Dr. Mehra.

"Can you tell us a bit more about this biotech company that can analyze the biopsy material?" asked Cynthia.

"The company is called CancerTech and was started about two years ago by some scientists from Stanford University and the University of California, San Francisco with venture capital funds. It specializes in deciphering alterations in the genomes of the cancer cell and then designing rational novel therapies. It's small, about thirty people, and is located in Foster City. Its chief scientific officer is Dr. Yacov Kaufman, who in addition to using genomic technologies, also specializes in the new science of cancer stem cells. He was educated in Israel, then spent many years training in leading scientific institutions around the world, and helped develop cancer drugs at a major pharmaceutical company. In 2001, a bunch of venture capitalists persuaded him to help lead the scientific program at CancerTech in the area of brain and breast cancers.

Dr. Mehra hastened to add, "I've no financial stakes in the company nor any association, other than helping to find new treatments for brain malignancies. I have met Dr. Kaufman at conferences, hosted him for a seminar at Stanford, and am very impressed by his innovative ideas and dedication to research. His provocative ideas that many cancers result from conversion of a normal cell to a cancer stem cell, which then is endowed with unlimited growth advantage, is a potential game changer. Part of the request to give CancerTech some biopsy material is to confirm that the cells growing in a petri dish have the properties of self-perpetuating stem cells."

After a pause to let the information sink in, he continued, "From the treatment point of view, the cancer cells growing in the petri dish can be used to test if available cancer drugs can kill them. Your willingness to give biopsy material can help not only you but many other folks in the future."

The couple looked at each other and said almost in unison, "No harm in giving some biopsy material to CancerTech, especially if that helps in finding new cures."

"Great. Ill inform Dr. Jabbar so you can sign a consent form, and I'll also alert Dr. Yacov Kaufman to arrange to get the biopsy material following surgery."

Though Graham was reassured to learn that one of the best neurosurgeons would operate on him to remove the growth in his brain, he remained anxious with the aggressive timeline because it added to the inevitability rather than some respite that he was hoping against hope.

Chapter 4

PREPARATION FOR SURGERY

THOUGH GRAHAM HAD MADE THE DECISION to undergo surgery to remove the mass propagating in his brain, he was nevertheless very apprehensive about the outcome. Would he ever be the same person before those episodes of dull but persistent headaches took over his life? Would he still be able to teach? Would he be able to run another marathon? Would he live to see his children get married and have their own children? Would he be able to hold his grandchildren in his arms? What would Cynthia do if he was no longer around?

Lost in these thoughts, he was jolted out of his musings when Cynthia informed him that she was going to the pharmacist to get the steroid pills prescribed by Dr. Mehra.

As Cynthia collected her purse, car keys, and was heading to the garage, he felt further disheartened by his dependence even to get his own medication. Though he had planned to go to the school in the afternoon, instead, he now called his colleague to substitute for him for the Friday afternoon tutorial.

He took the first of his many steroid pills before lunch and decided to take an afternoon nap. He was woken up around 4:30 p.m.by a phone call from Dr. Jabbar's office, the neurosurgeon who was originally recommended by Dr. Gordon.

"Hello, Mr. Bunker, I am the administrative assistant for the neurosurgery group at the Morgan Hospital and wanted to let you know that Dr. Jabbar would like to meet you next Tuesday afternoon in her office at the hospital and go over some of the details of surgery. Right now, we have a 4:30 P.M. slot open."

"Yes, that`ll work for us.".

Great, "We`re in Suite 260. Also, please check if the possible dates for surgery on either Friday, May 28th or Monday, May 31st are suitable for you. Please bring your insurance information as we do not have a record of it."

Graham responded by saying that either date would be fine but was again gripped with fear of the surgery and whether it was some sort of malignant tumor that was incurable. His stoic exterior was beginning to crumble.

Graham, whose emotions were bouncing like a yo-yo between fear and relief, pain and recovery, cupped his wife's face in his hands and said, "I know it will be fine, but it's all happening too fast to process my feelings of fear of the future."

They remained in that position for a while, and then he loosened his grip, got up, and started to look at his schedule for the coming days. He now wanted the surgery over with as soon as possible. Anticipating that the coming months would revolve around his disease and recovery, he wanted to send a note to the school principal for a leave of absence, but Cynthia persuaded him to wait until after meeting Dr. Jabbar.

"Perhaps I'd invite the girls for lunch or dinner tomorrow or Sunday if they're available. We'll then let them know about your possible upcoming surgery. I still think we should not alarm them and give minimal information, something like, 'Dad has been experiencing these very bad headaches, and the doctor thinks that there's a small growth in his brain, removal of which by surgery will bring Dad relief and back to normal life.'"

Graham agreed but added, "If the girls want to know more about my symptoms, the growth in the brain, prognosis, or recovery, we should be forthcoming. They're adults and can probably handle bad news well. We don't always need to shield them from adverse events in life."

"I know, I know, but Jessica is just coming out of a breakup and is looking forward to travelling with her new guy, so I didn't want to stress them any more than needed. They've always viewed you as a tower of strength, nearly infallible, available when needed, and will be devastated to know that something is wrong with their daddy," said Cynthia in a mother's protective tone.

"When shall we tell Nigel?" asked Graham.

"Probably after talking to the girls," responded Cynthia.

To get their minds off the events of the past few days, Cynthia rented a popular movie, "Sideways", recommended by some of her book club members, who described it as a funny satire about wine snobs. But she regretted her choice shortly after the movie started because one of the two lead male characters is a divorced, depressed, alcoholic teacher and an unsuccessful writer. Within half an hour of the movie, she saw Graham slumped and snoring on the cushion adorning the sofa. She continued to watch the movie for a bit longer then lowered the volume after the phone rang in the kitchen.

"Hi, Mom, I haven't heard from you for the last two days and just wanted to check if all was ok," asked Amber, one of the twins.

"Darling, I was planning to call you later, after finishing a movie, but Dad fell asleep during it, so it is a good time to chat," Cynthia said, feeling tired.

"What were you watching?" inquired Amber, and upon knowing its identity, added, "It got mixed reviews. Jessica's boyfriend says that sales of Pinot Noir have gone up at the cost of Merlot after the film came out."

"I haven't reached the point in the movie to know the rationale for this factoid. I was going to call Jessica and you to see if you're both free over the weekend to come over for lunch or dinner," pleaded Cynthia.

"Sure, love to, but let me talk to Jessica and see if she is free. You know, Mom, she is in LOOOOOVE…" said Amber with mischief in her voice.

"Okay, call me after you talk to your sister, and lots of love." Cynthia loved her daughters and felt blessed that they lived so close, especially now.

When she returned from the kitchen, Graham was awake, a bit dazed, and unable to decipher the storyline in the movie since he'd fallen asleep just after it started.

Cynthia turned off the TV and asked if he was hungry, which surprisingly he was and said, "Maybe it's those steroid pills. I'm famished."

Cynthia was delighted by his positive response and decided to heat up some pasta with the leftover chicken from the previous night's dinner, which he had barely touched. While she was cooking, Graham helped by preparing the tomato salad and set the table for dinner.

During the dinner, where both were trying to steer

the conversation away from his disease, the phone rang and Cynthia decided not to pick it up, but as the message started to record, she jumped up, picked up the receiver, and said, "Hi, Amber, were just screening calls from all those homeowner policies and cheap loan calls… Oh, great that both of you can come for lunch on Sunday… Anytime… Yes, yes, 1 p.m… will be fine. I'll make pumpkin soup and buy some jumbo shrimp for a salad… A plum pie. Yum, your dad would love it. Thanks, honey. See your sister and you on Sunday. Dad is waving hi! Bye-bye."

By the time they finished dinner and cleaned up, it was 9:30 p.m. Before taking his third steroid pill, Graham started to read on the internet about the usage of steroids, which he had previously associated with athletes, especially professional bicycle riders and sprinters. He was struck by the diversity of steroids and their widespread effects on the human body. The Decadron pill that Dr. Mehra had prescribed was actually a glucocorticoid, which was said to diminish inflammation and edema. It was one of the most potent biological molecules suppressing the immune function.

He was a bit concerned upon reading that ingesting steroid for sustained periods of time had numerous side effects, ranging from the dysfunction of many hormones, muscle wasting, skeletal, gastrointestinal, and even psychiatric disorders. At the same time, he was thrilled and very excited to read that over 70% of patients with abnormal growth in their brain show symptomatic improvement with just steroids alone.

That night he went to bed without the pronounced headache he had been experiencing for days and slept through the night till 6 a.m., when he woke up and took his fourth pill.

It was the first morning in days that he'd woken up without a throbbing head or feeling of nausea. He sat on his bed for a time, savoring the moment and recalling Dr. Mehra's words, "I'll prescribe Decadron, a steroid which will reduce the brain swelling, and you may feel recovered, but that is temporary, and long-term use of steroids have terrible side effects."

Graham briefly toyed with the idea of forgoing surgery in favor of continuous use of steroids but also realized how surgery would remove the mass and give permanent relief, further strengthening his resolve to undergo surgery.

When Cynthia woke up, she found her husband relaxing and reading the newspaper, a sight she had not beheld in over a month. He even volunteered to brew fresh coffee for her and again commented on his increased appetite.

It was a pretty clear day, slightly warm with a predicted high of 82°F, and Graham, after a hearty breakfast, suggested a drive and a walk on the beach. She was delighted to comply but was also worried that the effects of those steroid pills would soon wear off and leave Graham once again facing headaches, restlessness, and intense vomiting episodes.

They chose to go to the Half Moon Bay State Beach Park with its gorgeous views and easy access without going up or down the hills. After a forty-five-minute drive, they arrived at the beach, which was relatively empty except for some enthusiastic fishermen and a few joggers. Soon after their arrival and a short walk on the beach, Graham began to tire, sweat more than usual, feel a bit dehydrated, and wanted a place to sit.

Suddenly his ebullient mood withered, and a tired Graham with a note of dejection in his voice said, "I wonder if this is my last visit to this beautiful beach where I've spent so many happy hours over the last forty years."

Cynthia, now familiar with his changing moods, sat next to him on the sand, bit her lip, and said, "Perhaps we overdid it. No wonder you feel exhausted."

They remained seated quietly for the next few minutes, but for him, feeling agitated and restless, it seemed like an eternity. Suddenly getting up, he said, "Maybe we can have some lunch at the Main Street Grill, where they have moderately priced tacos and good salads."

Cynthia, whose moods, feelings, and even her appetite were now influenced by his symptoms, agreed and started to walk towards the parked car.

By late afternoon, they returned home, and shortly after that, she went shopping for the next day's lunch planned with their daughters. Graham felt better by evening and went to bed early after some light reading, but his mind was still fiercely in overdrive, charting scenarios of life with the disease that could cut his life short or worse, leave him dependent and a burden on his loved ones.

On Sunday morning, the magic of steroid pills was back, and he was less agitated, free of headache, and offered to help Cynthia prepare the lunch with their daughters.

She asked him to wash some of the jumbo shrimp she had bought at El Pescador, help set the table on the patio to keep him occupied with the mundane, rather than having to constantly ruminate about surgery, the mass, growth, benign and malignant brain tumors.

Amber and Jessica arrived together around 1 p.m. Amber went straight to the kitchen to put the plum pie in the refrigerator, while Jessica went to the patio to say hi to Dad.

Dressed in his casual shorts, a T-shirt emblazoned with the San Francisco Giants logo, and a cap with the

Golden State Warriors insignia, he was reading the newspaper when he saw the girls. Putting aside the newspaper, he got up to give Jessica a big hug when he saw her.

He asked, "How is Mr. Special? When do I get to meet him?"

Jessica demurred, "All in good time, Dad. I don't want to jinx it. He is away for a few days at a meeting in New Orleans."

"What is he like?" teased Graham.

"Like you, Dad. He reads a lot, watches sports. He's a fanatic Warriors fan, so I'm sure you will get along," Jessica said, smiling.

Before he could respond, Amber walked in to give him a big hug and a kiss and announced, "You look so much better since our sushi dinner after your MRI."

He did not want to reveal the secret power of his steroid pills, so he just smiled and said, "You must be hungry," and pointed her to the patio table set for lunch.

Everyone liked the pumpkin soup, and during the main course of stuffed jumbo shrimp, while Amber was talking about buying a new car, their mom in a solemn tone said, "Dad and I've some news to share." Suddenly the conversation stopped, and both girls looked anxiously towards their dad.

He cleared his throat, set the fork and knife down, and said, "You know that I've been having headaches, nausea, and on occasion, unexpected fits of anger for some time. You remember I had an MRI about ten days ago, when we went to the sushi place."

"Yes, at *Haiku* in San Mateo," recalled Amber.

"A few days ago, the doctor said that the MRI showed a big mass growing on my brain, pressure from which causes all these symptoms I've been experiencing in the last few weeks. The doctor has recommended surgery to remove this unwanted growth on my brain so I can get back my former life."

Panicked, Jessica said, "Oh my god, I hope it is not a tumor like Mindy's mother, our soccer coach in high school. Mom, you remember her, the big blonde lady, always in her sweatpants. She never came back, and later we learned that she had passed away and Mindy left for Oregon to live with her father. That was a terrible shock."

Their dad, now more composed, said, "My MRI shows an unruly mass on my prefrontal cortex," pointing to the anterior portion of his forehead, "and during surgery, the doctors will also find out if it is a benign or cancerous growth. In either case, they'll remove the mass, stitch my skull back, and send me home. Mom and I are scheduled to meet the neurosurgeon on Tuesday, and surgery is planned for Friday or next Monday. Both Dr. Gordon and the neuro-oncologist speak very highly of the neurosurgeon."

Amber, nearly in tears, said, "Dad, I had no idea that you have been having these bad headaches and vomiting episodes. I thought that you're just tired from the packed end of the school year activities and needed rest. Mom said that you were thinking of taking a short vacation in wine country. I really hope that there is nothing serious," and then went up to her dad and gave him a long and tight hug.

Cynthia tried to lighten the mood by saying, "We'll know more about the surgery after talking to the neurosurgeon, and I'll let you know the outcome, date, and time of the surgery at the Morgan Hospital in Redwood City. Now we better clean up the table so we all can taste Amber's luscious plum pie." Since they all opted for tea, Cynthia put the kettle on, took the pie out of the fridge, and soon Jessica cut a generous slice of pie for each of them, but Amber gave the largest piece to her dad.

Almost in unison, the girls asked if Nigel knew about the surgery.

"We will call him later today to let him know. Dad and I will also inform Grandpa David and Linda. Tomorrow I will call Grandma Karen since it's a bit late to call England."

The girls left around 3:30 or 4 p.m., after more hugs with Dad and words of comfort and solidarity, again asking if they could do anything, including coming back and staying with them.

Their mom and dad said, "Of course we'll call if we need you."

"Just seeing you makes me feel better," added their dad.

After the girls left, they remained seated on the patio, talking about their kids and how lucky they were that all were healthy, well- balanced, caring for each other and their extended family. Both the nice weather and hearty lunch propelled Graham to take a short nap, during which time Cynthia cleaned the kitchen and put away the leftovers, especially the pie to be enjoyed later.

While loading the dishwasher, she thought of the times, not so long ago, when Graham would have undertaken this task and reminded her, "I'm a champion dishwasher loader, not 1 mm of space is wasted…" Then there would have been the usual question, "Quick wash or regular wash?" She smiled thinking of this mundane conversation and was again engulfed by sadness.

She called their son, Nigel, at his apartment in Claremont, which he shared with two other students, who picked up the phone on the first ring and, hearing his mother's voice said, "What's up, Mom?"

"Oh, nothing major. Just checking to see how you`re

holding up under the pressure of final exams."

"You know, Mom, these finals aren't that big a deal. Most of our grades are already in, and the finals are just the topping."

"Your sisters were home for lunch. Did you know that Jessica has a new boyfriend?"

"Good for her, after that jerk who broke up with her. I never got along with him. I don't know why Dad was always so nice to him."

"You know your dad. He is much more tolerant than the rest of us."

"Did you meet the new guy?" asked Nigel.

"No, he is away at a conference, but Jessica seemed very happy." After a pause, she continued, "Nigel, since last month, your dad has been having these awful headaches and sometimes bad episodes of vomiting and restlessness, so he got an MRI, and the results show a small growth on his brain. Doctors think it's the pressure of this extra mass on the brain that is causing the symptoms."

Not hearing any response, she continued, "They have recommended surgery to remove the tum—" She immediately corrected herself and said, "the growth. Dad is thinking of getting the surgery done sometime next week."

"Next week! Mom, aren't brain surgeries dangerous? Are the doctors sure that the only way to remove the mass is through surgery? Aren't there pills to destroy this extra mass? This sounds ominous. Is Dad home?" inquired Nigel. Hearing yes, he asked, "Mom, can you put Dad on the phone please?"

"Sure." She called Graham, who came to the phone and immediately said, "Hey, buddy, how are you doing?"

"I'm fine. Dad, what's this business about brain surgery? It sounds so dire and dangerous. Are you sure you want to do this? Did you seek a second opinion? This is very worrying," said Nigel, who was considerably shaken with the news.

"We've consulted two doctors, including a neuro-oncologist, and the advice is the same: to remove the mass by surgery, which will alleviate the pressure on the brain, likely the cause of some of the symptoms I'm experiencing," said Graham a bit defensively.

"But, Dad, why did you consult a neuro-oncologist? You don't have a brain tumor," asked an alarmed Nigel.

"Dr. Gordon thinks that sometimes the mass on the brain tissue can be due to uncontrolled growth of cancer cells. My neuro-oncologist said that a biopsy will be taken during surgery and a pathologist will be able to identify if the extra mass in my brain has any cancer cells. I have to get the mass removed by surgery regardless of whether it is benign or a malignant growth, and the sooner the better, especially if it's cancer," said Graham.

"Dad, that's scary."

"Think of the positive side. If I'm hobbling or have a bandage on my head, your school administrators might give your mom and me the front seat at your graduation ceremony," joked Graham.

"Not funny, Dad," said Nigel, still shocked to hear the news of his father's upcoming surgery.

Hesitantly, Nigel probed, "What happens, Dad, if it's a tumor?"

"Your Mom and I are going to see the neurosurgeon on Tuesday and will know more about post-surgery issues."

"Dad, please call me after the meeting with the neurosurgeon so I can plan to be home when the surgery is performed," said Nigel, clearly upset by the news.

Graham thought about dissuading Nigel from coming to Palo Alto, especially during his finals, but he knew his son and thought better not to engage in a discussion.

"Sure, Nigel. Mom or I'll update you following the meeting with the neurosurgeon. We send our love, and good luck with your finals," replied Graham, trying his best to sound upbeat.

Nigel had barely put the receiver into the socket when the phone rang again. He answered, and it was his sisters, as usual on a speakerphone, who wanted to know if Mom or Dad had called him with the news.

"Yes, I just hung up after talking first to Mom and then to Dad. I think they're not telling us the whole truth to spare us, but why would Dad consult a neuro-oncologist if it was not a brain tumor? Survival prognosis from some types of brain tumors is very poor, only months after surgery. I want to be there when surgery is performed," Nigel said, clearly emotional.

"We, too, were shocked to hear the news," said Jessica, "but we think the best we can do is to support their decision and offer any help we can. Schools will be closed soon, so Mom will be home full-time, and Amber and I can take turns to give Mom some relief. I don't think Mom wants any full-time help. You know, Mom is very stoic, so we'd make sure that she doesn't get too exhausted."

Nigel said, "I haven't yet decided what to do after finishing college, so most likely I 'll be home for the whole summer to give Mom and Dad company. Keep me in the loop with any news from them. Being the youngest, they still want to protect me from any adverse events in their life." After a few more exchanges, Nigel said good-bye to his sisters.

It was now 8 p.m., and Cynthia was not sure if she should wait till the next day to talk to Graham's father and Linda. Even though the news of pending surgery was now out, she was quite sure that Grandpa David was unlikely to call any of his grandchildren on Sunday night. Graham agreed to wait, mostly because he was tired of repeating the same information multiple times.

The magic of steroids continued to wield its charm on Graham with another headache-free night and reduced restlessness, but he had increased muscle pain and fatigue. He also felt a bit bloated but was willing to try anything to get those headaches to subside.

Despite Cynthia's concerns, Graham decided to go to school in the morning, return all the assignments, and talk to the principal about his impending surgery with an uncertain outcome if the biopsy showed cancerous tissue.

The principal, an old friend, advised him to not worry about his responsibilities to the school and focus on his health. They could manage until the school reopened in September after summer vacations that started mid-June. To Graham's relief, his many colleagues were happy to share the load of his work over the next few weeks. He returned home a bit tired but excited and ebullient with the enormous support and affection of his colleagues.

Just before lunch, he called his father but got Linda on the phone, who asked him all about his birthday celebrations and their impending visit to Palo Alto in a few weeks and then handed the phone to his father, who was standing next to her, to get his turn to speak with his son.

The first thing his father asked was, "What are you doing home so early on Monday morning? Hope all is well with all of you!"

Graham then went through the same explanation he

had given his children, again making sure that the word tumor was not mentioned.

His father's first response was, "I hope you're getting the best care and going to the best doctors. Why didn't you elect to have surgery at Stanford Medical School?"

"Dad, Dr. Jabbar is a top neurosurgeon and was highly recommended by Dr. Gordon and my neuro-oncologist. Cynthia and I will meet her on Tuesday morning and let you know the date of the surgery," explained Graham.

"Is Cynthia home?"

"Yes, Dad."

"Can I talk to her?"

"Sure." He passed the phone to her, and she gently asked, "How're you, Grandpa? How is Linda? We're looking forward to your visit to Palo Alto in late July. Hope you'll stay with us, there are extra rooms since the kids have left the nest."

"I'm fine, Cynthia," replied Grandpa David. "How are you coping with the news of Graham's unexpected upcoming surgery? Do you need any help? Linda and I can be in Palo Alto within a few hours. How long will his recovery and rehabilitation be?" asked Grandpa in a rapid fire of questions.

"All this has happened so soon that I'm still processing the information. When I looked at the MRI that Dr. Gordon and the neuro-oncologist showed us, I was shocked to see the growth in Graham's brain. Its removal is the first priority, so we agreed to undertake the surgery as soon as possible," replied Cynthia.

"Spare no expense to get the best treatment for my boy," said David with a firm voice.

"Spare no expense to get the best treatment for my

boy," said David with a firm voice.

"We both really liked the young neuro-oncologist, Dr. Mehra, and felt very comfortable with his recommendations. Tomorrow we will meet the neurosurgeon, who will perform the surgery."

"Did you tell the children?" inquired Grandpa David.

"We had the girls for lunch yesterday and told them about their dad's upcoming surgery and later called Nigel to let him know. Not surprisingly, they were very upset and want to be with their dad when he undergoes surgery," replied Cynthia.

"Glad you told the kids. They're now quite grown up and mature enough to handle vexatious news. Do you want me to call Graham's mother? No, on second thought, why don't Graham or you call her. I guess she is probably at her county estate in Sussex. I gather Scott Jepson has pretty debilitating arthritis, so they may be in a warmer climate. I'm not sure where Adelaide is because she is shuttling between Africa and Asia. Please make sure to call us when you fix the date for surgery and keep up the good spirits," urged Graham's father.

"Thanks, Grandpa. One of us will call Grandma Karen and will keep Linda and you informed about the schedule for surgery," replied a subdued Cynthia.

She walked up to Graham, who was now sitting on the kitchen chair, put her arms around his neck, and told him, "How lucky we are to have such a caring family."

Graham held her hands in his hands, kissed them, and replied affectionately, "I'll do all I can to be around all of you for a long time to come."

After putting the phone down, Graham's father went downstairs, and Linda immediately knew from his ashen face that the news was not good.

He repeated the gist of his conversation with Graham

and Cynthia, slumped on his chair, and said, "I don't understand when all this happened. I got no indication that anything was wrong when we called him on his fiftieth birthday just a few weeks ago. Graham is always so fit and in such good health."

Linda detected fear and concern in David's voice and said in a comforting tone, "It looks like he's in good hands, and being in good physical shape, he'll cope well with surgery. Does Cynthia want us to be in Palo Alto so we can be helpful?"

"The date for surgery is not yet set, and we didn't talk about the logistics," said David, still shaken from the news about his son.

"Cynthia is a very strong woman, but she still relies on you, and somewhat on me, for emotional support since her parents passed away within months of each other. She has no siblings. We should make sure that we keep an eye on her well-being during the next few weeks when the focus will be on Graham's disease," advised Linda, who always held Cynthia in great affection and esteem.

Around 1 p.m., Cynthia called Graham's mother in England, where it would be around 9 p.m., but unfortunately, no one picked up the phone, so she left a detailed message to call her back. Neither Graham nor she was able to locate his sister Adelaide's current phone number in Singapore and hoped to get it from his mother when she returned her call.

Twenty-four hours ago, only they were privy to the growth in his brain and its consequences, but now the news had spread among other close family and loved ones. Graham, always self-reliant, which he attributed to his survival instincts after his parents separated when he was just nine years old, would have preferred to keep his illness and its treatment quietly personal. Cynthia, on the other hand, felt that in difficult times, it was important to have family support.

When her dad had been quite sick, her mom had kept it a secret to protect her from bad news. On the contrary, Cynthia would have loved to have helped her mother, spent more time with her dad, and has always felt shortchanged by her well-intentioned mother. Perhaps it was her mother's upbringing in a traditional Japanese family where stoicism was considered a virtue and tears were a manifestation of weakness.

A certain weight was lifted from Cynthia by sharing the news with the family, but it also made the disease and its consequences so very real.

Chapter 5

SURGERY

O N TUESDAY, MAY 24TH AT 3 P.M., Dr. Mehra met with the neurosurgeon, Dr. Sherri Jabbar, prior to her meeting with Cynthia and Graham Bunker. A stately six-feet-tall, strikingly beautiful woman with dark hair and green eyes, she was a second-generation Iranian who had grown up in Los Angeles in the tight-knit community of Iranian Americans.

"Dr. Jabbar, I've discussed with the Bunkers the use of some of the surgically resected mass from Graham's brain for research at CancerTech, a biotech company in Foster City."

"Oh, please call me Sherry. What's the primary focus of this biotech company?"

"Breast and brain cancer. If the biopsy from Graham Bunker's excised growth shows cancer cells, the scientists at CancerTech would be interested in determining any genetic changes that may be implicated in tumor formation. They would also want to grow the tumor cells in a petri dish to have an unlimited supply for future use," replied Dr. Mehra.

"Dr. Jabbar, I mean Sherry, the chief scientist at CancerTech, Dr. Yacov Kaufman, a highly respected cancer biologist, believes that most cells in malignant brain tumors have acquired the properties of immortal stem cells that can grow unchecked at will. That's why any tumor cells left behind after surgery can start proliferating, leading to reoccurrence of the cancer. Yacov and his colleagues are testing drugs that can impede the growth of these immortal stem cells."

"But we do not know if the mass in the patient's brain is malignant," responded Dr. Jabbar.

"Yes, you are absolutely right. We'll not know for certain until pathology is performed on the biopsy from the excised tissue," replied Dr. Mehra.

"How can we help?" queried Sherry Jabbar.

"Yacov is convinced that a small piece of fresh, unfrozen tumor tissue excised from the patient, deposited into a special solution kept in icy temperatures, and immediately used to make similar tumors in mice and immortal cell lines will give the best results," said Dr. Mehra.

"You mean immortal cell lines, like the HeLa cells that were generated from the cervical cancer excised from the uterus of Henrietta Lacks?"

"Exactly. If the patient's excised mass is cancerous, Dr. Kaufman thinks that the faster we can get the tissue, the better the chances are for viable transplantation into mouse brains and the generation of cell lines. He can send a technician who can wait outside the operating room to ferry the excised tissue in the chilled solution, expeditiously to CancerTech." Dr. Mehra added, "Graham Bunker will need to sign a patient consent form before the surgery to allow the transfer of small amounts of the excised tissue."

Sherry Jabbar agreed with Dr. Mehra that to make progress in the treatment of malignant brain tumors, it would be essential to do more basic research requiring human material. She assured him that the parts of the excised mass from Graham's brain would be dropped into a tube containing a special solution kept cold in an ice bucket and quickly delivered to the technician from CancerTech, along with the preliminary report of the pathologist.

He thanked her, and after a short chit-chat about the state-of-the-art facilities at their hospital, stood up, shook her hand, again thanked her, and left the room, gently closing the door behind him.

Cynthia and Graham spent the rest of Monday in limbo, hoping for the best but preparing for the worst. Despite her best efforts to ward it off, the word "tumor" was dominating Cynthia's thoughts, and she felt helpless, scared, and paralyzed. She loved Graham, saw him as a towering figure of strength, but now he was shrinking in front of her with worry and fear of the unknown.

In the past, they had given comfort and solace to other people who had been diagnosed with cancer. It was something that happened to other people. They were not prepared to be the recipients of sympathy or looks of genuine pity. He was the one in whom family and friends confided, laid bare their fears and feelings, but now he must muster the courage and inner strength to face the coming days with equanimity and hope. Cynthia felt that he was absent despite sitting next to her, lost in some distant thoughts, or perhaps he was feeling pity for himself and repeatedly asking," Why me?"

Just before lunch, while he was taking one of his many naps, his mother called from the island of Crete in Greece, where her second husband, Scott Jepsen, owned a lavish beach house and used it increasingly to avoid the cold and wet English weather that aggravated his arthritic misery.

Cynthia, who had picked up the phone quickly to avoid waking up Graham, heard his mother's panicked voice.

"Darling Cynthia, when did it happen? He'd recorded a lovely message on Mother's Day, and there was no hint of distress or disease in his voice," said Graham's mother, very distraught.

She relayed to her an abbreviated version of the events of the last few weeks and said, "Both his physician and the neuro-oncologist have recommended surgery as soon as possible."

Graham's mother asked, "When is surgery scheduled?"

"We're going to meet the neurosurgeon today around 4:30 p.m. and will know more about the details of the procedure. Tentatively, if all goes by the book, surgery may occur on Friday."

"This Friday? Oh, dear, is it that urgent?" asked Graham's mother with a panicked voice.

"The neurosurgeon will be leaving for Africa in two weeks, where she does charitable work, and had only a few windows open to do surgery," said Cynthia, hoping to assuage her mother-in-law's anxiety.

"Does David know about the seriousness of Graham's situation? How are the girls and Nigel holding up? This is all so sudden. Should I come?" inquired Graham's mother.

"The girls and Nigel know and are very concerned and a bit scared. Yesterday we also told Grandpa David, and he wanted to make sure that we have the best doctors and surgeons taking care of Graham," replied Cynthia.

"Should I come, Cynthia?" Grandma Karen asked once more.

"The situation is very fluid and will become clearer after Graham and I meet the neurosurgeon," responded Cynthia, noticing that Graham had woken up and was looking listlessly at her.

She cupped her hand over the mouthpiece and in a hushed tone said, "Your mother." Returning to her phone, she said, "Here, Grandma Karen, I will give the phone to Graham."

"Hi, Mum, where are you?" asked Graham.

"In Crete! Nice time of the year.' Hearing no response from his mother, Graham waited and continued, "Mum, I am still trying to process the events of the last few weeks. I'd been experiencing bad headaches, but I never thought that it could progress to having to undergo brain surgery… We won't know for certain until the biopsy results, but if one reads between the cautious description of the mass in my brain by the neuro-oncologist, I'm afraid the news isn't going to be good."

"Darling, I'm so shocked and so sorry to hear about what you're going through. Are you in good hands and getting the best advice? Please spare no cost to get the best treatment. Shall I come to help and give moral support to Cynthia and the children?" repeated his mother, clearly concerned and shaken.

"Mum, wait until after our meeting with the neurosurgeon. Right now, I am on steroid pills to reduce brain swelling."

"Oh yes, steroids should also reduce inflammation," said his mother.

"But they make me very thirsty and leave me with a

dry mouth. Let me just get some water." Graham handed the phone to Cynthia.

She reassured his mother that he was in good hands and that she would keep her updated. She got her email address and landline phone number in Crete. Cynthia also wrote down the latest contact number for Adelaide, Graham's sister, so they could also keep her informed of his health.

After a drink of water, he took the phone again and asked his mother about Scotty's health and how long they were staying in Crete. He said goodbye to his mother after promising to keep her updated about his surgery.

News of Graham's impending surgery spread like wildfire at the school. Many of his colleagues sent messages wishing him rapid recovery, keeping him in their prayers, and urging Cynthia and Graham to maintain positive thoughts. Only the Williamses, in whose house he had celebrated his fiftieth birthday just two weeks ago, came by in person for a short visit to offer their help and support.

Graham appreciated all the messages of support but also felt a sense of impending doom. Though the steroid pills kept the unbearable headaches and vomiting episodes to a bare minimum, they were beginning to exert their negative side effects. He was starting to perspire excessively and experience dry mouth, a bloated tummy, and needed laxatives. At least he was getting a good night's sleep.

Tuesday at 4:25 p.m. they were in the outer office of Suite 240, which had consulting offices for the three neurosurgeons practicing at Morgan Hospital. After filling out the required insurance forms and some health questionnaires, they waited to be taken to meet Dr. Jabbar.

Around 5 p.m., they were ushered into her office,

where they sat on two comfortable chairs and surveyed the wall where many framed degrees and memberships in professional organizations were prominently displayed. Dr. Jabbar got her MD at the University of California, Los Angeles, completed her residency and specialization in Neurosurgery at UC San Francisco, and was also a member of the American Board of Neurosurgery.

As they were examining the triptych of colorful drawings of nerve connections by the famous Spanish neuroanatomist, Santiago Ramon Y Cajal, hanging on the wall, Dr. Jabbar entered, made a quick introduction, and sat behind her desk on a large black chair facing sideways from Cynthia and Graham.

They were struck by her youth, height, and delicately chiseled face. Her likely very long hair was bundled under a sky-blue cap, and she wore matching scrubs. She turned on her computer and displayed the MRI scan of Graham's brain onto the large screen on the wall. After knowing a bit more about Graham, his health, and the medications he was taking, she began to explain the surgical procedure that he would undergo either on Friday or Monday, depending upon the availability of surgical suites.

"Perhaps Dr. Mehra already explained to you that you have a three-to-four-centimeter mass on your prefrontal cortex," which she highlighted with a green laser pointer. "Fortunately, it doesn't look like it has spread anywhere else."

Noticing several small white areas over other parts of his brain on the scan, Graham asked, "How do you know it has not spread? What are those white areas?"

"Oh, many of those are artifacts, but if there are very small areas where the mass has spread, it is difficult to identify by MRI, even with the contrast dye," replied Dr. Jabbar, sounding slightly condescending.

Cynthia thanked her for agreeing to perform the surgery on Graham, considering how busy she was before leaving for Africa in a few weeks, and then asked, "What does brain surgery involve?"

"I will perform a craniotomy, which is the surgical removal of part of the bone from the skull to access the brain underneath. We`ll have three dimensional images of Graham's brain to precisely pinpoint the region where the abnormal mass is located. I`ll excise a small part of this abnormal mass, freeze it at -80°C, and send it to the pathology lab to determine if the cells in the mass are cancerous."

Jolted by the prospect that the mass may actually be cancerous, even though both of them were mentally prepared for this diagnosis, Graham asked, "How long does it take for the pathologist's report?"

"Within thirty minutes or so, the pathologist will indicate if it is malignant and roughly what subtype of tumor it is. If the indications are that it is cancerous, I`ll use special microsurgical tools and other instruments to remove all the tumor tissue as thoroughly as I can, which may take up to two hours. Once all the mass is removed and the dura, the thick skin around the brain, is stitched back together, I replace the bone flap, which is then attached to the surrounding bone and secured using staples, screws, and clamps to allow them to fuse. About a week or so after surgery, these accessories will be removed," explained Dr. Jabbar.

"How long will the whole surgery take?" asked a frightened Cynthia.

"Between four to six hours from the time the patient is wheeled in and out of the surgical room," guessed Dr. Jabbar.

"What happens once the surgery is over and the skull is sewed back together, as you mentioned?" inquired

Graham, slightly dazed and shaken by all the information.

"Following surgery, which of course is done under general anesthesia, you'll be taken to a recovery room for one and a half hours, where you will wake up and be monitored by nurses for the level of your consciousness, breathing, blood pressure, heartbeat, etc. After that you will be moved to the neurosurgery ward where your condition will be monitored for twenty-four to forty-eight hours by highly trained nursing staff. During this time, your close family can visit you for short durations."

"When can Graham go home?" asked Cynthia, still trying to come to grips with the details of the surgical procedure.

Swiveling her chair to face Cynthia, she carefully and calmly explained, "About three to four days after surgery, the incision wound will be covered with dressing, and staples will be removed seven or eight days after surgery, following which you can go home. Of course, it is surgery, and sometimes there are complications, like excessive bleeding, infections, cognitive impairments, but, Graham, you seem to be in excellent health, a non-smoker, no extra pounds, and aren't using any other medications, so I think your surgery will be very routine and you'll come out with flying colors."

Graham sighed and said, "There's a lot of information to process. In the last two to three weeks, my life and my family's life has been turned upside down. At least with surgery, I see some closure to this nightmare. I am of course most concerned that the mass in my brain is a tumor that is growing as we speak. If it's a malignant glioma, from what I can read, life expectancy is only twelve to fourteen months, even after subsequent radiation therapy and chemotherapy."

"You're right, Graham, but if it's a tumor, the pathologist will precisely classify the tumor and then your neuro-oncologist, Dr. Mehra, will help you in charting an appropriate recovery and a course of treatment. New medical modalities are being continuously developed to treat malignant brain tumors, and in that regard, I wanted to make sure that some of your biopsy material will be donated to CancerTech for research. I gather from Dr. Mehra that you've agreed to sign a letter of consent before the surgery?" said Dr. Jabbar.

"Yes, I agreed to sign the consent form because the excised mass can be used for research purposes and testing of new drugs." Cynthia asked the doctor about the post-recovery process and when Graham could resume a normal life.

She carefully responded, "If the surgery is normal without any complications, patients are usually up and about in six or eight weeks, during which time they can do gentle exercise, including walking without excessive exertion. Before I see Graham after six weeks or so after surgery, my office will arrange a CT or MRI scan, so I can see if the mass is entirely excised. If, on the other hand, the biopsy points towards malignancy, your neuro- oncologist will recommend radiation and chemotherapy."

The word *"malignant"* still rankled him and sent chills through his body, and he instantly held Cynthia's hand as her anchor and rock.

Sherri Jabbar looked directly into Cynthia's eyes before turning her gaze onto Graham and said, "I know this's a very hard situation. It seems so unfair, completely upends one's dreams, the future becomes uncertain, and fear takes over one's life. I want to assure you that the neuro- oncologist, my staff, and I are always available for any consultation or questions to make this journey easier."

"Thanks, Dr. Jabbar, for clearly describing the procedure and post-op care. You may know that I have been taking 4 mg pills of Decadron every six hours since Friday, which have temporarily alleviated some of my symptoms like those monstrous headaches, but clearly, that can't last," asked Graham.

"Yes, and that makes me think that surgery on Friday may be better, or we will have to reduce the dosage of the drug dramatically to avoid its side effects, some of which I'm sure you've already started to experience."

Graham nodded positively and said, "Yes, I feel very lethargic."

"Can you be ready for surgery if I can secure an operating room for Friday morning?" inquired Dr. Jabbar.

Graham looked at Cynthia, who concurred with a discrete nod and said, "Yes, the sooner the better."

"I suggest that you also have some routine lab tests performed to ensure that there are no surprises. Since you will have to fast overnight, probably tomorrow will be good to draw blood, and I can ask the diagnostic lab in the basement to put in a rush order, so we will have the report before the surgery. My office staff can also arrange, if you like, a meeting with the anesthesiologist and prep nurse for any preoperative questions and instructions so everything goes smoothly on the day of the surgery," suggested Dr. Jabbar.

"Thanks again. I agree, it will be a good idea to have a preoperative meeting. If possible, might we be able to combine that with a visit tomorrow to the clinical lab for blood work?" asked Graham.

Hearing no further questions from them, she got up, shook hands with them, and said, "Let me see if we can get an operating room on Friday, if need be, by postponing an optional surgery. My office will call you and also arrange a preoperative meeting with the anesthesiologist if he is available. Otherwise, we'll relay to you any additional instructions related to surgery."

As the doctor stood up to leave her office, both of them stood up, offered a warm handshake, and profusely thanked her for her help.

They slowly exited from her office, each engulfed in a flood of emotions in reaction to the numerous uncertainties. By now he was accustomed to the news of a mass on his brain, so knowing that surgery would be done in the next seventy-two hours came more as a relief than the fear that had been building up for many days.

They stopped for an early dinner at a bistro on their way back home and discussed the logistics if surgery was performed on Friday.

Cynthia said, "I know everyone has good intentions and wants to be here during your surgery, but it'll get very hectic. I'm not sure if everyone recognizes that they may not be able to see you for more than a few minutes during the first few days of your recovery. I am also worried how they may react if it turns out that you have cancer. We've known about this possibility for some days, and it's been very hard to come to grips with it, but we're now prepared and can cope with it."

"Nobody wants you to be alone during and after my surgery," reflected Graham; while distractedly stirring the small amount of cream he had put into his coffee.

"I know. The girls will surely want to be in the hospital during surgery, though Amber has some kind of a design show at the Asian Art Museum on Friday evening. Nigel will insist on sitting outside the surgery room with his earplugs and computer. If he has no exams on Friday, he can come for the weekend. Your father and Linda will also want to be here, but I think it'll be better if they came later after the surgery during the recovery period. I`ll let them know once we hear from Dr. Jabbar's office regarding the date for the surgery. Speaking of Dr. Jabbar, what do you think of her?" inquired Cynthia.

"I was impressed with how clearly, she explained the procedure without sugarcoating the hazards of surgery, the possibility that the biopsy may point towards a malignant growth, and her determination for maximal removal of the aberrant growth tissue. Too bad I will be half asleep all this time when a beautiful woman will be spending four to six hours in such close proximity to my mangled skull," chuckled Graham.

Cynthia rolled her eyes and in jest said, "Good to see that you haven't` lost your sense of humor, but don`t forget that Dr. Jabbar will be wielding the sharpest knife in her hand right next to your face."

Back home, they heard the message on the voice mail from the nurse in the neurosurgery suite, confirming that surgery can be scheduled for Friday morning as the "first start" case at 7:20 a.m.

"When you come tomorrow for a blood draw for lab diagnostics, maybe you can stop by the preoperative clinic for some instructions before the surgery. Because you have no heart or chest issues, the doctor did not recommend EKG or chest X-rays."

The die was cast, and there was no retreat from surgery.

Graham perversely thought that as the scalpel cut his skull, it would also be the death knell of those lawlessly marauding cancer cells. An image of Dr. Jabbar holding a can of Raid spraying mercilessly on a mound of ants on a tiny sugar speckle flashed in his head.

Graham later called the principal of the school to say that his surgery was slated for Friday the 28th and suggested that Barry could cover for him for the remainder of the school year.

The principal wished him luck and a speedy recovery. In an attempt to lighten the severity of life-threatening cancer that Graham was facing, he attempted to cheer him up by reemphasizing that the school needed him when it reopened in the first week of September.

After arriving home, he made sure not to eat anything before the blood work the next day. Cynthia left a message for their daughters about the day and time of Dad's surgery.

Following his mother's call, Nigel insisted on being at the hospital during the surgery, and since he had no major obligations on Friday, he suggested he come home on Thursday night.

"No, no, Mom, don't worry about picking me up. You will have plenty on your mind the night before the surgery. I can ask a friend to pick me up from the airport. Keep me informed if anything changes. See you soon. Love you, Mom," spoke Nigel in a hurry as his friends were waiting to go out for dinner.

The conversation with Graham's father was a little harder because he wanted to be at the hospital during surgery. Cynthia tried to explain to David that it would be more helpful if Linda and he could come a few days after surgery, when the girls would be back at their jobs and Nigel would return to school. She could take a break after the surgery if Linda and he were in town.

"Let me talk to Linda, and then I will call you. Tell my son that we're constantly thinking of him."

The following day she drove Graham to the hospital for the blood draw at the diagnostic lab and then joined him to talk to the nurse at the preoperative clinic, where one of the senior nurses asked him again about any medications he is taking, any allergies, diet supplements, any hints of diabetes or high blood pressure, any heart or respiratory illnesses.

Hearing none, the nurse in a practiced voice said, "Don't take any aspirin, continue your Decadron pills, and arrive at 5:20 a.m. for check-in on Friday morning. If there is anything unusual in your blood tests, we'll let you know. Any questions?" Hearing none, to reassure him, the nurse added for good measure, "Dr. Jabbar is an excellent neurosurgeon. You are lucky to have her perform your surgery."

For a moment, Graham thought that the aberrant lab report may yet offer a reprieve from surgery and subsequent diagnosis. Shook his head and quietly said to himself... *just get it over with...*!

Since he had not had anything to eat or drink since last night, he stopped at the hospital coffee cart on his way out and ordered coffee and a bagel with cream cheese. Cynthia only wanted coffee but did take a bite from his bagel.

His silence on the drive back home was wrapped in memories of good times, family travels, whims and moods of adolescent children—pride as the girls stood one and two on the podium after a swim meet, the death of their family dog, a stray who had followed eight-year-old Nigel home, and for a whole week, despite multiple postings all over the neighborhood, nobody claimed. Nigel had cried when Graham suggested taking the dog to the pound, so instead they'd kept him and named him Lucky.

Perhaps this diagnosis and upcoming surgery was all a nightmare, and the mass on his brain would just be a benign, benevolent mass -a mere nuisance to be expelled.

Lost in her own thoughts, Cynthia was soon turning onto their street and opening the electronic garage door to park their bright red SAAB 9000.

After tidying up the house a bit since they had left home early for the blood test, Cynthia went to the study and turned on her computer. There were several messages of good luck, keep strong, any help, and best wishes to Graham for the upcoming surgery by their colleagues at the school, where the principal had informed many staff members about his upcoming surgery. Some mentioned that they would pray for him, while others suggested that Graham's strength would vanquish any disease.

Uncertain about the international time differences, Cynthia, instead of calling them, sent emails to Graham's mother in Crete and his sister Adelaide in Singapore, informing them of his surgery early Friday morning.

As she was coming out of their study, the phone rang, and it was Graham's father, again offering to come during the surgery but to come later because that's what Linda had also suggested. He ended the short call by saying that he would call Graham tomorrow evening to wish him best of luck.

She detected concern but no fear in his voice, unlike her own thoughts that were laden with dread, anxiety, and despair.

In just a couple of hours, there was a response from Graham's mother with an offer to come and a note to her son, wishing him the best from Scott and her for a successful surgery.

She told him about the call from his father, response from his mother, and all the solicitous messages and prayers for his good health.

She was preparing lunch when he solemnly remarked, "In two days, I'm going to go through a major surgery under general anesthesia, and though the doctors assure us of the safety of the surgical procedure, there is still great risk. We have no last will or probate in case things take an unexpected bad turn."

"Please, this is too morbid a subject, and I don't want to talk about it," said Cynthia, clearly upset by his words.

"I'm serious. There are horror stories of descendants fighting for paltry financial sums," said Graham.

"Do whatever you want. I have plenty on my mind," said Cynthia, rattled by this suggestion.

"Ok, I`m just going to write a handwritten will. I think it is called a holographic will, which is legal in California," said Graham a bit defensively.

"Whatever. Leave me out of it. I don't want to go to any lawyers now," replied Cynthia with some exasperation.

"No, no, in California we don't need lawyers or even witnesses. I was going to designate you as the sole heir of all our properties and assets anyway," explained Graham.

After lunch, he read a bit more about brain surgery procedures at other institutions, most of which employed similar processes described by Dr. Jabbar. He also took intermittent naps, and again a general malaise overwhelmed him. In two days, his fate would be scaled—he would either have cancer or not, live or die.

Cynthia also called the Williamses, their closest friends, about the date of surgery, and they decided to come by in the evening. They brought some takeout Indian food, which was Graham's favorite. Cynthia was happy to have company to take his mind off the impending surgery, and it worked for a while until he clammed up again and started to brood and stare into space.

During the Williams' visit, like Nigel, both girls called

to say that they wanted to be in the hospital during the surgery. Nigel would fly in early Friday morning, and Amber on her way would pick him up from the airport and drive to the hospital. They all asked how Dad was doing, and Cynthia had the same response.

"As well as he can. I think he's both worried and relieved, but mostly he wants it to be over so he can get his life back. You know your dad. He doesn't like being fussed over. I hope he doesn't go stir-crazy being in the hospital for seven days. I'll see you at Morgan Hospital in the neurosurgery ward. It is in Redwood City, just off the highway. It's a brand-new building. You can't miss it. Besides, I`ll have my cell phone with me. Love you."

Despite her best efforts, she tossed and turned all night while Graham was knocked out under the influence of a sleeping pill previously recommended by Dr. Mehra. She did manage to fall asleep in the wee hours of the morning, and when she woke up, Graham was already in the kitchen with coffee, nursing a "drug-induced" hangover that many people experience after taking benzodiazepine-based sleeping pills.

He offered her a cup of coffee and said, "My last day of normal life. It may all change tomorrow. Today I may be carrying a tumor in my brain, and tomorrow the unwanted intruder will be removed and banished from my body."

She engulfed his head in an embrace and murmured in his ear, "We want your old brain back."

"Wonderful as that Indian food was, the steroids don't like all that curry, so I am feeling bloated and hope my Metamucil will work. I need to take it easy and fast for at least eight hours before the surgery."

She did some household chores, went to buy some food since Nigel would be staying home, and when she came home, Graham was putting some clothes in a bag for his hospital stay, along with his toiletries and bed slippers. He also packed pajamas and a bathrobe; in case he had to share a room with another patient.

While passing the study to make Nigel's bed in his old room, she heard the pinging sound on her computer announcing the arrival of a new email. She stopped by and saw the message was from Adelaide, Graham's sister:

My Dear Cynthia,

I was so shocked to get your email regarding Graham's brain surgery this morning (we are fifteen hours ahead in Singapore, it's Friday here). Graham has been a paragon of good health and is like a rock, so I can't even imagine him being sick. When I last saw him at the millennial party that Dad had hosted a few years ago, he was talking about his exercise regimen in advance of the Boston Marathon. When we were kids, he was the fastest runner in the school, fastest swimmer, and was very protective of me, even though I was two years older than him.

I talked to Mum earlier, and she is also quite shaken but feels that Graham, with your help, will pull through. If you remember, we have been talking about leaving Africa and moving to Singapore, where Roger had an offer to be a senior partner in an investment firm. After several trips to Singapore, we finally moved here two months ago and are still awaiting the arrival of our household goods. It is forever hot here, but otherwise, life is very comfortable and safe.

Please let me know if we can be of any help during this difficult period. I can easily come to Palo Alto to be with you during the surgery. Give my love and best wishes to Graham for a very successful outcome of the surgery and a speedy recovery. Love to my two nieces and Nigel, who must be, just now, finishing college.

With love and affection,

Adelaide

P.S.: I enclosed Uncle Jonathan's email address in Windhoek, Namibia, where he is currently posted. Mum told him about Graham's impending surgery.

Scrolling through her emails, she saw a cryptic email from Uncle Jonathan wishing Graham the best of luck with surgery. She printed both emails and took them to Graham, who was putting away an envelope addressed to Cynthia in his desk drawer. Later, Cynthia would find out that this was the last will written by Graham on Thursday, May 27th, at 12 noon, a day before the surgery.

During lunch on Thursday, Graham said, "After surgery, if all goes well, we should visit Adelaide in Singapore and Uncle Jonathan in Namibia before he retires and moves back to a country cottage in England. He never married, and Roger and Adelaide never had any children and spent a good part of their lives in Africa. Mum said that Roger sold his share of the diamond business in Botswana and became fabulously wealthy and now is at the investment firm."

Graham reminisced a bit more about his early life in England and the games Adelaide and he played at their grandparents' house. One that he always remembered was The Pirates, where he would be the knight with a sword protecting Adelaide from all invaders entering the palace. She would then give him gold-plated nuggets for saving her and the kingdom.

Later, Cynthia would not remember how she and Graham spent their afternoon and evening that day, except that they went to bed early since the alarm clock was set for 4 a.m. for a 5:20 a.m. check-in at the surgical ward at the hospital.

Chapter 6

BRAIN TUMOR

Friday, May 28th, 2004

Operative dictation

Preoperative Diagnosis: Irregular mass on right frontal lobe of the cortex

Postoperative Diagnosis: Same

Procedure: Right frontal craniotomy for resection of right frontal mass

Surgeon: Dr. Sherri Jabbar, MD

Anesthesia: General Endotracheal

Estimated Blood Loss: 250 ccs

Mr. Graham Bunker is a fifty-year-old male who had progressively worsening headaches, multiple vomiting episodes, unsteady gait, restlessness, and emotional distress. An MRI scan with contrast performed preoperatively showed a mass on the right *frontal lobe with irregular mar-*

gins, consistent with a suspected malignant neoplasm.

The patient was well apprised of all objectives, benefits, risks, and potential complications of the procedure, including but not limited to: worsening of current status, the possible need for further procedures, the risk of infection, headaches, CSF leak, seizures, hemorrhage, stroke, loss of language function, loss of sensory and motor function, paralysis, coma, and even death. Informed consent was obtained and secured in the chart after the patient voiced his understanding of these risks and decided to proceed with the operation.

The patient was transferred to the operating room at 6:05 a.m., he was given preoperative prophylactic IV antibiotics, sedated and intubated without difficulty by the anesthesia service. His eyes were taped shut after ointment was applied to prevent corneal abrasion. The mass appeared soft with areas of necrosis. A small sample was sent to pathology for a frozen section. The pathologist confirmed the mass to be a high-grade glioma.

As soon as the diagnosis of a malignant glioma was conveyed to Dr. Jabbar, she'd let Dr. Mehra know of the outcome, who in turn informed Yacov Kaufman to soon expect the arrival of the tissue samples.

Thirty minutes after bits of tumor tissue from Graham's brain had been deposited into a plastic test tube in an ice bucket, the technician raced north on Highway 101, reached CancerTech in Foster City at 10:37 a.m., and deposited the precious cargo labeled as Patient X to Yacov's team assembled in the small conference room. Few days prior, Yacov had carefully assembled a small team of scientists and technicians and prepared them to expect cancer tissue samples from a fifty-year-old male (Patient X) with glioblastoma.

He had already drawn on the whiteboard four unevenly spaced, empty boxes, which he now started to fill after guessing that the excised tissue brought by the technician was a little over 3-4 cm3 (about 1/10th of the tumor):

Box 1: Roughly a quarter of the material to be sent for genomic sequencing and RNA analysis

Box 2: A quarter of the material to make immortal cell lines

Box 3: Enough tissue to make xenografts and, if possible orthotopic xenografts

Box 4: Keep the remainder of the material at -80C

One of the younger associates on the team asked if some mice should be injected with only ten to a hundred cells of the tumor tissue to confirm that in the brain tumor most cells are stem cells capable of generating new tumors.

Yacov readily agreed with this suggestion, added it to the list in box three, and designated the team leaders responsible for carrying out and coordinating the mission listed in the first three boxes.

Through sheer coincidence, a board member of CancerTech was visiting Yacov Kaufman in connection with a family member recently diagnosed with glioblastoma multiforme (GBM) and happened to be in the conference room where Yacov, like a general in the army, had commandeered his troops into three different directions to combat the enemy.

The inquisitive board member, a distinguished financier who professed having minimal knowledge of biology, asked, "Dr. Kaufman, how will the research you are conducting on the tumor of Patient X help you find a cure for treating brain tumors?"

Yacov paused, reflected for a while, and then explained, "We want to find out the changes (mutations) in the DNA obtained from the tumor tissue of the patient and compare them to changes that have been recorded in the genomes (DNA) of other patients with glioblastomas. This information is available in a public database created by scientists supported by government funding. If we can find some common changes, we can decipher the nature and type of the tumor. Depending on the mutations, we can design patient-specific treatments". After a pause, he continued, "We also know that certain mutations affect the outcome of survival. It's not foolproof but still very helpful for the prognosis and treatment of the disease. We do not do this analysis at the company but outsource it for efficiency and cost- effectiveness. In the case of Patient X, we'll work with the neuro-oncologist, Dr. Mehra, who has an ongoing collaboration with scientists at Stanford University Medical School."

The board director interrupted to ask, "How do you know that all changes in the genome of a cancer cell are meaningful for treatment?"

"You are right—we don't know. However, if the changes are the same in tumors of different patients, it's reasonable to assume that they're significant. We, however, also undertake another analysis where we find out if there are aberrant amounts of messenger RNAs, which make the proteins to carry out various functions of a cell. The holy trilogy of biology is DNA-RNA-Protein, so if we see altered amounts of RNAs, that is a clue that something is wrong in the cancer cell, and this becomes a target of opportunity to exploit for drug development. Again, for efficiency and speed, we also outsource this analysis," explained Yacov with a teacher's flair.

"In box two, you have written cell lines. Is this to

make sure that you do not run out of the cancer tissue?" asked the board director with some hesitancy.

"Biduk (Exactly), responded Yacov." "The excised cancerous tissue from Patient X given to us is minimal in amount, and we cannot use it for further studies or drug testing. If instead we can grow the tumor cells forever in petri dishes, they're referred to as cell lines and in many ways are surrogates of the tumor excised from the patient, which can be used for not only testing drugs but also to identify unique signatures of a cancer cell."

"Of course, they do have limitations. Most significantly, they may undergo additional changes (mutations) during the process of growing them in petri dishes. It takes about fifteen to sixteen hours for most cancer cells to divide. For a thousand cancer cells in a petri dish to become 2,000 cells, it takes fifteen hours, and to become a million cells, it will take about a week. During this week, cancer cells would have divided ten times, and during these divisions, new mutations can occur, which are not seen in the original tumors and hence can give false information.

Ensuring that the distinguished director was still following his logic, Yacov again paused and then added, "Another problem that's just surfacing is that not all cancer cells in a given tumor, like the one from Patient X, have the same mutations. It is possible that we make a cell line from one region of the tumor tissue, which has a particular mutation, and from another part of the tumor, the cell line we make has a very different mutation. Thus, it's possible that a drug we test could kill one cell line and not the other so we may have to generate two separate drugs: one killing one cell line, another killing the other cell line made from the same tumor excised from the same patient. But this is the best system we have, and it has been gainfully employed by the Pharma industry to generate drugs. To overcome some of the limitations, we're taking a new approach that I have listed in box three," explained Yacov.

"Dr. Kaufman, pardon me for asking these basic questions, but when you write words like 'xenografts' and 'orthotopic xenograft, what do they mean, and how will they help in finding cures for this disease?" inquired the board member, who again emphasized his background as a financier lacking basic knowledge of modern biology.

Yacov walked up to the whiteboard and, with a red magic marker, drew the outlines of a mouse. He said, "We take a tiny bit, about 1 mm3, of the patient's tumor tissue, roughly the size of a sharp pencil point-and inject it under the skin of a mouse. Because we are injecting human tissue into mice, it will be immunologically rejected. To overcome this hurdle, scientists have generated mice with compromised immune systems, so that human tissue can be engrafted without rejection. Sometimes these immunodeficient mice are also called 'nude' mice because they are hairless... If we inject 1 mm3 of tumor tissue into the mouse, by six to eight weeks, a big palpable tumor appears, which still retains most of the characteristics of the starting tumor.," explained Yacov patiently.

"Regarding your second question about the orthotopic model, it simply means the tumor cells are directly injected into the mouse's brain to capture the environment from where the tumor was excised. We will treat the messy and bloody tumor tissue with some enzymes to break it up into individual cells and inject a hundred thousand cells into the brain of the mouse. About six to eight weeks after the injection, the tumors can become very large, and if not excised, can kill the recipient mouse," added Yacov.

The board director looked very puzzled, so Yacov

added, "We are trying to recreate the environment in which the human tumors grow, so putting the tumor cells from the patient back into the brain of the mouse is the closest approximation that we can mimic the way human brain tumors may grow. We aren't sure if this will really work, but we have to try, to find out one way or the other."

The board member asked about the prognosis of someone with a malignant tumor like that of Patient X and how prevalent was such a cancer. Yacov reflected briefly and said, "The median survival time of patients with stage IV GBM that Patient X has been diagnosed with is twelve to fourteen months after surgery, radiation, and chemotherapy treatment. Approximately 20,000 Americans die every year of brain cancer. It is a terrible disease, and since becoming the chief scientist at CancerTech, I'm consumed by finding ways to extend the life of the patients with this lethal disease."

The board director thanked Yacov for the clear and concise explanation, wished his team good luck, and parted by confiding, "Would it be ok for my older brother, who was diagnosed with GBM and is being treated at a hospital in Houston, to call you to get information on state-of-the-art treatments and discoveries?"

Taken aback by the GBM diagnosis of the board member's brother, Yacov said, "I'm sorry to hear that. Of course, your brother can call me anytime." Before Yacov could thank the board member for his interest and support, the company CEO whisked him away to his waiting limo. After putting the plan in action with his team, Yacov returned to his office and placed a call to Rakesh Mehra to inform him about the arrival of the tissue and his plan for how Graham's precious tumor tissue was to be used.

The administrative assistant picked up the phone and after greeting Dr. Kaufman said, "Dr. Mehra is with a patient, but he'll be done in ten minutes and can then call you back."

While waiting for the call and fiddling with a pencil sharpener on his desk, Yacov's mind wandered to the day in October 1976 when he had joined his parents to go to the Hadassah Medical Center in Ein Kerem, to visit his dod (Uncle) Shmuel, who had suddenly taken sick and rushed to the hospital. He had been shocked to see how old, exhausted, and thin his uncle looked, since he had last seen him some three months prior. He recalled hearing Dr. Levy, a renowned oncologist who had migrated to Israel from Boston, explained to his aunt, "I've completed most of the tests and the news is not good. Your husband has pancreatic cancer, which unfortunately has spread to other tissues, so we can't remove it by surgery. The difficulty with this cancer is that if one detects it too late then all one can do is to administer chemotherapy and sometimes radiation treatment." He could still picture his aunt, her eyes red from crying and lack of sleep, asking, "How long does my Shmueli have?"

Yacov vividly remembered Dr. Levy's response, "It's hard to say because each patient responds differently to drugs. The average time left for someone at this stage of the disease is between six months to a year, but if the chemotherapy works, then it could be longer. The tumor is surrounded by a thick wall which prevents the drugs from getting in and killing the cancer cells. We'll do our best, but I wish science had made more strides in understanding and treating pancreatic cancer. More research is needed."

As he had intensely listened to Dr. Levy, he understood the last statement to mean that cancer doctors will continue to administer the same futile treatments until one understands the true nature of the disease.

On the drive back home on the winding road from

Jerusalem, his mind had raced between becoming a doctor who treated the disease or a researcher who uncovered the cause of the disease. Doctors treat and save a few dozen patients, but a researcher could provide answers that could save hundreds, if not thousands, of patients and might even find clues to prevent the disease from occurring in the first place. He'd also doubted if he would ever have the courage to pronounce life and death judgments as Dr. Levy had that morning sitting not far from his sick uncle. That is when he decided he wanted to be a cancer researcher.

The loud ringing of the phone broke his reverie. It was Dr. Mehra returning his call.

"Rakesh, would you like to participate in determining the genomic sequence of the tumor from the GBM patient with your collaborators at Stanford, or should CancerTech consider outsourcing to a company in the UK?"

"I've talked to my colleagues at Stanford, and they are happy to collaborate, as long as they can put the data on a public website. They may also require some funding to purchase a new DNA sequencer and supplies," replied Rakesh.

"Who's the contact at Stanford regarding logistics, so I can have our legal folks get in touch with them?" inquired Yacov. "And how long do you think it'll take the Stanford group to prepare the first rough draft of the sequence?"

"If the tissue sample is in good condition, probably a month at the most. Also, I know of a good Affymetrix-associated service provider to do the microarray analysis," responded Rakesh.

Yacov, with his usual gusto, replied, "Great, and thanks. I'll have the project leader of genomics at CancerTech contact you right away. I'm also hoping that by early next week the pathologist's final report will be available to confirm the diagnosis of GBM. Rakesh, I'm thrilled with the speed we're moving with the analysis of the tumor samples from Patient X.'.

"I'm also excited, especially as you know I'm also the attending neuro-oncologist for Patient X. I've gotten to know his wife a bit as well, and they're a delightful couple. You'd enjoy meeting them."

Before closing the flap of his mobile phone, Rakesh thanked Yacov for keeping him in the loop and wished him and his family a good weekend.

Back at the hospital, Dr. Jabbar informed the family that the surgery had gone without a hitch, with no excessive bleeding, and that she was able to excise nearly all the tumor tissue. She said, "I'll meet you around 3:45 p.m. in the consulting room next to my office," and left while untying her surgical mask.

At about 1:30 p.m., Graham was transferred to a recovery room where he slowly woke up from the anesthesia and was closely monitored by two nurses for arm and leg strength, level of consciousness, breathing, blood pressure, and heart rate.

A little over an hour later, Graham was awake, groggy but coherent, and asked for water. He was very thirsty.

Instead, the nurse gave him an ice cube to suck on. By 3 p.m., he was wheeled into a neurosurgery ward and moved into a room with a single bed.

First to enter the room was Cynthia, who blew him kisses and gave a thumbs-up sign. A few minutes later, she left and the three children walked in with smiles, waving at their dad who tried to reciprocate but realized that he lacked the strength to raise his arm with ease.

At about 3:45 p.m. Cynthia and the children assembled in Dr. Jabbar's office, and after brief introductions with the children, she said in a solemn tone, "The mass on Graham's brain was a tumor, a high-grade glioma that grows very rapidly—"

And before she could finish her sentence, Cynthia inhaled and exhaled loudly, swallowed, tears welling her eyes, haltingly in a choked voice said, "I was worried from the first day that Graham had cancer. Oh my god, your dad has brain cancer." She looked at her children, and seeking support, reached for Amber's arm who was sitting next to her.

After a brief pause to let the news sink in, Dr. Jabbar assured them with confidence, "I was able to excise nearly all the tumorous material."

As she was removing her cap and a heap of jet-black hair was tumbling down, Nigel asked, "How long will it take before Dad can go home?"

"It is hard to say because each patient responds differently, but since surgery went without any major complications, your dad's chances of recovery are excellent. If all goes well, he should spend his next weekend at home," assured Dr. Jabbar.

She said to Cynthia, "I'll see your husband before he goes home and then again after his recovery in about six or seven weeks when I'm back from Africa." She wished them well, signed a few papers, and left the room.

Jolted by the definitive diagnosis of cancer in Graham's brain, she was still in shock when Nigel asked in a tone that sounded slightly accusatory, "Mom, did you know that Dad had cancer and you didn't tell us?"

Distraught, she replied, "No, I was not certain. Neither were his doctors until the pathologist confirmed from the biopsy that the mass in your dad's brain was malignant. I was hoping against hope that it would not be cancer, but in the back of my mind, I had this sinking feeling that the news wouldn't be good. I've been living under the sword of Damocles since I saw that fuzzy white mass on the MRI of your father's brain some three weeks ago."

Jessica and Amber, sitting on adjacent chairs next to Cynthia, now in tears, got up and buried their faces in their mom's breast and started sobbing.

Cynthia, trying to control her emotions, put her arms around her daughters and said, "It'll be ok. You just heard the surgeon say that she excised most of the cancerous tissue, so Dad will be cancer-free and he can go back to being the old Dad that we knew."

Nigel just sat in the chair, looking angry, in disbelief, and helpless.

They stayed like this for a while until Nigel put his arms around his mother, teared up, and said, "Mom, we'll all be there to help Dad get better." Later she would think of this very personal and touching family huddle often over the coming months, and it would give her solace, strength, and comfort.

As the family was about to leave the conference room, Dr. Mehra peeked in, said hello to Cynthia, introduced himself to the rest of the family, and reiterated that surgery went well and that Graham's vital signs and reflexes were normal, and his cognitive functions appeared to be undiminished.

He added, "I just saw Graham in the neurosurgery ward where he was comfortably resting under sedation. You all have been up since the crack of dawn, so I advise you to go home and rest. Most likely late tomorrow or Sunday, Graham will be transferred to the neurological nursing unit, barring any complications."

He homed in on Nigel and added for good measure, "Your dad is in very good physical shape and should weather the surgery well to be home in a few days. I'll talk to you again before your father is discharged to go home."

Before Dr. Mehra could leave, Nigel asked, "When will they know what type of brain cancer Dad has? I've read that the treatment and prognosis depend on that."

"The detailed pathologist's report will take a week or so, along with some genomic analysis we are undertaking at CancerTech will precisely identify the subtype of brain cancer that your Dad has," responded Dr. Mehra. He added, "Probably Dr. Jabbar already told you that she was able to remove nearly all the tumor tissue, which of course lessens the chances of recurrence."

Amber hesitantly asked, "Does Dad know that he has cancer?"

"No, not yet. He`s under heavy sedation and asleep. I'll make the rounds tomorrow morning, and if he is awake and coherent, I`ll then let him know."

"Can I be there when you break the news to him?" urged Cynthia.

"Sure. Around 9:30 a.m. Will that work for you?" asked Dr. Mehra.

"Of course, I'll make it work. See you then," replied Cynthia.

Hearing no further queries, he wished them well and slowly walked out of the room, gently closing the door behind him.

They were all exhausted and wouldn't be able to visit Graham more that day, so they trooped out of the conference room to the parking lot. The sisters decided to go home and transferred Nigel's backpack to their mother's car. They all agreed to meet the next day at noon at the hospital.

Nigel offered to drive, but his mother said, "You were probably up at 4 a.m. to get to LAX to fly to San Francisco and have probably eaten nothing, so let us first stop at the corner cafe and get something to eat, and then we'll drive home."

Both were indeed very hungry and felt much better after a filling meal and steaming cups of coffee. During their drive home, Nigel wanted to know all about his father's disease, when it started, and what to expect in the future. He also wondered if there was a hereditary link, which made him susceptible to brain tumors.

Back home, Cynthia said, "I need to call Grandpa David and Linda because I'm sure they are sitting near the phone wanting to know how the surgery went. I have to compose myself to tell Grandpa without falling apart that the mass in Graham's brain was malignant. He'll be shattered by the news. I'll send an email to Grandma Karen and Aunt Adelaide instead of calling them because it's late there."

Nigel volunteered to send the email to Grandma and his aunt while his mother relayed the news to Linda and Grandpa David.

Predictably, conversation with Graham's father was very emotional. Though she sensed that he had done his homework and was prepared for the bad news, he was concerned that Graham's vital signs and cognitive functions may have been compromised and whether the surgeon had removed the last bits of cancerous tissue.

"When could Linda and I come to see Graham?"

"Probably best when he's home, which if all goes well, will likely be another five to seven days, but we'll know more after he's moved out of the ICU to the nursing unit. When we visit him tomorrow at the hospital, I'll ask the nursing staff if he can receive a short call from you and Linda."

Knowing that his grandson Nigel had been at the hospital but was now home, he wanted to talk to him, but Cynthia said, "He's sending an email to let Grandma and Aunt Adelaide know about the events of the day. I`ll have him call you."

"Please do. I know he must be quite upset right now," acknowledged Grandpa David.

"Oh, yes, Nigel was quite overwhelmed with the news but has acted very mature and responsibly. I`m so glad he is staying the weekend with me," replied Cynthia, feeling tired and exhausted. She bade goodbye to Linda and David and went to the bathroom to take a long hot shower.

In the meantime, Nigel wrote:

Dear Grandma and Aunt Adelaide:

Today was a very tough day, but Dad did come out with flying colors and is now sedated and resting in the ICU. The surgeon and the neuro- oncologist both said that surgery went well. Yes, the mass on Dad's brain was cancer, but the surgeon said that she removed most of it. The surgery took nearly six hours, and Dad has a big bandage around his head that will come off in a week. We saw him in the ICU, waved at him, and he barely waved back, which required some effort. The surgeon, a very impressive woman, said that there was very little bleeding and all cognitive functions are intact and that Dad will heal just fine and will be back to normal soon. She also told us that she sent a small amount of the excised tumor to a biotech laboratory for research purposes. I think that is very good.

I am staying with Mom until the weekend because on Monday I have my Chemistry final, a subject I have not done well in. Strange that Grandpa and you were chemists and I am floundering. Please send me some of your "magic."

Aunt Adelaide, I did not know that you had finally moved to Singapore and Uncle Roger is now at an investment firm. I missed my chance for a safari by not visiting you when you were still in

Botswana.

That is all the news I have and will keep you updated on Dad's recovery. Now I must take a big shower because I have been in the same clothes since 4 a.m. when I left home to get to the airport in LA. Grandma, please give my best to Scotty, and Aunt Adelaide, say hi to Uncle Roger. More tomorrow. Stay tuned…

Mom and I send our love,

Nigel

He saw a note from his mom asking him to call Grandpa after sending the email, which he did, and though the subject matter was somber, he slipped in some comments about the Golden State Warriors, their favorite team. After promising to visit Linda and him in Vancouver Island, Nigel said goodbye to his grandpa and put the phone down.

He ordered pizza and watched part of a movie with his mom, largely to avoid thinking about how his dad would react to the news that he had brain cancer. But the day's exhaustion overtook him, and he fell asleep, leaving a partially eaten pizza on the kitchen counter. Cynthia looked at her son, saw Graham in him, gently put a light blanket on him, then glided her hand through his dense and disheveled hair, and retired to the bedroom, thinking how terribly unjust it would be if he were to lose his father.

Chapter 7

POST-SURGERY

DESPITE THE APPROACHING WEEK-END, the scientists whom Yacov had designated to make cell lines and xenografts immediately started the process. The lead scientist, a very experienced cancer biologist who had come along with Yacov from a previous biotech company, was considered to have golden hands when it came to manipulating cells and tissue culturing methodologies. Tall, thin, with her whitish-grey hair pulled into a bun and her long fingers-perhaps more suited for playing the piano-clad in latex gloves, Erica Hagen, in her late fifties, was a delight to watch—how meticulously she minced the cancer tissue and added a mixture of enzymes to force the stubborn mass to break apart into single cells, so they could be plated onto plastic petri dishes, which were stacked like a multistory building. She then placed roughly 100,000 disseminated cells into ten petri dishes, filled them up with ten milliliters of a special red solution, and stacked them in a 37°C incubator. Erica saved a small portion of the disseminated tumor material for direct injection into the brain of the immunodeficient mice.

Satisfied with her work, Erica cleaned and disinfected the work area by squirting alcohol and wiping it up with sterile tissue paper. She removed her coat, threw the gloves into the wastebasket, washed her hands, applied cream to them, and turned on the UV light to further sterilize the room.

The group designated to make xenograft models injected the cancer cells that Erica Hagen had kept aside under the skin of only two immunodeficient mice due to the paucity of the tissue from Patient X. The technician designated to inject just ten to fifty cancer cells into various regions of the mouse brain had to leave early on Friday, so instead came on Saturday to finish the work. As the technician was leaving, he ran into Yacov, who was coming in to make sure that the planned experimental approach was underway because he knew that there would be a race against the clock—if it was a GBM, the tumor would likely reappear in the patient probably within six to nine months.

He wrote an internal memo to the CEO of CancerTech to request extra resources to speed up the genomic analysis. He then wrote another memo to the business development officer to contact Stanford Medical School about sequencing the genome of the cancer tissue of Patient X. He also wrote a note for his admin assistant to remind him to call the company that Rakesh had recommended to determine the changes in messenger RNAs (mRNAs direct the synthesis of proteins) in cancer cells compared to normal brain cells. Could it be that some proteins made in cancer cells differ from those normal brain cells? And if so, could drugs be made to eliminate or inactivate the function of such proteins and thereby debilitate the cancer cell's ability for further mischief? Satisfied that he was moving expeditiously, Yacov decided to go home before lunch and hoped the family could go to see the popular movie, *The Terminal*, playing in San Mateo.

The next day, when Graham woke up, his head hurt.

The nurse in the ICU raised the headboard of the bed to reduce the pain due to swelling and increased the dosage of painkillers into the IV drip.

His face was also quite swollen, and a plethora of tubes were coming out of his body, linked to instruments with flashing and beeping lights.

His head was heavily bandaged to cover the wound, which added further pressure on his brain. After all, his head had been drilled into, his skull cut, and brain tissue manipulated to excise the tumor. The dura mater covering the brain had been restitched, and the bone flap cut to expose the brain had been sutured back. It was no surprise that his head was swollen and appeared a bit grotesque.

Though the brain itself has no nerve endings to feel pain, the skull and skin are rich in nerve endings, making Graham acutely sensitive to even a slight movement of his head. Instead of the promise of feeling better after surgery, for now, the pain was unbearable, and there was a limit to how much painkiller could be added to the mix of medicines that already contained steroids, anticonvulsants, and salt solutions to replenish his balance of electrolytes.

Graham was extremely tired from the surgery and pain and was semi-asleep when he saw the hazy outlines of Cynthia and Dr. Mehra's faces through the glass window in his room. They were accompanied by a neurosurgery resident.

Cynthia blew a kiss to Graham, went near his bed, held his warm hand in both of hers, and asked how he was doing. He made hand gestures indicating a throbbing head and motioned for her to sit on his bed.

The nurse said that Graham had had a good sleep and that a headache after the lengthy surgery was quite common but should subside as swelling goes down, perhaps within a day or so.

"Other than that," she confided, "the patient is doing well, especially his cognitive functions."

Dr. Mehra, now sitting on a tall stool next to Graham's bed, introduced the neurosurgery resident who was also present during the surgery.

With great empathy, he said, "Graham, your surgery was extremely successful. The mass on your brain was cleanly removed, but the pathologist confirmed that it was malignant." Then, he let the news sink in.

Graham's eyes darted towards Cynthia as he tightened his squeeze of her hand, and nobody spoke a word for the next few moments, as if time had frozen. Cynthia did her best to suppress her emotions and simply kept squeezing Graham's hand. She did not want to minimize the enormity of Dr. Mehra's announcement that her husband had cancer, so she avoided making a banal statement like, "It will be ok."

Dr. Mehra, always sensitive to patient and family emotions, thought that it would be best to leave the couple alone to process the diagnosis, so he got up and said, "I'll see you later," and left with the young resident following.

She remained seated on his bed, holding his hand until the nurse started to again adjust his pillow to keep him a bit more upright. Soon he closed his eyes, fell asleep, and after a while, the nurse left.

Cynthia stayed at the hospital until 11:30 a.m.., when her three children arrived to see and hesitantly greeted their father. The first question Nigel asked his mom was, "Does Dad know that he has cancer?"

"Yes, this morning Dr. Mehra told him in my presence. Your dad was not shocked and accepted the diagnosis with equanimity, partly I believe, because in the back of his mind, he expected that and was prepared. Of course, he was also still under some sedation and heavily bandaged."

Seeing her dad from the window of his room, Jessica remarked, "Dad's bandage looks like a *gele*, an African woman's head wrap that one sees in the pictures in National Geographic."

Amber agreed but remarked that his face appeared quite swollen.

He saw his family peering at him through the window and beckoned them to come in. The twins stood next to their dad's bed with forced smiles to make him feel good, but they were scared, wondering if their dad would ever look normal.

They asked him if he was in pain, and he slowly and with difficulty said, "It`ll soon get better."

The nurse said, "See, your dad's brain is functioning fine. One of the neurosurgery residents was visiting your dad earlier, asking questions, and was satisfied that your father's speech was normal and unaffected by the surgery. The swelling should go down by evening."

"What type of questions?" asked Nigel.

"Like his date of birth, present location, response to basic commands, such as moving his arms, legs, and indicating where he is experiencing pain," volunteered the nurse.

Later, the head nurse at the ICU told Cynthia that a physiotherapist would get Graham out of bed to assess his strength, balance, mobility, movement, and sensation.

"If that goes well, he will be moved to the neurosurgical nursing unit, most likely tomorrow afternoon. Then you all can spend more time with him."

Nigel said, "Dad, we`ll be out there if you need anything," a gesture that was acknowledged by a slight nod of Graham's head.

Satisfied and relieved but unable to spend more time with Graham, other than for him to know that he is not alone, Cynthia suggested taking the children to lunch at a Vietnamese restaurant she had passed by while driving to the hospital.

It was a small family-style restaurant, but the food was exceptionally fresh and tasty. The conversation was centered around Dad and plans to spend more time with him during his recovery.

Cynthia said, "Perhaps I'd need part-time help, so I can spend more time with Dad, and cut down some of our community obligations. But you know your dad. He gets fully engrossed in whatever he does—there are no part-time jobs for him."

Nigel wanted to know more about the company where the cancer tissue was donated and if he could help out in the summer when he is home.

Of course, they all quizzed Jessica about her new beau and asked when they would meet him.

Jessica smiled, skirted the issue, and remained non-committal.

Despite the friendly banter, the underlying thread of worry and concern about Dad was palpable. He had been the center of their lives while they were growing up, always dependable, strong, and tall, and here he was in the hospital, so vulnerable, weak, and helpless. The sisters did not want to know too much about the nature of his cancer or its prognosis, partly because they did not want to face the facts. All of this was happening too rapidly.

After lunch, they trooped back to the hospital to re-assure Dad that they were all there and saw the nurse taking his vitals and adjusting the network of tubes emanating from his body.

Graham smiled weakly and motioned for them to come in.

Seeing no objection from the staff nurse, they rushed in and asked inane questions about how he was doing, if he was in pain, and when he could come home, all the while hoping that he would say everything was fine because they were not prepared to deal with his disease.

Chapter 8

ENCOURAGING RESULTS

THOUGH IT WAS THE WEEKEND, CancerTech kept humming with the comings and goings of scientists, technicians, and physical plant supervisors maintaining vigil over all the delicate equipment and precise temperatures of dozens of freezers, cold rooms, water baths, and incubators.

Late afternoon on Sunday, Erica Hagen drove her battered and antique Volkswagen to the parking lot at CancerTech, exchanged a few words with the security guard, put on her lab coat, pulled out a new pair of gloves from a box marked 'Large', and turned off the UV light source. She opened the door to the room containing half a dozen incubators kept at 37°C, and went straight to the incubator marked 'D', where she had placed ten petri dishes in two stacks of five each, containing tumor cells from Patient X.

In several petri dishes, the red-colored solution containing ingredients on which plated cells survive, divide, and thrive that she had added some forty-eight hours prior had now turned pale yellow—a sure indicator of the voracious growth of tumor cells. And in some cases, they had clumped together to look like small spherical balls. Pleased that the tumor cells were viable, she carefully removed the yellow solution by suction, added a new batch of red solution, and put the stack of petri dishes back to the incubator.

The lead scientist involved in transplanting small bits of tumor tissues excised from Patient X into mice was less fortunate. One of the attendants from the animal quarters working on weekend shift had left a message that three of the five mice, which had bits of the excised tumor tissue transplanted into their brains, had died.

The dejected scientist hoped that the remaining two mice carrying the tumor cells would survive because there was very little tissue sample left to repeat the protocol to further propagate the tumor cells. He had a very uneasy night.

* * *

Two days after surgery, on Sunday afternoon, the physiotherapist helped Graham take a few steps and felt that he was strong enough to move to the neurological nursing unit. The swelling must have decreased because the intensity of his headache had considerably diminished, and he was proclaiming to be very hungry and thirsty, courtesy of the daily 16 mgs of glucocorticoid in his system. He was lucky to have no memory or other cognitive issues, in part because his tumor had been located on the frontal lobe and easily accessible without causing damage to normal brain tissue.

His new room was large with two beds, a large TV

jutting out of the wall, a few chairs, and Graham was the only occupant. He was still heavily bandaged but in less pain. The TV remote control was in his hand when the family came by. Everyone gave him a hug and asked how he was feeling.

With his face much less swollen, Graham looked more normal, a bit relaxed, and ready to go home. His speech was strong, and his hand gestures more fluid, though his choice of words to form sentences still needed a bit of effort.

The twins were sitting on two chairs on his right, and Nigel on a high stool on his left when Cynthia took out her cellphone and connected Graham to his father, who had been anxiously waiting to talk to his son since the surgery.

"Hi, Dad," said Graham haltingly. "I`m feeling better since my head is not hurting as much as yesterday… Yes, I`m on painkillers but want to reduce their use, in part because they cause constipation and I feel bloated… Yes, I still get exhausted easily. Hope to talk to you more when I`m home… Hi, Linda.… I'm doing my best to get better… Oh, good that you`ll be coming with Dad to visit us… Yes, how can I resist your pecan pie? … Thanks. Will see you soon… Love to Dad and you." He gave the phone back to Cynthia, who exchanged a few more sentences with Linda and then ended the call.

Nigel held his dad's hand and said, "Grandma Karen sent an email wishing you a speedy recovery and wants to come to see you as soon as Mom and you are comfortable enough to have visitors. Also, Aunt Adelaide said that she can hop over from Singapore to San Francisco on a nonstop flight and be here in fifteen hours."

Graham said, "I'll write to them once I'm home and allowed to use my computer," pointedly looking at Cynthia.

Realizing that Dad was getting tired, they got up, gave him short hugs, said bye, and promised to see him soon, except Nigel who said, I have to leave tonight for my chemistry final tomorrow, but I'll be back home when the school year is over in early June." Good luck," Graham said and gave him a thumbs-up.

Cynthia hugged each of her children, thanked them for being there for Dad and her, and gave Nigel her car key to transfer his backpack to Amber's car as she was going to drop him at the airport. Returning the keys, he again gave his mother a long and tighter hug before going back to join his sisters.

She stayed on into the late afternoon till Graham was taken for a CAT scan to ensure that the surgery had removed most of the mass and the swelling had subsided.

When Cynthia arrived home, she was alone in the house for the first time since the surgery while Graham was lying in the recovery room. She distracted herself by eating some leftovers, and browsing TV channels, and then decided to sleep in Jessica's old room rather than sleep alone in the master bedroom. She would be overwhelmed with memories.

Monday, June 1st, Graham woke up without a headache and felt much better. When Cynthia arrived, he was in a relaxed and jovial mood, with a less puffy face and more fluid body language.

Dr. Jabbar had come early in the morning to examine him. She had told him, "The CAT scan shows that most of the mass in your brain was successfully removed without any visible signs of any detectable mass in the brain. Additionally, brain swelling has substantially diminished, and there's no sign of hemorrhage or excessive bleeding."

"Thanks, that is good news."

"Yes, I`m glad. Dr. Mehra will probably see you later today or tomorrow to chart the post-recovery and treatment course. I'll order an MRI after six weeks from now to ensure that there are no hints of recurrence."

"Recurrence that soon?" inquired Graham, unduly alarmed.

"Unlikely, just to be on a safe side."

Barring any additional queries, she told him that he could go home Wednesday or Thursday, wished him good luck, turned around, and walked out of the room.

Graham had an unbecoming, prickly grey and white stubble on his face, making him look more disheveled than he felt. Cynthia gave him his electric razor and held the mirror, so he could slowly pare it. The smell of his aftershave lotion uncovered a sense of normalcy that she had so craved over the last few days.

She told him of the steady stream of emails from his sister, mother, and many friends enquiring about his operation and wishing him a speedy recovery. She asked him if he would like her to buy an English library chair with distressed leather, the type Russell Baker sat on while introducing Masterpiece Theatre, so he could have a comfortable chair to sit in, read, and even *pontificate*.

Graham smiled and said, "What's wrong with my current chair? And besides, I intend to get back to work as soon as I feel well and not sit around in some stuffy, comfortable chair."

Soon the nurse came to take his vitals, check his meds, clean the wound, put on a fresh dressing, and commented on how well the wound was healing. As a result of the reduced swelling of the brain, his bandage no longer looked like an African wrap.

Right after the nurse left, an aide wheeled in lunch

in a trolley and placed the foldable tray laden with un-inspiring food onto Graham's bed, across his body. To Cynthia's astonishment, Graham ate his food with gusto and even finished the dessert, which consisted of utterly unappetizing Jell-O.

Dr. Mehra came by to see him and appeared satisfied after gleaning the information on the chart hanging next to the bed.

He said, "Graham, your recovery is progressing very well. If you can go to the bathroom without the need for a catheter, I think you can be discharged by Thursday afternoon at the latest. I'll come around 11 a.m. tomorrow to discuss the follow-up treatment with you. Cynthia, will that work for you, since it would also be good for you to know about the treatment plan?"

"Of course. I'll make sure to be here at 11 a.m." replied Cynthia.

By sundown, Graham was beginning to feel weary after a full day of being awake and walking a couple of times to keep his circulation going.

Cynthia stopped to shop on the way home to stock up for his return and possibly a visit from Linda and Graham's dad. She talked to Nigel and the girls to give them an update, and they were all delighted to know that Dad would be coming home from the hospital.

The girls offered to help, but Cynthia said, "For now, I can manage but will call if I need help." She again chose to sleep in Jessica's room but woke up many times, thinking of the new adjustments and new reality that her husband was a cancer patient and the fear of living with the uncertainty of recurrence. She shuddered at the thought of life without Graham, curled up in a fetal position, and tried to blot these thoughts out of her mind.

Rakesh Mehra was woken up early when he heard his wife, Lakshmi, vomiting in the bathroom. He jumped out of bed to go to her aid, only to be rebuffed.

"Go back to bed. I am fine." A few minutes later, he heard the toilet flush and then the sound of water splashing in the sink, followed by Lakshmi returning to bed. Rakesh put his arms around her and heard her say, "I've missed my period for over two weeks, and now this. I might be pregnant." Startled to hear this news, he turned and sat up, but Lakshmi quickly added, "Let us go back to sleep. It is probably just another false alarm. It's not the first time I've missed my period. Maybe I'll buy one of those pregnancy kits."

While Lakshmi, after turning and tossing a few times in the bed, fell asleep, Rakesh got up, went to the kitchen, and heard the clock chime six times. As he turned on the kettle to make tea, his thoughts went back to his parents' visit some four years ago in Cambridge. They had vehemently opposed him marrying Lakshmi because she was divorced and not from the same region of the country as he came from. His mother had made a big fuss, and to show their displeasure, his parents had returned early to India. They had broken all contact with him, despite his many attempts at reconciliation. Perhaps the news of Lakshmi's pregnancy and the prospect of a grandchild would change their attitude. He was sure that if his parents were a bit more open-minded, they would have fallen in love with Lakshmi, just as he had.

She was still asleep when he was ready to leave for the hospital. He penned a short note, *"Hope you caught some sleep and are feeling better, Love,"* and left it on the kitchen counter.

As he was driving to the hospital, he started to think about how life would be with a child at home. While navigating the dense traffic going north, it struck him that while he was thinking of a new life, soon he would be seeing Graham, who was fighting a terminal disease, threatening to extinguish life.

Such was his state of mind when, an hour later, he sat on the opposite side of Graham's bed, across from Cynthia, and started the conversation by expressing his satisfaction with his recovery following surgery and with Dr. Jabbar's dexterity in the nearly complete excision of the tumorous mass.

"Graham, when you go home, take as much rest as you can, at least the first few days. Walk short distances but avoid any strenuous tasks. Report back immediately if you experience sustained headaches, increased pain around the incision site, vision changes, trouble with breathing, chest pains, speech impediment, or any seizure activity. Keep in touch with the lead neurosurgery registered nurse," Dr. Mehra instructed.

"In about six weeks, depending on how you're progressing, you`ll have another MRI as a standard follow-up and then we`ll start radiation." "How long is the treatment?" asked Cynthia.

"After planning sessions to make the 3D mask for radiation therapy treatment, which may take several hours, subsequent treatments will be much shorter, and you`ll be in and out of the radiation facility in about an hour for each session. Typically, treatments are given once a day, three to five days a week for five to seven weeks. The radiation beam is focused at the precise site from where the tumor was removed to avoid any radiation-induced toxicity in normal brain cells. This radiation therapy is an additional insurance against any tumor cells that may have escaped Dr. Jabbar's scalpel and suction tube."

"But you`d also mentioned chemotherapy?" inquired Cynthia.

"A week or so after finishing radiotherapy, you'll be treated with a chemotherapeutic drug called Temador that comes in capsules that can be taken orally. One capsule every day for five days then a break for twenty-three days for a total of six months. All along, we'll monitor your health through regular checkups every three months or more if needed and by MRI to detect any recurrence of the tumor," Dr. Mehra patiently explained to the attentive but worried couple.

Graham asked, "What are the side effects of radiation and chemotherapy?"

"They vary from patient to patient," replied Dr. Mehra. "But generally, there are few serious side effects. For instance, some patients may suffer from nausea, fatigue, hair loss at the site of the treatment, or headaches. Side effects from chemotherapy depend on the dose, but again, depending on the patient, they may additionally endure constipation, increased risk of infections, or general malaise.

"From the genomic analysis at CancerTech of your excised tumor tissue, we will soon find out if there is a mutation in a gene that helps the chemotherapy drug that I mentioned before to be more effective at lower doses that can mitigate the side effects."

"Can I continue to teach during radiation and chemotherapy?" Graham pleaded.

"Most likely, but we'll have to see how you respond to the treatment. Your age and good health will definitely favor a return to normal life," assured Dr. Mehra.

Cynthia added, "If radiation therapy started in the first week of July, by the time the school reopens in early September, darling, you'd have completed the whole radiation course and started chemotherapy capsules. Let us hope you have minimal side effects of these treatments."

She then asked Dr. Mehra, "Can the radiation and chemotherapy treatment be given simultaneously?"

"There is a big debate on this issue, and at meetings I hear about studies where simultaneous treatment may be more beneficial, but it's not a standard practice and will require changes in protocols for treatment, which can take some time. I'll, however, keep a close watch for any new developments in this area," replied Dr. Mehra.

They profusely thanked Dr. Mehra for all of his help and support and urged him to keep them informed of any progress in research at CancerTech. They also expressed their desire to meet Dr. Yacov Kaufman, who was keeping Graham's cancer cells alive in a petri dish and trying to find ways to kill them.

On Thursday, June 3rd, about a week after checking in for surgery, Graham was wheeled out of the hospital without the extra mass on his brain but with the knowledge and dread that the little dregs of the extraneous tissue that may have escaped the watchful eye of the surgeon had the potential to reincarnate back into the same unruly monster with an insatiable appetite to multiply.

Graham's homecoming was bittersweet.

There was a handmade poster of *WELCOME HOME, GRAHAM* from the neighbors taped onto the front door, and a giant card saying *SPEEDY RECOVERY* signed by hundreds of students and faculty from Menlo-Atherton High School, was prominently displayed in front of the fireplace. There were several bouquets of flowers on the kitchen counter, including two matching beautiful orchids sent by his sister and mother.

Graham did not like to be the center of attention and felt uncomfortable with all the displays of affection and concern for him. He felt that having cancer or its removal did not deserve such attention and instead took it as a sign of pity from others. He sat on his favorite chair with a big sigh while Cynthia turned on the kettle to make some tea.

The message light was flashing on the answering machine. Most of the messages, Cynthia said, were best wishes for surgery, and that she had not erased them in case he wanted to hear them.

"Later," said Graham with a dismissive motion of his hand.

There was also a stack of mail piled high on the credenza in the living room, with multi-colored envelopes likely containing Hallmark Get Well greeting cards.

He would have preferred a no-fuss, quiet return, in part because he knew that his disease-free status was only a temporary reprieve—his type of cancer often strikes back.

While she was busy making tea and putting some odds and ends away, Graham, exhausted from the drive home and trying to cope with all the information provided by Dr. Jabbar and Dr. Mehra, started to nod off, closed his eyes, and fell asleep in his chair.

A short time later, he woke up with a shudder at the tail end of a dream where he was running on an open road in a hospital gown with the IV drip bag on a stand trailing him while the doctors and staff in flowing blue, green, and white coats were running after him, furiously flapping their hands and shouting, "Stop! Stop!"

While dazed and trying to reconstruct his dream, he heard Cynthia ask if he wanted tea or if he was hungry, she could make soup or prepare some pasta dish.

"Maybe tea with a biscuit," Graham replied and then added, "I hope you took good notes from the conversations with the doctors because my mind was still in a blur from those painkillers."

"Yes, I did, and also, they gave us a packet with some of the same information and instructions."

"I`m feeling a bit feverish and have chills. I`d like to go to bed and lie down for a while," said Graham as he tried to get out of the chair but sat down again because his legs couldn't support him. She gave him the extra lift to stand up and helped him to the bedroom, where she propped up several pillows so his head with the bandage would be slightly elevated. She then covered him with a light blanket, dimmed the lights, and left the room.

Two hours later, Cynthia heard some movement in the bedroom and went in to see if he was ok.

He was exiting the bathroom and appeared less uncomfortable with a steadier gait. In a conspiratorial voice, he confided to her, "Darling, I never knew that constipation could be such a nuisance. Hopefully the laxatives will do their job."

He sat on a chair at the dining table and proclaimed that he was hungry, ravenously hungry, and that his bandaged head was not hurting.

She took out a container of pappardelle pasta, heated it, added ragù Bolognese sauce, and prepared a salad of sliced tomatoes, cucumbers, and diced onions.

Graham, cautious not to overdo it, still managed to have a few extra servings, all along saying how good the home-cooked food was after the hospital food.

She mused, "That is hardly a compliment."

"Come on. You know what I meant," retorted Graham.

After talking a bit more about recovery in the coming days and possible visits of the family members, Graham said, "Let me take the plethora of pills given to me by the neurology nurse, and hopefully I will have a good sleep. Maybe I should get one of those pill organizers that your mom used to have."

Even though they shared a queen-size bed, she felt that Graham, with his bandage might find it easier to have the whole bed to himself, but she also worried that if he needed help to go to the bathroom at night or any other help, she would be too far away if she slept in Jessica's room. Despite his initial protest, she decided to bring in the rollaway bed from the garage. After readjusting some furniture, she unfolded it next to the master bed.

"It is only temporary. I'll be fine."

This indeed was a good plan because Graham needed help at night to go to the bathroom and refill the water carafe to quench his thirst, a consequence of all that medication.

Friday, June 4th was an overcast day, and Cynthia was up early with a stiff back while the recovering patient was still in deep slumber. She heard pinging noises on the computer, went to the study, and read several messages from the girls, Nigel, Grandpa David, Adelaide, and the last one was from his mother, asking to speak with him when he is able.

Around 10 a.m., the nurse from the hospital called to check how Graham was doing and inquired if someone from her staff should come to change the bandages on his head.

Cynthia gave her an update and said that the hospital had provided her all the required materials and that she could change the bandage herself. Satisfied, the nurse again reiterated that if they needed any help, they should not hesitate to call.

After he woke up, she helped him get ready, making sure that his wound remained dry during a shower. Afterwards, she changed the bandage on the rapidly healing wound, though it was still quite raw and unseemly in its appearance.

"I am sure that in a few days the wound will completely heal, and you`ll only need to don a cap to protect it from the sun." "And not scare the onlookers," added Graham for good measure.

During the late breakfast, they fell into their old routine, him reading the newspaper and her solving the crossword puzzle.

Graham observed, "Everything looks so surreally normal—a middle-aged couple, comfortable in each other's company, enjoying a leisurely breakfast. But the reality is that I'm merely in remission, marking time until cancer rears its ugly head again."

"We`ve to enjoy every day and keep the monster at bay as long as you can. No harm in being an optimist," Cynthia said, cheerfully adding, "Got this eight-letter word…ELEVATOR."

He went back to reading the newspaper and said, "Honey, I`m still having trouble with my vision. It's blurry. Perhaps I need new prescription glasses. Can you please pick up a pair of those cheap reading glasses from the pharmacy when you next go shopping? My current glasses are +125, so maybe I should try +150."

"OK," Cynthia said and then continued, "Maybe next time we`re at the hospital, we should set up an appointment with the optometrist in the eye clinic to get a proper eye exam."

"What's wrong with Lens Crafters? They are cheap, need no appointment, and are in the shopping mall," replied Graham.

This mundane conversation that makes daily life tedious is exactly what they were enjoying after days and days of dealing with the grimness of his disease.

After the sumptuous breakfast, Graham sprawled out on the sofa in the living room with his bandaged head comfortably resting on a bank of cushions and started to read some of the instructions given to them before his discharge from the hospital. But he was unable to focus, so he set them aside and closed his eyes.

He woke up while the phone was ringing, and not seeing Cynthia around, picked it up and uttered a sleepy hello. "Graham, my boy, how are you feeling?" The voice at the other end was that of his father.

"Ok, Dad. Sorry. I fell asleep after breakfast. Just a minute, Dad. Let me get a drink because my mouth is so dry from the meds I'm taking."

"No problem. I'll wait," said his dad.

While in the kitchen, he saw a note on the counter from Cynthia that she went out to run some quick errands and would be back soon. After a brief pause, he picked up the phone again and said, "Sorry, Dad."

"I just wanted to say hello and see how you're doing upon returning home from the hospital. Also, I wanted to let you know that Linda and I are planning to come tomorrow midday and spend Saturday and Sunday with you. Will that be, ok?" Graham's father asked, then inquired, "Is Cynthia home?"

"She has momentarily stepped out and will be back soon. But, Dad, I get tired easily, nap and sleep a lot, and won't be good company." "We just want to see you, won't interfere with your recovery, and may be able to lend a hand to Cynthia, who alone has largely been caring for you during your hospitalization," urged his dad.

Just then, Cynthia arrived from the garage with some grocery bags, put them on the kitchen counter, and upon Graham's urging, took the phone and said, "Hi, Grandpa, how're you doing?"

"Ok, but my heart and mind are in Palo Alto. Linda and I were thinking of coming down this weekend to see Graham."

"Of course, Grandpa, come anytime you want, but I warn you that Graham tires easily and takes frequent naps. You should stay with us." "Thanks darling, but we`ll stay at the Hyatt. We don't want to be in your way, especially when Graham is recuperating. Cynthia, you also need time to recover. Let Linda and me help with shopping or other needs while you take care of him," proposed his father. "Thanks for the offer. I may take you up on that. When will you arrive?"

"We plan to arrive tomorrow around 2 p.m. or so, rent a car, check in, and probably be at your place around 5 p.m." "Great, see you tomorrow, Grandpa, and love to Linda."

She put away the groceries and handed Graham a blue-colored weekly pill organizer and a pair of black rimmed +150 reading glasses, which he immediately tried and said, "much better."

Late in the afternoon, Amber and Jessica called to say hi and welcome home to their dad. They wanted to come by to say hello but learning that Linda and Grandpa would be in town, they agreed to instead come on Sunday and have lunch together.

Nigel called after dinner and inquired about Dad, but he was already in bed. His mom told him that grandpa and Linda were coming the next day to see Dad.

"Shoot, I have at least another ten days in college to get my degree. The original plan was for all of you to come for my graduation on June 19th, but now Dad can't really fly, and it would be a great strain on him to drive this long distance, so maybe Amber, Jessica, Linda, and Grandpa could come."

"That sounds like a good plan."

I'll talk to Grandpa tomorrow when he is at your place. Say hi to Dad. Love you, Mom," said Nigel in an uncharacteristically affectionate tone.

Graham was steadily gaining strength, could walk without any assistance, and felt no pain around the incision site, except for itchiness around the wound. Most importantly he had respite from the persistent, dull headache and was generally feeling less fatigued.

By the time Linda and his father came around 5:30 p.m., however, he was beginning to tire and again experience the beginnings of that tightening around his bandaged head, which he knew would become a full-blown headache.

He got up from the chair, greeted Linda with a big hug and kisses on each cheek, and said, "You look so good. Thank you for coming." Then he gave his dad a bear hug, sat down on the nearest chair, and admiringly said, "Dad, looks like you're working out. I can feel your biceps."

"Oh no, you're just weak from surgery. Otherwise, you could squeeze me like a lemon," chuckled his dad and added, "Plus you've been on hospital chow. We need to fatten you up."

"I agree. Brain surgery is too drastic a treatment to try to lose weight," said Graham with a mischievous smile. Cynthia offered to make some dinner, but Linda and David said firmly, "We can fend for ourselves."

"You've been so busy in the last weeks, and the last thing we want is to encumber you with more work. Honey, you take care of your husband, and don't worry about us. We'll come tomorrow and chat more," said a very friendly and solicitous Linda.

"The girls are coming tomorrow around noon, so

why don't you also come then. I'll whip up some lunch," said Cynthia.

"We will pick up lunch from The Village Cheese House, one of Graham's favorites," said his father. He then asked, "Are there any dietary restrictions for Graham?" "Not that anyone mentioned," replied Cynthia.

"Please, Dad, no Jell-O," said Graham with a twinkle in his eye.

She was pleased to hear that her husband's sense of humor had not deserted him.

Sunday morning, Graham woke up from a long sleep without any pharmaceutical aid but was very stiff, especially his neck, probably because he had lain in the same position for a long time, trying to protect his bandaged head. He felt less tightening around his head, indicative of less swelling, and asked Cynthia to change the bandage after his shower. Except for a small blood smear on the bandage, healing in the main was progressing as expected.

To reduce itching, the nurse had suggested applying some ointment, which Cynthia did, and bandaged the wound like a pro.

"I'm sure that you`re well taken care of," said his mother.

"Oh, yes, I am being very well cared for, and Cynthia has been an angel. Linda and Dad are here and will soon come for lunch along with Amber and Jessica."

"Graham, you have just undergone a big surgery, so don't exhaust yourself," implored his mother. "Yes, I`m taking it very easy. I don't have much energy and tire easily, not uncommon, for the type of surgery I went through. The neuro-oncologist has told me that it`ll take four to six weeks to fully recover before starting radiotherapy. Of course, we'll be delighted to see you," said Graham and then his mother told him her plans.

"What? In another two weeks, around Nigel's graduation? Oh, Mom, Nigel will be thrilled, and I should be well into my recovery by then, but let me pass the phone to Cynthia since she has all the dates on the calendar and is a lot more organized. Say hi to Scotty." He then passed the phone to Cynthia, who was watering the indoor plants.

She put down the watering can, dried her hands, took the phone, and cheerfully said, "Hi, Grandma, how is Greece? Is it already getting hot?"

"Not in Crete compared to Athens. I`m so glad that Graham is recovering and seems to be in good spirits."

"He tires easily, which is not surprising, considering what he went through," responded Cynthia.

"From Nigel's email, I gather that the neurosurgeon did a great job removing vast amounts of the cancerous tissue. He mentioned that some of the excised tumor tissue was sent to a biotech company for drug testing. I am very curious about the plans of this company. If it is nearby, maybe I can visit them when I come to Palo Alto in a few weeks," suggested Grandma Karen.

"The company is called CancerTech and is located in Foster City, about half an hour's drive from our place," said Cynthia.

"Also, I wanted to check with you about combining my plans to visit Graham with attending Nigel's graduation. Tentatively, I am planning to arrive late evening in San Francisco on Tuesday the 15th, spend the 16th and 17th with Graham and you, and then leave the afternoon of the 18th for Los Angeles to attend the graduation ceremony on the 19th. I can fly back to Greece the following Sunday from Los Angeles. You know, Scotty's arthritis is pretty bad, and despite having a good housekeeper, I know he needs me for simple tasks of even changing his clothes."

"Sorry to hear about Scotty's advanced arthritis. Of course, we fully understand your need to get back soon to Greece to be near him."

"Thanks. Some days the flare-up of his arthritis is excruciatingly painful. By the way, I talked earlier to Adelaide, and she`s also coming to see Graham and attend Nigel's graduation. She wanted to coordinate with my visit and is planning to arrive on June 16th in the morning. I'm sure she will call you once I get off the phone," said Graham's mother.

"That's great. Graham and I would be delighted if Adelaide and you would stay with us during your visit," entreated Cynthia.

"Thanks, Cynthia, but with jet lag, waking up at odd hours, and roaming in the kitchen to make tea in the wee hours of the morning, we`re not exactly the type of guests you need while Graham is recuperating from such a major surgery. I talked to David earlier, and he said that staying at the Hyatt is a good compromise for Linda and him, so Adelaide and I can also stay there when we come."

After some additional chit-chat about the girls, a possible visit from Jessica and her new boyfriend, to England and Europe, Cynthia said good-bye and put down the phone.

It immediately rang again, and it was Adelaide confirming the plans laid out earlier by her mom.

At noon sharp on Sunday, the doorbell rang, and as Cynthia opened the front door, in came Linda and Graham's dad carrying two large paper bags embossed with the logo of The Village Cheese House. They placed them on the kitchen counter.

Well-shaven, wearing an ironed green Polo shirt, crisp white shorts, and looking perfectly normal, except for the bandage on his head, Graham put down his newspaper, got up, and exchanged greetings with Linda and his dad, despite their protests that he should remain in his chair.

"You're looking a lot better than when we saw you yesterday," said his father.

"Yes, the magic of good sleep and relief from constipation," said Graham, pointing to his stomach.

The front door opened, and Amber and Jessica walked in with a gift bag and placed it on the side table next to where their dad had been sitting.

As he always did, Graham's father put his arms around his granddaughters, proclaimed them to be the most beautiful princesses, and proceeded to give each one a kiss on their cheeks. The girls then exchanged hugs and kisses with Linda and their dad, put their big handbags down on the floor, and asked their mom if she needed any help in the kitchen.

After lunch, Graham wanted to know what was in the gift bag. Amber took it out and removed the wrapping paper. It was a single-tone blue cap with Golden State Warriors written in yellow letters and an image of a portion of the iconic Golden Gate Bridge.

"Dad, when the bandage is removed, you will need to protect the wound before it is completely healed. Amber and I thought that you may like to wear the cap of your favorite team, the Golden State Warriors," said Jessica.

"Oh, thanks, honey, that is so thoughtful," Graham said and took his daughters in his arms and planted a kiss on each of their foreheads.

The family talked about Nigel's graduation and Graham's inability to be at the ceremony, but he left the door open by saying, "It's still two weeks away. Maybe I'll be well enough to go by car but would need permission from my neuro-oncologist."

Linda firmly said, "Look, you all should be at Nigel's graduation, especially Cynthia, so I'll stay with Graham if needed during that time.

No ifs, ands, or buts. End of discussion."

By late afternoon and early evening, Graham again succumbed to the feeling of being very tired and started to doze off in his chair.

Grandpa David offered to take his granddaughters to dinner at the Jing Jang Szechwan restaurant on Emerson Street and promised to order their favorite Dan-Dan noodles, the best in the world. Cynthia stayed back while they all left around 6 p.m.

Graham woke up an hour later, had a quick bite of some of the leftovers, and retired to the bedroom.

While cleaning up, Cynthia was again surprised and relieved at how normal the day had been, with good food, laughs, light conversation, and planning for the graduation and upcoming visits with Graham's sister and mother. His disease was not the focus of conversations and had almost been forgotten.

Just like a thick cloud cover hiding the burning sun.

Chapter **9**

NEW RESEARCH STRATEGIES

AFTER SOME TECHNICAL AND ADMIN-
ISTRATIVE SNAGS several days after Graham's surgery, an arrangement was executed
with a laboratory at Stanford University Medical School
to receive bits of the excised tumor tissue to determine
the sequence of its genome. Dr. Mehra had agreed to
coordinate the project since he'd spent nearly a year in
2002 / 2003 as a neuro-oncology fellow in the same laboratory. Samples had also been sent to the Affymetrix
service labs for quantification of messenger RNAs, the
tell-tale signs of what novel protein may be made in the
cancer cells.

Now they had to wait, one of the hardest parts of
being a scientist.

Another week passed before Dr. Mehra received the
preliminary data from genomic sequence analysis done
at Stanford. After a quick survey of the data, he forwarded it to Yacov with a cryptic note:

loss of some chromosomes and gain of others that had previously been reported in other patients with GBM.

MGMT gene altered; may not make the MGMT protein, which would have favorable consequences for the treatment with chemotherapy.

Yacov shot back an equally cryptic email.

Thx, lunch on Wednesday at noon?

How about at 12:15? Will be wrapping up a mtg at noon, Rakesh replied.

On June 9th, Yacov and Rakesh met at a small soup and salad place not far from CancerTech to talk about strategy and new ideas for finding treatments to extend the life of patients with GBM.

Before they delved into the diagnosis and prognosis of Graham's disease, Rakesh, barely able to contain himself, announced, "Lakshmi is pregnant. We are going to be parents."

"Mazel tov," said Yacov, shaking his hand and asking, "When is the baby due?"

"In early March."

"How is Lakshmi doing?"

"OK, except for the morning sickness. But she is very tough. I just have to get used to a whole new situation," replied Rakesh.

"Good she is tough. I remember when Nurit was pregnant with our oldest boy, Yinon, who is now twenty-four and doing his doctorate at UC Los Angeles. We had just moved from Toronto to Los Angeles. She was miserable for three to four months. Luckily her mother came over from Israel to help, and that was a godsend," recalled Yacov. "Do you`ve family who can help?"

"Yes and no. But that is a long story for another day," said Rakesh, whose demeanor changed from ebullience to sadness.

After a brief and awkward pause when both were silent, Yacov started to recount the details of how the excised tumor tissue was being used.

He repeatedly queried Rakesh on the near-certain propensity of recurrence, the most troubling and vexing aspect of this disease.

Rakesh reminded his friend, "It was during your talk at Stanford in the fall of 2002 that I first became aware of the fact that tumor cells in GBM may actually be stem cells capable of immortality, ruthless growth, and shepherding the recurrence of the tumor. Theoretically, even if the surgeon removes 99.999% of the tumor, the remaining few tumor cells will divide mercilessly to form a new one. It was not long after your talk at a mini symposium on brain tumors that I heard a famous surgeon at his plenary talk proclaim that he had operated on maybe a thousand patients with GBM and there was rarely a survivor after eighteen months. My first impression was that he was a terrible surgeon. But this admission lays bare the facts of the course and outcome of this unrelenting disease that marches on despite the best efforts of modern medicine."

"You have a good memory." Yacov then urged Rakesh to try the gazpacho, the signature dish of the restaurant.

As soon as the waiter left, an ebullient Yacov said, "Rakesh, I am convinced, if we can stop the proliferation of stem cells, we can checkmate this tumor in its tracks." After a brief pause, he resumed the conversation and delved into the possible origins of GBM and whether it could be detected without invasive procedures.

Rakesh said, "I too have been thinking a lot about early diagnosis and am planning to submit a grant proposal in collaboration with a bioengineer at Stanford in this area."

Yacov, who had hardly touched his soup, except nibbling on the warm sourdough bread, reflected, "In the last fifty years or so, cancer, all kinds of cancers, have had the same three treatments: surgery, chemotherapy, and radiation. We've to start thinking of new modalities to treat it." That's why I am so excited about your ideas for going after the stem cells that may not be affected by any of the current therapeutic approaches," said Rakesh.

Now busily eating his soup from the bowl, Yacov said, "Oh, this is really a good soup, especially on an unusually warm day. Today almost feels like Santa Ana. We have them in Israel, and we call them *Khamsin*, which in Arabic means fifty, a period of fifty days in spring or autumn when dry, hot, sandy local winds blow with vengeance. Some historians have speculated that it was these fierce winds that parted the Red Sea for Moses to cross from Egypt to the land of Canaan."

Rakesh said, "In Punjab, where I grew up, we also had similar days, and we call them Andheri, probably an Urdu word meaning darkness. All I remember is running into the house, closing all the windows, doors, and bringing in all the hanging laundry to prevent it from being sullied in the massive dust storm. Oh, it was a mess for a few hours outside, and then it was gone."

Getting back to the main topic, Yacov inquired if a formal arrangement could be established between Morton Hospital and CancerTech to obtain a steady stream of excised tumor tissue from patients with brain tumors.

"I've been thinking about it as well and have talked to the chair of the surgery department, and he was very supportive. I`ll raise the issue again and see what is needed to formalize the arrangement."

"CancerTech has an arrangement with Stanford Medical School to obtain breast cancer tissue, we can use that as a template for an agreement with your hospital. I`ll ask our external relationship group to initiate the process." Yacov then went back to busily devouring the contents in his salad bowl.

Just as he was ordering coffee, someone tapped him on his back and said, "Hope you had gazpacho, best on the peninsula."

He turned back and said, "Bill, how are you? Haven't seen you for a while."

"I was very busy signing the deal on our breast cancer program with the Pharma company, whose Chief Scientific Officer you introduced me to at the ASCO meeting in Chicago. They loved your presentation, and hopefully we`ll soon announce the deal since the board approved it last Friday. Yacov, I've been meaning to come by and talk to you about some of the details of the agreement. I`ll ask Cindy to set up a time to chat."

Yacov then introduced Rakesh to Bill as the neuro-oncologist from Morton Hospital getting involved in his GBM program.

Bill warmly shook Rakesh's hand and said, "Great. I`m afraid that our focus may shift more to breast cancer after the deal is announced, but we`ll continue to support the GBM program. In fact, I just approved Yacov's request for additional funds."

Before Yacov could say thanks, Bill was already extending his hand to another acquaintance to say hello and had moved away from their table. During coffee, they talked about their families and agreed to go out for dinner together with their spouses.

Back in his office, Erica knocked cheerfully at the door and excitedly asked Yacov to come to the tissue culture room to see the first successful cells growing from the tumor tissue of Patient X.

* * *

Over the few weeks following his surgery, Graham steadily improved, regained his strength, appetite, and even took short walks around his neighborhood. But for Cynthia, it was not the recovery but fear of recurrence that began to haunt her.

As a graduation gift for Nigel, his parents decided to buy him an Apple MacBook since his current computer was quite old and unreliable.

Though Nigel was a good student, about to finish his college degree in four years, his mom was concerned that he had no future plans. Graham was much less worried because, after his undergraduate studies at Princeton, he, too, had no concrete plans, though he had met Cynthia and his future revolved around her.

It had taken some cajoling from Graham, but Cynthia had agreed to go to Nigel's graduation and let Linda stay behind to be around him if he needed any help.

His mother and sister came to see Graham on the afternoon of Wednesday, June 16th - and were very pleased to see him now nearly normal, except for the Golden State Warriors cap covering the remnants of his surgery.

He had jumped out of his chair to first give his mom and then his sister a big hug and kisses. He had not seen Adelaide for some time and said, "Adelaide, you look younger than the last time I saw you, and your hair is much shorter."

"Singapore is nearly always hot, so best to keep my hair short," Adelaide replied then added, "and you look very good, after what you've gone through."

His mother also said, "I, too, am relieved to see that you're recovering so well, though you've lost some weight."

"My medication has been substantially reduced, and soon I'll be able to do some physical exercise but am not yet allowed to drive or fly."

He volunteered to make tea, and Adelaide followed him to the kitchen and said, "How about we make real English tea?"

Graham rummaged through the pantry and came back with a box of Darjeeling tea that had an expiration date of March 2004. They looked at each other, shrugged their shoulders, and went ahead to use the contents of the box.

While the kettle was turned on to boil water, he also boiled some milk and said, "If only we had some scones and cream." "You know, we have proper English tea at several hotels in Singapore," said Adelaide tongue- in- cheek.

"Speaking of Singapore, how is Roger and his new business venture? Does he miss the hustle and bustle of Botswana?"

"Roger had been shuttling between Johannesburg and Gaborone, the capital, and it just became increasingly unsafe, especially in South Africa, where he was spending more and more time. I had mentioned to Dad and you about the opportunities in investment firms in Hong Kong or Singapore. I know you favored Hong Kong because of its vibrancy, but with China's increasing meddling in Hong Kong's politics, we felt Singapore would be a safer bet. It turned out to be a good decision."

In the meantime, his mother and Cynthia were sitting on a sofa, chatting about the grandkids and Karen's shuttling back and forth between Crete and the country home in Essex.

Adelaide carried the tray with tea, and her brother took a plate of chocolate chip cookies, placing them on the table in front of the sofa. Cynthia, pouring the tea through a strainer, commented, "Real English tea with hot milk."

"Of course. Not those ubiquitous tea bags. This is real Darjeeling tea," said Adelaide with a straight face.

Taking the teacup from her daughter, Grandma Karen said, "Lovely. I have a slight preference for Darjeeling tea since one of my maternal uncles was a manager of a tea plantation in Bengal, India, and always spoke about great Indian teas and their comparative aromas. Uncle Henry didn't like the way we make tea in England. He especially disliked the small bags swimming in hot water. He would animatedly describe how proper Indian tea is brewed."

Graham dismissively said, "That's too much work for Americans." After a pause, he asked his mother about Scott's health.

"Not very good. His arthritis is getting progressively worse. His rheumatologist in England wants him to try some of the new biologics that just got approved, but Scott wants to wait to see if they are safe."

Adelaide, who had only vague memories of her time in Palo Alto, said to Cynthia, "Driving from the airport to the hotel, I couldn't believe the dense traffic and number of new buildings and giant shopping centers."

She quickly added, "But compared to Singapore with its tropical environment and perpetual hot weather, I`m very happy to be in cooler Palo Alto."

Cynthia, who had not seen Graham's mother for nearly two years, thought that she looked a bit more gaunt and tired, perhaps due to the long flight and jet lag. She had always been awestruck by the dynamism and good looks of Karen Bunker and thought that Adelaide was her spitting image.

Like her mother, Adelaide was tall, well proportioned, with a long neck, smooth skin, peach complexion, light blue eyes, and dark hair. Adelaide's hair was just cropped shorter than her mother's neck-length hair. By any standard, Adelaide was a very attractive woman and had impeccable manners.

Graham's mother had brought a jar of his favorite native Greek black olives, now being shared by all, along with tea and cookies.

Around 6:30 p.m., Cynthia noticed that Graham's mom was trying to stifle yawns, so she suggested an early supper.

"I`m not sure if I can eat anything yet. I'm just happy to be here with Graham, Adelaide, and you," said Karen.

"But you will be up at 3 a.m., with pangs of hunger. I'll pack a few sandwiches. You could have easily stayed here with all the space since the kids have left," said Cynthia.

"Yes, you`re right, but we worried having house guests would add to your burden," said Graham's mother. "But you are family," responded Cynthia.

Graham's mother then put her arms around her and said, "Darling, I know that. We just didn't want to be an additional bother."

Cynthia heated some vegetable soup that she had bought earlier and, with Adelaide's help, set the table while Graham chatted with his mother about chemo and radiation therapy.

Around 8 p.m., pleading long travel and fatigue, both Adelaide and her mother decided to leave and drove to their hotel.

The next day, which was now nearly three weeks after his surgery, Adelaide, her mother, and Cynthia took Graham for a short ride but decided to have lunch at home because he was not yet comfortable in a room full of strangers and loud noises.

In the afternoon while he rested, Cynthia took Adelaide and Karen to visit CancerTech. Since Yacov Kaufman was out of town, it was Erica Hagen who gave them the tour of the facility. She told them about their efforts to grow cells from tumor tissue excised from Graham's brain.

Graham's mother said, "I was a chemist and the chief scientist in the oncology division at British Pharma before it was sold to a major pharmaceutical company based in Basel. For a while, we had a large lab in Menlo Park where we synthesized novel chemotherapeutic entities. We also experimented on combination therapies. Some of the drugs we synthesized, like the derivatives of Carboplatin, are still in use to treat certain leukemias."

Erica warmed up to Graham's mother and quickly told her of the plans that Dr. Kaufman and Dr. Mehra had with the tumor samples obtained from Graham's brain in their attempt to find drugs to prevent the growth of the tumor cells.

They chatted for a few more minutes before Graham's mother realized that both Adelaide and Cynthia were anxiously looking at their watches.

She said to Erica, "Thanks for the tour. Maybe next time I'll have an opportunity to meet Dr. Kaufman."

They stopped on the way back for some groceries so Linda would not need to do any shopping during her stay with Graham.

On Friday afternoon, after dropping Linda at the house in Palo Alto, Graham's father drove Cynthia, Adelaide, and Karen to the airport in San Francisco, where they were joined by his two granddaughters for a flight to Los Angeles.

The graduation was an impressive ceremony held the next day where 382 degrees were awarded and the famous anchorman, Walter Cronkite, gave the commencement speech. Cynthia choked up when Nigel Bunker's name was called, largely because Graham, who was so close to his son, was not in attendance. Everyone in the family was cognizant of Graham's absence, but no one wanted Nigel to feel it, so they all kept a very upbeat mood.

Later that night, they celebrated with a Mexican botano platter with Nigel's friends and some of his teachers. He introduced his family to Dr. Elaine Adams, who was from Australia, under whose supervision he had been doing research on the effects of environmental pollutants on the coral reefs.

Both sisters tried hard to find out about Nigel's girlfriends from his friends, especially details about a girl called Miranda whose name he had mentioned, but they had little success.

Cynthia gave Nigel his gift. His eyes lit up when he saw the new MacBook, and he gave her a big kiss and lamented, "I really missed Dad at my graduation ceremony."

Over the next few weeks, Graham continued to regain strength, slept normal hours, was less fatigued, and extended his walks to nearly an hour at a stretch. He also started to organize hundreds of family pictures taken during their trips and family gatherings. This was a huge task since color slides had to be first converted into prints. Going through old family pictures gave Graham a chance to reminisce and remember wonderful moments in his life, which gave him further strength to overcome his disease. There were so many wonderful things in life to live and fight for. *"I won't let my family down."*

* * *

Peering through the microscope, Yacov could see a beautiful layer of cells whose innocence belie their deadly attribute of relentless growth. It was too early to know if they were immortal, but the important step of getting tumor cells from Patient X appeared to have met success.

"Wow." Without lifting his eyes away from the microscope, he said, "Looks like the tumor cells from Patient X can be grown in a petri dish, so we may be able to generate large quantities of cells to do subsequent drug testing."

Erica was more circumspect because it had only been six weeks, and she needed more cell divisions to be sure that they were truly immortal and would continue to divide, mimicking the original brain tumor.

At their weekly group meeting on Wednesday afternoons, the technician who had injected the tumor cells from Patient X under the skin of two mice, one of which had died due to inadvertent flooding in the cage from a leaky water bottle, said, "Last evening before leaving the animal quarters, I checked the mouse cage with the surviving mouse and could feel a mass developing at the site of the injection. It's early but promising. I`ll keep an eye on this special mouse before any further misfortune befalls it."

The scientists who had transplanted tumor cells and tumor tissue directly into the brain of several mice nearly a month prior had little to report other than to wait. They wished that CancerTech had a small MRI machine to identify any growing mass, just as had been used to detect the mass in the brain of Patient X some two months ago. It was an expensive piece of equipment and unlikely to be available to the scientists at CancerTech, they just had to wait until the transplanted mice showed enlarged heads, indicating the presence of a large mass. This wait was nerve-racking and disconcerting because if the experiment failed, they had no more available cancerous tissue from Patient X allotted to them.

"Three nude mice, see how they run..." The younger of the two scientists involved in the experiment chuckled, presumably referring to the immunodeficient status of the injected mice, which have no hair on their skin.

Sometimes Dr. Mehra attended the group meetings by telephone, and during one such conference call, he said, "The results from the more complete draft of the genomic sequencing data reconfirm and support the conclusions of the pathology report that Patient X has grade IV Glioma (GBM). The previous results on *MGMT* are in doubt and will have to await confirmation from the results to be delivered by Genechip, an Affymetrix subsidiary, later in the week."

"I'm a bit disappointed because if the product of this gene is not functional, it improves the chances of more successful chemotherapy with Temodar." Sensing that some of the scientists and staff in the conference room were confused by why inactivity of the *MGMT* gene should influence chemotherapy, he gave a lengthy scientific explanation. "About 30% of patients with GBM have the product of this gene nonfunctional, which is what we are hoping for our Patient X."

Anticipating no additional questions, Yacov ended the meeting by saying, "Keep up the good work. See you next week. Let me know of any critical developments as soon as they happen."

Mid-July brought the results from Genechip in a FedEx envelope containing a single flash drive with a notation, Patient X. Presumably, the entire data regarding the amounts of messenger RNAs, the entity that makes all the proteins in a cell from the tumor samples of Patient X, was encrypted in this three-inch-long flash drive.

The envelope marked 'Urgent' was addressed to Dr. Yacov Kaufman and was opened by his administrative assistant. There was a disclaimer that *the patient's data was compared to brain data obtained from non-diseased people but not to the normal brain cells from the patient, so some apparent changes may be due to individual variation rather than specific for the tumor cells of Patient X.*

Since Yacov was on a family vacation in the Sierras, the admin was uncertain as to the importance of the package, and in any case, it was hard to reach him in the remote mountains. She asked some of the senior colleagues working with him, but no one knew about it, and she was hesitant to ask Dr. Mehra, even though he was now spending a lot of time with him, mostly on the phone. She put the FedEx packet into her top desk drawer.

Fortunately, Yacov called a day later to check if all was well in his absence and if there was anything that he should know.

The admin affirmed everything was fine and asked about his vacation and if his kids were enjoying hiking. "Great, I'm thrilled that all of you are having a good time. It's not easy to keep two teenagers happy." Before saying goodbye, she told him about the FedEx packet, and immediately his tone changed.

"When did it arrive? Why didn't you call me right away? Please check if Nick, head of our bioinformatics program, is available."

She quickly apologized, and after placing him on hold, she was able to get Nick on the line right away. She transferred his call to Nick's office line. "Thanks, Nick, for taking my call. I`m sorry to interrupt your meeting with the staff, but it's kind of important to enlist your help in deconvoluting the data we`ve just received from Genechip regarding a patient. We`re in a time crunch."

Aren't we all?" joked Nick.

"I know, but this is really urgent. Will you be able to work on it in the coming days so when I`m back, we can go over the results and design new experimental strategies if warranted?" urged Yacov.

"I'll try, do my best, but my group is up to its neck in dealing with the data on breast cancer patients sent to us by our collaborators at the University of North Carolina. When are you back?" inquired Nick.

"Presently we`re planning to be back by the end of the month. Hopefully, that gives you enough time?"

"Have your admin deliver to us the flash drive sent by Genechip. As I said, we`ll do our best to mine the data. Enjoy your vacation and say hi to Nurith," proffered Nick, who then transferred the phone back to the admin.

Yacov gave her explicit instructions on how to handle

the information.

"Ok. I'll personally deliver the package with the flash drive to Dr. Ostrove," and immediately left her office, climbed the staircase to find Dr. Ostrove's office on the second floor.

* * *

As in the past, Cynthia had driven her husband to his latest appointment with Dr. Mehra and joined him during the conversation on July 6th. The doctor had been very pleased with his recovery and decided that Graham was ready to start radiotherapy. He'd ordered another MRI to ensure that there were minuscule or no traces of tumor tissue at the site of the surgery.

He next scheduled the Bunkers to meet the radiologist, who took them through the details of the procedure of using Intensity Modulated Radiotherapy (IMRT) to kill any residual tumor cells that may have escaped Dr. Jabbar's scalpel. The radiologist informed them that this type of treatment required making three- dimensional images of the brain to accurately locate the area from which the tumor had been removed and pinpoint radiotherapy to that area.

"Our whole goal is to destroy any remaining cancer cells and minimize the killing of any normal brain cells. "he added, "We'll have a multidisciplinary team of specialists that will include Dr. Mehra, myself, a radiographer, a medical physicist, and a technologist to ensure the best treatment for you. We'll make a stereotactic mask around your head, which will ensure that the radiation beam is focused precisely on the site of surgery."

"How do you make this mask?" asked Cynthia.

"The therapist will place a warm, wet sheet of plastic mesh over your face while you are lying on the table, and then shape it to fit around your head. This process of simulation will also require two tattoos the size of a pinhead on either side of your head just above the ears. These tattoos will be used as guides to position you correctly each day of your treatment. Since the mask is made up of plastic mesh, there`re many holes in it to allow normal breathing. You`ll get treatment with radiation five times a week for about five to six weeks, and each visit will take no more than an hour or so." the radiologist explained. "Isn't radiation treatment dangerous?" inquired Graham.

"Yes, you`re right, but the whole idea is to give focused radiation to the minimum region, in your case the beam focused around the area from where the tumor was excised. This type of localized radiation is nowhere near the doses leading to death," advised the radiologist. He then asked them if they had any questions.

Graham said, "Yes, my first question is, when can I start the treatment? And how long will it last?"

The radiologist examined a calendar on his desk and said, "Let us see…today is July 13th. We can have the radiation mask and 3D maps completed this Friday. You can then have your first treatment on Monday, July 19th, and the last on August 28th. As I mentioned before, treatment will be five days a week, Monday through Friday."

Cynthia asked, "What kind of side effects should Graham watch out for?"

"Generally, they`re mild," said the radiologist. "The most common symptoms are dizziness, dull headache, some hair loss, from time-to-time nausea, and in the long run, there is scar tissue at the site of radiation due to dead cells. I`ll also recommend that Graham not drive during the radiation treatment."

On Friday, July 16th, a stereotaxic mask was created for Graham along with the 3D maps of his brain. He proudly showed Cynthia his two tattoos and was ready for his radiation therapy on the following Monday morning at 10 a.m. Much like what he had to do for the MRI, he was taken to a dressing room, changed into a hospital gown, laid on his back on patients table, and was slowly slid into position in the linear accelerator where a high- energy beam could be pinpointed on cancer cells by the radiation therapist. The treatment lasted between fifteen and thirty minutes, after which Graham exchanged his hospital gown for his street clothes.

It felt anticlimactic to Graham that those days of preparation and weeks of anticipation led to a short fifteen- to thirty-minute session.

Cynthia drove him home, and all day he expected to have some reaction to the radiation treatment. But other than a feeling of burning on his skin on his skull where the external radio beam had been focused and perhaps some short-lived nausea, he felt quite normal.

Cynthia applied some cream to his head to prevent the scratching or burning sensation.

After a light lunch, she urged him to take a nap to lessen his fatigue, an expected common side effect. In the evening, he felt a bit nauseous and dizzy, but nothing compared to what he'd felt before the surgery.

The first five days of treatment ended on July 30th with only minor issues of dizziness and increased fatigue. Cynthia regularly applied cream to Graham's head after each treatment. She remained vigilant for any unexpected side effects that might exhibit or experience.

Chapter 10

BREAKTHROUGH

ON MONDAY, AUGUST 2ND, upon returning from his vacation, Yacov, who lived in San Mateo, drove south in his slightly battered but comfortable Lexus, planning and organizing his day. An all-day meeting with scientists from a big Pharma company interested in CancerTech's breast cancer program would occupy most of his day. The following day, he had to be in Los Angeles at the farewell party of the founder and CEO of his previous company. It wasn't until late Thursday afternoon on August 4th that he had a chance to call Nick to see if his group had been able to look at the data sent by Genechip.

"Yes, Yacov, we're just about done, and if there is no further push to get the recent data on breast cancer to the Pharma folks, we can meet tomorrow afternoon in the conference room next to your office."

"Perfect."

"Aren't you coming to the dinner tonight with the

leader of our partner's breast cancer program?" inquired Nick.

"No, I had already told Bill that it was Nurit's birthday and the family was going out for dinner. Let us meet at 3 p.m. tomorrow, and I`ll also invite Dr. Mehra, the neuro-oncologist who is helping us on this project."

"Tell Nurit happy birthday." Nick had known the Kaufman's from their Los Angeles days. In fact, it was Yacov who had been instrumental in urging him to join CancerTech a year before.

When Yacov arrived in the conference room the next day, Rakesh was already there, peering at the screen of his laptop placed on the large oval table, with a large coffee cup in his hand. Yacov walked up to him and asked how his wife was doing.

"Thanks. She can keep food down a little longer, and the episodes of morning sickness are less frequent, but some foods and drinks, especially coffee, make her nauseous, said Rakesh. "How was your vacation?"

"Great, the Sierras are spectacular. The only thing is that my kids climbed those high mountains effortlessly, while I struggled. Nurit was able to keep up with them. I've to lose weight and get back in shape."

As he was settling down, Rakesh asked, "How were Graham's tumor cells doing in culture?"

"They`re growing very well, and they`re being expanded. Maybe Erica can give you a glimpse of these cells under the microscope after the meeting."

Before Rakesh could respond, Nick Ostrove, accompanied by one of his young baby-faced assistants, entered the room with reams of paper and an open laptop, which he quickly hooked up to the overhead projector.

After short introductions, Nick dove into the data and reiterated the cautious warning, "There are no proper controls because we don't have the normal brain tissue from the patient. The comparisons are with data obtained from an average of several normal brain tissues, so some of the changes that I highlight may be due to genetic variations among individuals. Keep this in mind as we go through the data."

"Despite the limitations of the data obtained from Genechip, I can confidently state that some of the changes in the levels of messenger RNAs from the patient's cancerous tissue when compared to normal tissue are very, very significant. Dmitry"—Nick pointed to his young assistant sitting next to him— "has made a list of top fifty hits, by which we mean that at least fifty different messenger RNAs from the patient's tissue are significantly higher in amount than those expected from a normal or noncancerous tissue."

Dmitry, who had migrated from Russia some ten years prior, passed a printed paper to Yacov and Rakesh and in a thick Russian accent said, "Nick has the same list projected on the screen as you have on this printed page." He went on to say that a survey of the literature shows that most, if not all, of the changes are in the genes that are involved in the immune system.

Before Dmitry or Nick could say another word, Yacov literally jumped up from his seat and uncharacteristically blurted out, "Holy shit, these are major immune response genes controlled by *NFkB*! This is amazing, incredible! I…I can't believe it!" Then he started to draw ovals with his pen around some of the hits on the list.

Rakesh didn't understand why Yacov was so excited and said, "I don't get it. What does it mean?"

Yacov walked up to the whiteboard, wiped it with an eraser, fumbled to find a colored pen, and in a slightly breathless and excited voice said, "In the mid-eighties when I was a postdoctoral fellow in Toronto, I remember reading papers from the laboratory of a famous Nobel Prize- winning American scientist about the discovery of a family of proteins that controlled many aspects of our immune system. Rakesh, think about the fact that Dmitry, Nick, you, and I are constantly being bombarded with millions of unseen bacteria, viruses, and other unknown pathogens, and yet we are not getting sick because our immune system defends and fights against these invaders. This family of proteins, upon sensing the invasion, activates the response task force, which is normally sitting dormant until given the marching orders to wake up and fight."

"What has that got to do with glioblastoma?" quizzed a puzzled Rakesh.

As Yacov was trying to formulate a response, Dmitry handed a few extra sheets of paper to both of them that listed several genes in descending order of the magnitude of difference between the patient's sample and the controls.

While they were surveying the list, Dmitry said, "Analysis of the data shows that there is an enrichment of genes involved in stem cells and—"

"What do you mean by stem cell genes?" Yacov almost shouting with excitement he again jumped out of his seat.

With his laser pointer directed at the screen, Dmitry said, "See the lower left corner which has data from the normal brain?" "Yes?" Rakesh and Yacov answered simultaneously.

"Now compare it to the data from the tumor samples on the right side, the ones that I've highlighted in yellow. What immediately jumps out is much higher numbers of stem cell- associated genes in the tumor—"

Yacov rolled back his chair as he exploded with another uncharacteristic expletive. "Oh my God, this is a perfect example of brain tumors being stem cells! Hence any cancer cell left behind after surgery will regrow to become a tumor. This is exactly what I have been saying about these lethal brain tumors, and experts in the field just shrug me off." He put his hand on Dimitry`s shoulder and exclaimed," I can't believe it. It's too good a result!"

Nick, ever cautious, again reminded Yacov that the data is from one patient and added for good measure, "One swallow does not a summer make."

"Yes, yes, I know. We don't have enough material from Patient X to even repeat the experiment. But as soon as we get a sufficient number of the patient's tumor cells growing in the petri dish and in the mice whose brains were injected with the tumor tissue, we`ll immediately repeat the experiment to confirm the results."

"We`ll still have to grapple with the limitation of not having the patient's normal brain tissue as a control," cautioned Nick.

Rakesh added, "It further emphasizes our earlier conversation about the need to obtain the surgically excised cancer tissues from more patients with GBM. If we recapitulate the results obtained from the tumor tissue of Patient X with tumors from other patients, we'll be on a much firmer ground to pursue our hypothesis that all or the majority of cells in GBM are stem cells."

He agreed with Rakesh for the need to have more samples and thanked Dmitry and Nick for their help in the analysis of the data, while collating the sheaf of papers Dmitry had given him. He then had a short chat with Nick about the breast cancer data and the ongoing negotiations with the Pharma company as Rakesh packed away his laptop and the loose sheets of paper with the gene data.

Before taking Rakesh to the laboratory to look at the growing cells from Graham's tumor tissue under the microscope, Yacov, with his belongings in hand, reminisced, "At the Brain Tumor Society meeting in Tucson earlier this year, I was nearly chased off the podium when I pointed out that most of the cells in GBM were stem cells. I didn't have the molecular data to support my claim. It sometimes takes decades to change the minds of people who have for so long championed a certain hypothesis." He then quoted the population geneticist JBS Haldane who had famously described, "The four stages of acceptance of new scientific ideas: 1. This is worthless nonsense. 2. This is an interesting but perverse point of view. 3. This is true but quite unimportant. 4. I always said so."

"Did you know that JBS Haldane was a confirmed socialist Marxist who left the UK because of his leftist policies and became an Indian citizen?" said Rakesh.

"*Eh'meth*, really true, I never knew that," replied Yacov, using a Hebrew vernacular response.

* * *

Erica was now more certain that the tumor cells growing in the petri dish would survive. She had platted them several times, and each time they grew and looked murderously healthy. She now had well over several billion tumor cells growing in petri dishes. She started to scrape tumor cells from some of the petri dishes with a rubber spatula and stored them in a special solution at -80°C for future use.

Rakesh Mehra was impressed by the mounds of petri dishes in the incubators held at 37°C and thrilled to observe them under a microscope. Some cancer cells obtained from Graham's tumor were dividing to become two cells just as he was watching them under the microscope, which was both thrilling and scary to see right before his eyes.

Yacov asked Erica if he could have about ten million cells grown from the tumor of Patient X. He wanted to send them to Genechip for a similar analysis performed on the tumor tissue.

"Sure. When do you want them?"

"If possible, Monday so we can ship them that afternoon."

He turned to Rakesh. "If results from these cells growing in the petri dishes are similar to what Dmitry and Nick discussed this morning, I think we will have a very good starting point to search for inhibitors that interfere with the growth of the stem cells. Maybe some of the members of the *NFkB* family of proteins are essential for cancer stem cells to divide in addition to activating the innate immune response."

"Could it be just a coincidence?" asked Dr. Mehra.

"Possibly, but I have my hunch," responded Yacov with a practiced flair of someone who often got things right.

"When will you know if mice injected with Graham's tumor cells will form tumors?" asked Rakesh.

"I know that the cells injected under the skin are growing because there is a big unseemly bump, and we should soon know if tumors are forming in the brains of the mice injected with the patient's cancer tissue," said Yacov, surveying the dates when injection protocols were initiated.

"Good. Then we'll also send samples from these tumors to Genechip for analysis," said Rakesh.

Before he left, Yacov asked if his wife was feeling better and if they would like to go out for dinner the following Saturday at a newly opened Middle Eastern restaurant in San Mateo.

"Sure," said Rakesh. "Let me check with Lakshmi. I am sure she would like to meet your wife and you. It would be a good change for her because she's been feeling a bit lonely since I`ve been very busy with patients and writing grants to get funds to start my laboratory."

In the end, the dinner did not materialize, and they postponed it for a later date. Yacov's wife, Nurit, had to fly home to Tel Aviv on a very short notice because her mother had broken her hip during a fall in the bathroom of the assisted living home.

He later told Rakesh how difficult it had been for Nurit to deal with her mother's advanced Alzheimer's since the death of her father some three years before.

"Does your wife have other siblings living in Israel?" inquired Rakesh.

"Nurit has an older stepsister from her father's first marriage who is estranged from the family, and her only brother, who was injured in the 1982 war in Lebanon, has been fighting drug dependence for years, in and out of rehab centers. Being 7,500 miles away, Nurit feels helpless and guilt- ridden."

I have been encouraging her to bring her mother to the US and find a good home in the Bay Area where she can be taken care of. At least Nurit and the grandkids can visit her, even though I gather she hardly recognizes her own daughter when she went to see her at the hospital."

"Alzheimer's is an insidious disease. Loss of memory and dementia robs one of all reasons. In cancer at least we have some tools of treatment, but with Alzheimer's, we have no clue what to do except wait, wait, and see the loved ones slowly decline and lose their dignity…"

Rakesh said, "I`m really sorry to hear about the agony Nurit must be going through."

"Yes, we all have our crosses to bear," reflected Yacov.

*** * * ***

The second week of treatment was uneventful, except that Nigel was home and drove his father to the radiation treatment to give his mother a break.

Graham's radiotherapy was proceeding as planned without any serious hitches or side effects. However, he had begun to feel claustrophobic and wanted to do something different other than going for treatment, coming home, and waiting for the next day's treatment.

Cynthia did not feel like socializing and was reluctant to accept lunch or dinner invitations from friends and colleagues, which made Graham feel particularly bad for her. Her life was now tied to his disease, driving to the hospital, worrying about his health, and not attending many of her social activities like her book club, cooking classes, or biking with friends.

Graham did not want his disease to totally overwhelm their lives, so he proposed to Cynthia that they take the weekend after his third treatment to travel to Napa Valley to walk in the vineyards, even though he had stopped consuming alcohol before the surgery.

Cynthia jumped at the idea. Right after radiation treatment on August 13th, she drove them to Napa Valley where they stayed the weekend at a very elegant boutique hotel overlooking the Napa River.

For Graham, this was the first night away from their

Palo Alto home or the hospital since early May when those debilitating headaches had started. He was thrilled to be in a new environment, away from the hospital, doctors, treatment, and the disease.

They had a wonderful dinner, walked in the town, slept late, and had breakfast in bed, interrupting the tedium of the last many months.

While Cynthia was also excited to be away, she was unable to shake the feeling that Graham was on borrowed time. Every time she looked at him, she had the sinking feeling that it was all a show, and soon the curtains would come crashing down. Could he be one of the lucky 5% of GBM patients who escaped the sentence of recurrence and lived a long time? She wanted to keep the upbeat mood because Graham was really happy and acted as someone who had untied from the anchor that tied him to his disease.

Back home in time for the fourth round of radiation, Graham started to toy with the idea of going back to teaching, initially part-time, to regain a small measure of his former life.

Cynthia, however, reminded him that a week after completing his radiotherapy treatment at the end of the month, he would have to undergo a regimen of six months of chemotherapy. Although his chemotherapy did not require hospital visits because the drug was delivered orally, they still could not anticipate the extent of its side effects. Cynthia instead suggested going away for a short trip after finishing radiotherapy and before the start of chemotherapy.

When Graham proposed delaying chemotherapy by a week so that Cynthia and he could take a short break, he was relieved that Dr. Mehra raised no objection and agreed to see them soon to set up a schedule for chemotherapy.

On Tuesday, August 24th, Cynthia had sent an email to Dr. Mehra, asking if on Thursday, a day before Graham's last session of radiotherapy, they could stop by his office after the radiation treatment.

Dr. Mehra responded positively but asked them to stop by before the treatment, as he had an off-site meeting in the afternoon. Cynthia gently knocked at the partially open office door.

Dr. Mehra looked up from his large brown leather chair and said with a bright smile, "Well, hello, come on in. I've just been reviewing some of the latest reports from Dr. Kaufman's team at CancerTech."

The Bunkers took their seats in the chairs on the other side of Dr. Mehra's desk. "Thank you for seeing us on such short notice," said Graham.

"Before we discuss the chemotherapy regimen, I have some very good news to share with you."

"Really? What`s it?" responded Cynthia eagerly as she leaned forward with curiosity.

Looking at Graham, Dr. Mehra said, "Scientists at CancerTech were able to grow cells from your tumor in petri dishes and now have an inexhaustible supply for testing drugs that might kill these tumor cells." His eyes darted eagerly between the two of them as he waited for a response.

Graham smiled and said, "That's fantastic news!"

"And there's more," Dr. Mehra added enthusiastically. "The genomic data from your tumor suggests that the chemotherapeutic drug would be unhindered in its maximal potential to kill tumor cells because an enzyme that reduces the potency of the drug isn't being made."

Graham and Cynthia both sat quietly for a moment with puzzled looks on their faces until Graham inquired, "What exactly does this mean?"

"In practical terms, it means that the dosage of the drug Temodar can be lower because your body will be less likely to mount a resistance to it. Also, lower amounts of the drug result in fewer side effects," replied Dr. Mehra.

"That's great. Are the side effects of this drug similar to those expected from radiation therapy?" asked Graham.

"Yes, usually very similar: nausea, fatigue, dizziness, mild headache, sometimes diarrhea. Overall, the side effects are quite mild. We do recommend periodic blood work to ensure that your normal blood count is not compromised. You escaped most of the side effects of radiation therapy, and I'm hoping for similarly smooth sailing from chemotherapy," said Dr. Mehra.

"Can Graham fly? We're thinking of flying from San Francisco to Jackson Hole, Wyoming, a flight of about two hours, and some places in Yellowstone Park, maybe over 7,000 feet high."

"Oh, that should be ok, so long as Graham doesn't indulge in strenuous activity. He'll fatigue easily and may experience some dizziness," cautioned Dr. Mehra. "Graham, when were you planning to start chemotherapy?"

"We're planning to return on Thursday, September 2nd, so I'd start my first twenty-eight-day Chemo cycle the next day on the 3rd," replied Graham.

"Great. I'll have the nurse send instructions to your house and will call the pharmacy for Temodar capsules. The important thing is to make sure that you take your pills on an empty stomach with at least eight ounces of water to reduce any nausea or urge to vomit. If you prefer, you can also take the pills before going to bed, making sure that there's a decent interval of one to two hours after dinner," advised Dr. Mehra.

Graham nudged Cynthia and grumbled, "There goes my nightly slice of cake."

Cynthia again wanted to make sure that the gap between radiation and chemotherapy wouldn't be detrimental to the planned treatment. "Dr. Mehra, are you sure there isn't an issue delaying the chemo for a week? I want to do what is best for Graham's health."

Rakesh clasped his hands and leaned forward, placing his elbows on the table, then in a conspiratorial tone, said, "No, Cynthia, it'll be ok. The purpose of both therapies is to kill any leftover cancer cells. This is really a one-two punch. Any bad guys who escaped surgery and radiotherapy will now have to deal with the third foe, chemotherapy. You should take a few days for a relaxing vacation. It'll do you both some good."

"Thanks. We had a weekend in Napa a few weeks ago and loved it," said Graham.

Rakesh got up, shook hands with the couple, and said, "Have a good trip, and keep me informed if there are any serious side effects from chemotherapy."

As soon as they returned home, Cynthia got on the internet to secure two seats on a flight to Jackson Hole, Wyoming and was lucky to get a cottage at the Jackson Lake Lodge in Grand Teton National Park.

She then arranged a rental car, all within an hour of arrival at home, leading Graham to comment, "You're amazing. Have you thought about setting up a travel business?"

Cynthia smiled, waved her plastic American Express card, and replied, "It's magical powers!"

Later in the evening, she sent emails to their children, Graham's father, mother, and sister to inform them of their upcoming trip, lest they worry if no one responds to phone calls or messages. Everyone was thrilled by their plans and wished them a great trip.

Right after the last zapping of any wayward tumor cells in his brain with focused beams of high energy electrons, Graham changed into his street clothes, thanked the radiation technologist, walked out of the building, and was picked up by Cynthia. They drove to the San Francisco airport for their flight, first to Denver and then to the smaller airport in Jackson Hole, Wyoming. They drove to the Jackson Lake Lodge, a distance of some thirty miles, and had to wait as a herd of moose, indifferent to their surroundings unfazed by the couple's urgency to get to their lodge, lazily crossed the road, taking nearly 15 minutes.

Graham, feeling free from the shackles of driving back and forth for hospital appointments, said, "Look at the vastness of this place. As far as the eye can see, there's open land."

She added, "I too feel liberated. It's wonderful to be away from the densely populated urban areas with traffic, all that honking and road rage."

"Only rage to worry about here is the wayward elk, moose, or that lone bear," added Graham with a sly smile.

Cynthia fell into silence and again started to brood about the future, a future where Graham might not be sitting next to her.

They made it to the lodge just in time to see through the giant glass windows in the lobby the glow of the setting sun on the jagged peaks and deep canyons of the Teton range, rising abruptly from the valley.

The evening was getting a bit chilly, and after a light dinner, they abandoned the idea of a short walk and instead went to sleep early in their heated lodge.

The next day after breakfast, they drove for about an

hour and a half and made a beeline to the most talked-about tourist attraction, Old Faithful, in the nearby Yellowstone Park, whose eruption intervals are fairly reliable, sometimes within ten to fifteen minutes of the predicted times. While entering the park, the ranger told them that the next eruption was predicted for 11:55 a.m., so they made it to the parking area near the visitor center and joined hundreds of other tourists sitting on aluminum benches, waiting to behold the eruption of Old Faithful.

Graham, wearing a windbreaker, his trusted Swiss backpack with water bottles sticking out of the netted side pockets, and his favorite cap with the logo of the Golden State Warriors, whispered to Cynthia about the great diversity of the tourists and multiple accents, dialects, and languages being spoken.

Amazingly at 11:54 a.m., a small plume of steam emerged from the disarmingly quiet geyser. Minutes later, it erupted, shooting the steam as high as fifty to seventy feet for the next four to five minutes, eventually dying down to just a few feet and back to a small plume of steam. It indeed was faithful, reliable, and a spectacular show.

As much as Cynthia wanted to not be reminded of her husband's disease during these blissful days, she couldn't help but compare the eruption of the geyser to the recurrence of a tumor from the dormant cells. One moment it was quiet, and then there was an eruption, first slow then gaining momentum and shooting upwards. Her whole body shuddered, and she instinctively tightened her grip on Graham's arm.

They went back to their lodgings in the early evening and charted some easy hikes for the following day in the Grand Teton Park.

Though Graham had visited Yellowstone Park in the

mid-sixties with his school, he hardly remembered any of the beautiful vistas, just Old Faithful and an encounter with a grizzly bear who had wandered into their campground and was trying to open the bear-proof trash cans. The frustrated bear had then slowly ambled into the nearby woods.

Cynthia couldn`t remember such a relaxed and enjoyable vacation. If only all of life could be so simple and beautiful. But soon it was time to pack up and get back to Palo Alto. The drive from the San Francisco airport to home was somber and quiet as they passed through Redwood City, a reminder of Graham's disease, surgery, radiotherapy, doctor visits, the fear, and future.

Arriving back home on Thursday, September 4th, they found a fat envelope from the hospital in the mail that contained all of the instructions for chemotherapy and a note saying that the prescription for a five-day supply of Temodar had been sent to the pharmacy. Cynthia immediately called the pharmacy to ensure that the prescription was ready for her to pick up.

The letter from the hospital had suggested a dose of 300 mg/day for five days for the first cycle. Since the capsules of Temodar came in 5, 20, 100, and 250 mg doses, the prescription was for fifteen capsules of 100 mg each. The prescription also included an antiemetic, Meclozine, in case of nausea or vomiting. The letter also advised that Mr. Graham Bunker should get a blood test before starting chemotherapy to ensure normal blood counts.

Early the next morning, Cynthia drove Graham to the hospital to get the blood test and on the way back stopped at the pharmacy to get the prescribed medication.

In the afternoon, the nurse from Dr. Mehra's office called to inform Graham that his blood count was fine, and that he could start his first cycle of chemotherapy. She again urged him to immediately inform the hospital if there were any serious side effects.

Graham took his first three capsules with a full glass of water at 9 p.m., some two hours after dinner. Not knowing if he would experience side effects, he decided not to take the anti-nausea tablet.

He woke up in the middle of the night feeling that he might have to throw up, but it passed a few minutes later and he went back to sleep. Though he woke up multiple times thinking he may vomit, again nothing transpired.

Surprisingly, Cynthia remained asleep, unaware of Graham's concerns. By now they had developed a pattern where each partner made sure that the other wasn`t disturbed and got maximal rest.

When he woke up the next morning, Cynthia was ready to go to school as a substitute fourth- grade teacher, at the last-minute request of the principal.

Even though his school principal expected Graham to be back in September, he was not ready and extended his medical leave of absence. He had, however, left open the possibility of part-time teaching if his health permitted, especially if he tolerated the chemotherapeutic drug without any side effects.

He felt a little nauseous mid-morning, but again the moment passed, and he had a late lunch when Cynthia arrived home.

"How did you hold up on your own since I was gone so long?" asked Cynthia while putting her purse on the kitchen counter.

"I read the paper, shaved, showered, had a cup of tea, and started to read Ron Chernow's Alexander Hamilton'…boy, he writes so well. I just finished lunch," replied Graham.

"So, you didn't miss me…" said Cynthia a bit playfully.

"Well, I didn't say that," said Graham with a mischievous smile.

The first cycle of chemotherapy ended on Tuesday, September 7th when Graham took his thirteenth, fourteenth, and fifteenth pill. Except for one minor vomiting episode, he had had no discernable side effects. He'd even kept his daily one-hour walking schedule and made no changes to his diet.

Dr. Mehra was very pleased and told him over the phone to maintain the same dose of Temodar for the second cycle, which would start twenty- three days later on October 1st. He again emphasized that Graham should call him if he felt debilitated due to any side effects of chemotherapy.

Dr. Mehra supported Graham's desire to go back to teaching, since all outward signs were that he was coping well with treatment of his disease.

The school principal was delighted with the news and promised to start with a lower load of teaching one period of history to ninth graders and gradually move to also teaching the tenth graders.

Graham was thrilled to get back to work and to see his colleagues after nearly four months of being away. His colleagues were sensitive to not talk about his disease, merely solicitous of his health. No one could have guessed that Graham had gone through brain surgery, radiotherapy, and was in the midst of chemotherapy. He was a bit thinner, slightly gaunter, more thoughtful, more agreeable, and generally more considerate. He had not lost his sense of humor and remarked to a colleague that he had left the school with a bigger brain and returned with a smaller one.

Chapter 11

THE "KILLER" MOLECULE

BETWEEN MID-SEPTEMBER TO EARLY OCTOBER, Yacov and his team had successfully utilized the tumor tissue from Patient X to make cell lines to produce an unlimited number of tumor cells and generate tumors in the brains and under the skin of the mice. They confirmed the high representation of immune genes and enrichment of stem cell genes in the immortal brain tumor cells growing not only in the petri dishes but also in the tumor tissues obtained from the mice. Most assuredly, the data obtained from the tumor tissue of Patient X could be replicated in substantial measure in the tumor tissues obtained from four additional patients diagnosed with GBM, similar to the one excised from Graham's brain.

Armed with this consistent and very strong piece of evidence, Yacov and his team started to comb the existing literature to find ways to block the activity of the family of *NFkB* proteins. The primary premise of the team was *No NFkB activity, no stem cell growth, hence no cell proliferation, and NO TUMOR!*

One of the younger members of the team dug up an old paper published many years prior where scientists had used a small chemically synthesized molecule to show that the activity of *NFkB* can be severely curtailed. It was commercially available.

"Order this compound and let us see if it stops the growth of the cell line generated from Patient X," proposed Yacov. He then asked one of his senior scientists to take the lead in ensuring that the material was ordered as soon as possible and immediately initiating the experiments he'd just proposed.

"I`m going to be very busy in the coming days with the breast cancer team from our Pharma collaborators who are demanding more and more of my time and involvement in the project. Bill, a few days ago, asked me to curtail my time on the GBM project and is reluctant to fund the additional technical support I had requested. But once he sees the data we have accumulated, he`ll realize that we have had a major breakthrough to find ways to combat this deadly disease. So, guys, let us order this 'killer' molecule and get the data as soon as possible!" thundered Yacov.

A week later, 100 mg (an amount equal to about four rice grains) of the "killer" molecule, costing over $9,000, arrived and was immediately handed over to the team leader who then gave it to Erica. She weighed a minuscule amount, dissolved it in a special solution, and added different amounts to petri dishes containing cell lines made from cancerous tissue of Patient X. Erica called her favorite cell line, XY50, because the patient was male (XY chromosomes) and fifty years old, a secret only shared with Yacov and Rakesh.

Seventy-two hours after Erica added the solution containing the "killer" molecule into the petri dishes containing half a million XY50 cells, they were plainly unhappy, unable to grow, dying, disheveled, and decaying. In contrast, siblings of the same XY50 cells that had escaped encounter with the "killer" molecule were thriving and had increased in number by at least fivefold.

The "killer" molecule had indeed halted the growth of XY50 cells. But did it mean that cancer cells in Patient X could be eliminated by this "killer," or as Erica preferred, "miracle" molecule? She sent the detailed report of these results by email to Yacov, who was on a business trip to the East coast, in connection with the breast cancer project.

Excited about her news, he wrote back and instructed her to repeat the experiment in mice injected with cancer cells from Patient X.

The scientists working on this project reminded him of two limitations: 1) the "killer" molecule may not be able to get into the brain where the tumor resides. They can conduct the proposed experiments only in the mice where tumor cells from Patient X were injected under the skin, and 2) there was only a limited supply of the "killer" molecule with which to perform any additional experiments.

Yacov assured the team that he would talk to management for the allocation of additional funds to buy more of the "killer" molecule and urged them to do the proposed experiments in mice as soon as possible with all the remaining material.

* * *

The second cycle of chemotherapy started on Friday, October 1st, and it was good that it was on a weekend because, on Saturday afternoon, Graham had multiple episodes of vomiting, which led him to have little or no appetite for the rest of the day. At times, the vomiting was so violent he felt his innards would be expelled. But by noon on Sunday, his appetite resurfaced, and he ate bagels with lox, tomatoes, and cream cheese, followed by a large fruit salad.

They said goodbye to Jessica, who was on her way to England and Europe for ten days with her new boyfriend, whom no one except Amber had met.

Graham asked Jessica when she was going to see Grandma, and she replied, "After arriving in London, I`ll take a bus to Cambridge and spend the first few days in Elsworth with Grandma, then join Adam in London for a few days, after which we are going to spend three days in Amsterdam, my favorite city."

"Adam…at least we now know the name of the mystery man…Give my love to Mom and say hi to Scotty," and before he could put the receiver down, Amber said, "Dad, after I drop Jessica at the airport, I`ll swing by to see how you`re doing and have something to eat. Next week is going to be very busy for me."

"Great. Your mom will be delighted to see you and I `m sure you will make your favorite pasta."

During dinner, Cynthia said, "Grandpa David wants to celebrate his seventy-fifth birthday at his place on Vancouver Island. But I was thinking that with all the travel required to go to Vancouver Island and the time we have taken off from the school due to Dad's illness, I wonder if we should combine it with Thanksgiving dinner here and invite Aunt Adelaide."

"Great idea, Mom," Amber replied, and Graham nodded his head in agreement. "Okay, let me explore it with Linda first," said Cynthia, pleased by their reactions.

* * *

Graham swallowed the last three capsules of Temodar for the second cycle of chemotherapy at 9:30. p.m. on October 5th, as he was fiddling with the TV remote control, he read the fast-moving horizontal news ticker: *"Golfer Tiger Woods marries Swedish model Elin Nordegren, Comedian Rodney Dangerfield dies at eighty-two, DNA Discoverer and Nobel Laureate Maurice Wilkins dies at age "eighty-eight".* Wilkins had been a friend of his mom and stepfather.

With no recent discernable side effects, aside from the single bout of nausea from the chemotherapy, Graham extended his teaching hours to include a period with tenth graders and, for the first time since his fiftieth birthday, decided to jog a short distance in the soccer field adjacent to the school. It felt good, really good. His disease now seemed distant, though not forgotten.

Cynthia was more prudent and continuously worried about the future. She was still haunted by the fear that the cancer would return, a common occurrence in this disease.

* * *

"I like the idea of combining David's seventy-fifth birthday celebration with Thanksgiving," Linda told Cynthia over the phone one afternoon in mid-October. "David and I will come a few days early, help with shopping and cooking the turkey. David would love to have all of his family, especially his grandchildren, around him for the celebration. It'll be great if Adelaide and Roger were able to join."

"Shall we also ask Grandma Karen and Scotty to join?" asked Cynthia.

"Sure, but I think Scotty's arthritis is really bad, so I'm not sure if he can come, but we'll leave that to Karen," replied Linda.

"I'll ask Graham to write to his mother," she replied and then said goodbye to Linda. She circled November 20th on the calendar and wrote underneath it: *Order Fresh Turkey and Order Birthday Cake from Gayle's Bakery.*

Graham later sent an email to his mom inviting her to the Thanksgiving dinner and his dad's seventy-fifth birthday party:

Dear Mom,

I gather that Jessica had a good time with Scotty and you. She is still talking about the high tea you took her to in Grantchester Village. We still have not met her mystery boyfriend.

I am now in the midst of my second twenty-eight-day chemotherapy cycle and have escaped any serious side effects. Jessica probably told you that I have started to teach again, though only part-time. Amazing to think that I am being treated with chemotherapy drugs in California similar to those that you started to synthesize at Synthetico in Menlo Park some forty years ago. Little did you realize that one day your son would be benefiting from them.

Dad will turn seventy-five on November 5th, and Linda and Cynthia decided to combine the celebration with Thanksgiving dinner on November 25th. All the children will be home, and I am going to write to Adelaide and Roger to also join us. We would all love it if Scotty and you could also join us for the celebrations.

Hope Scotty's arthritis is under control. Lots of Love,

Graham

Before Graham could send an invitation to his sister, a response came back from his mother.

My Dear Graham,

I am so glad that you are doing fine with little or no side effects of chemotherapy. The drugs we made in the sixties were very toxic and often made the patients very sick. The drug Temodar that you are taking gets into the brain easily, so doses are quite low, hence less toxic.

I should have realized that David would soon be seventy-five because I am only a few months younger…a big one for me next year.

Scotty is in quite poor health, so it won't be wise for me to leave him, even with the part-time caretaker that we now employ. I will make sure to call David on his birthday and give my best wishes.

I was also wondering if the children, Cynthia, and you would like to spend Xmas with us in Elsworth. I know it would be a long way to travel but would be a good break for all of you. Think about it.

We had a lovely time with Jessica. She is now such a mature, lovely young woman. She was so gentle and considerate to Scotty, who is now practically wheelchair- bound.

Give our love to Cynthia and the grandkids, Your Loving Mother,

Karen

Graham liked the idea of celebrating a real winter Christmas like his childhood in England. However, like Cynthia, the specter of recurrence of his cancer was now deeply rooted in his mind, even though he was feeling pretty normal and in better health than several months ago. Dr. Jabbar had said that she took out the tumor tissue from his brain, but what if there were still some recalcitrant cancer cells left unscathed?

What if these few hardened criminals also escaped the

dragnet of chemoradiation? Could they have escaped to other parts of the brain, unreachable by current chemotherapy and waiting to strike again? But when will they make the end run? Without openly admitting it, he feared that it could be his last Christmas.

* * *

A few days before starting his third cycle of chemotherapy on October 29th, Graham went for his blood work. Except for a slightly lower count of white blood cells, those that fight infection, everything was within the normal range. Dr. Mehra's office called to say that the dose of Temodar could be increased to 400 mg/day, and they had called the pharmacy for twenty capsules of 100 mg each for the five-day treatment. Despite the increased dose, Graham experienced few side effects, mostly a feeling of mild nausea, vomiting, and occasional diarrhea.

On November 5th, they both called his father to wish him a happy seventy-fifth and were disappointed to learn that Adelaide and Roger would not be able to join them for Thanksgiving due to previous commitments.

There was a very eerie normalcy to life these days. At times, Graham and Cynthia just looked at each other without saying anything, and at other times, they averted their gazes because of the fear that they were together on borrowed time.

While Cynthia maintained a cheery disposition around him, Graham felt that she was walking on eggshells, ready to please him. He desperately wanted the old Cynthia back, not hiding her true feelings but sharing what was on her mind. Strangely, the physical manifestation of Graham's disease was considerably under control, but the emotional toll was often more palpable.

Cynthia just couldn't shake off the dread of some impending doom.

To avoid being alone, they often invited friends to visit them. Cynthia, who loved to read, could no longer concentrate, and Graham, who loved to watch sports, now continuously changed channels on the TV. In a way, it was a godsend that they both could work part-time. They desperately loved each other, and neither could bear the thought of being without the other. Their silence spoke volumes.

***

In early November, the mice injected with tumor cells five weeks prior had enlarged tumors, while those treated with the "killer" molecule showed little or no symptoms of the disease. A quick analysis of the treated and untreated animals showed that the "killer" molecule prevented the growth of cancer cells obtained from the brain tumor of Patient X.

Yacov realized that this was one of those eureka moments that most scientists crave for but rarely experience. He would later lament to Rakesh how he wished he had been there to witness this rather than be on a plane for yet another business trip for the breast cancer program.

Upon his return, Yacov gathered the entire GBM team in the large conference room for a complete review of the project and an action plan to move forward in the coming year.

They waited a few minutes for Rakesh to arrive before Erica presented the results obtained from the "killer" molecule and the ongoing experiments with tumor tissues from four other GBM patients.

She finished her talk and pleaded, "We need additional amounts of the 'killer' molecule, along with more detailed studies of its toxicity and pharmacologic properties."

Andy, one of the members of the team who had joined CancerTech only a few months before, said, "I know of a small and struggling biotech company on the east coast that was using the 'killer' molecule for combating inflammatory bowel disease. But it turned out to be quite toxic."

"What kind of toxicity," asked Yacov?

"I think its extended use had liver toxicity and some platelet reduction. But a lot of those adverse events were mitigated with lower doses and better dose management."

"Why did they not do trials with lower doses?"

Another member of the team said, "Not very effective at low doses. Unlike cancer, the long-term safety profile for chronic diseases is another ball game. The investors get jittery."

Andy chimed in, "Would it be productive to have a dialogue with them to see how far they had progressed with its manufacture, purity, toxicity, and efficacy?"

Yacov immediately said, "Excellent idea. Can you get me some particulars of this company, so I can get our business group to contact them before the onset of the holidays? It would be ideal if we could collaborate rather than try to duplicate, especially if they have extensive safety and toxicology studies. Thanks, Andy. Great lead."

After the meeting was over, Rakesh and Yacov chatted more about the logistics and how Graham was doing now that his chemotherapy treatment and six weeks of radiation were coming close to an end.

Rakesh said, "I saw Graham earlier this morning, and he's asymptomatic, in good health, and doing some teaching. He just finished his fourth round of chemo and has plans to go with his family to England for the Christmas holidays before he begins the next round. Everything has gone well for him, and I'm really pleased with his progress. I gather he is back to running."

"Well, it sounds as if he's doing wonderfully and feeling well enough if he's started running again," responded Yacov.

As he was packing up his battered briefcase with the loose sheafs of data, Andy popped in to give him the contact information of the small biotech company in Waltham, Massachusetts using the "killer" molecule for their lead product.

Yacov took the information, thanked Andy, and started to walk toward the office of the CEO. On his way, he stopped by the business office and asked Sandy, their business development officer, to look into the biotech company that Andy had mentioned.

Bill Hollander, the CEO, was just winding up a meeting and motioned for Yacov to come in. He was packing up to leave for the weekend but said he could spare a moment for his most famous scientist.

However, as soon as Yacov brought up the GBM program, it was very clear from the onset that Bill had little or no interest in talking about the recent strides that he and his team had made with the "killer" molecule.

"Look, Yacov, we've just signed a very lucrative deal with a big Pharma on our, actually your, breast cancer program, and that should now be the priority. I agree that data from one patient is impressive, but it's years away from bringing it to the clinic. On the other hand, with this Pharma support, we can be in Phase 1 clinical trials for the breast cancer drug by early 2006."

"That is really very optimistic, considering we haven`t yet fully completed the preclinical part of the protocol. We don't really know the toxicity of the inhibitor they`re pushing us to take to the clinic," said Yacov with some skepticism.

"But remember, they`re now footing the bill for over 80% of our activities, so we really need to double our efforts to get it to the clinic by the end of next year. If that requires hiring new employees, so be it. We can afford it," asserted Bill Hollander firmly.

"You haven`t yet approved the hiring of the new technician that I requested. We`ll either have to slow down the work or cut corners, and we may not get to our goal before the patient succumbs to his disease."

The CEO was not impressed and kept packing his briefcase with papers strewn all over his desk.

"Look, Bill, we`re not asking much, just 80-85 grand for a trained animal technician who can also be used later for the breast cancer program," urged Yacov.

"What about this 'killer' molecule you are talking about? Where will you get it from, and how much will it cost for a full-blown toxicology study without a partner? I just don't see how we can continue this project on brain cancer," said Bill, betraying some exasperation.

"We`ve just located a small biotech company that is using this small molecule for some inflammatory diseases, and I`ve asked Sandy in the business office to call them to find out if there's room for collaboration. Apparently, they`re in Phase 1 trials, so they must have done the extensive preclinical safety and toxicology studies. I agree that tox studies are expensive and time-consuming, and there are no partners for the brain cancer program."

"That's the problem, we have no partners for your GBM program."

"I'm a bit disappointed that I was unable to persuade our new Pharma collaborator to also invest in the brain tumor program. I guess their equation was that there are probably ten times more patients with breast cancer than brain cancers. Maybe I should've fought more because glioblastomas are excellent examples of stem cell tumors, the reason I joined CancerTech," reflected Yacov, feeling defeated and a bit guilty.

"Now come on, Yacov, the real reason why the Pharma company is investing in us is because of their faith in your hypothesis that many cancers harbor stem cells which must be eliminated to achieve long-term cure. You`re the star, buddy!" said Bill while putting his arm around his shoulder.

Yacov, who had now slumped down onto the sofa in the CEO's office after a bit of reflection, said in a pleading voice, "Bill, let Sandy talk to her counterpart at the biotech company in Waltham to see if there is a possibility of synergy between us. I really think we're onto something important. Give us a chance."

"Sure, try it, but we may have to clear it with our new Pharma partner since they now practically own CancerTech," replied Bill and left.

As he was walking back to his office, Sandy poked her head out and said, "Yacov, I had a quick look at the website of the company in Waltham that you mentioned. It is called Immune Bio, started four years ago with technology licenses from Yale and MIT and has support from angel investors. They`re in Phase 1 clinical trials and are in some financial crunch. We may need to make some upfront payments, which could be hard to swing by Bill."

"Yep, I know."

"I`ve nevertheless placed a call to their CEO, whom I met last year at the JP Morgan meeting. Probably will know more in the next few days."

"Thanks, please keep me informed."

* * *

It was Cynthia's free day, and Graham was on his way back from the school when Linda and Graham's father arrived in the late afternoon, on Tuesday, November 23rd, after checking in at the Hyatt Hotel.

After hugs and kisses, Cynthia turned on the tea kettle and opened a pack of chocolate- covered Belgian biscuits.

Graham said, "Dad, do you remember Grandfather Weiss having an unlimited supply of Belgian chocolates that he brought back from his trips to Antwerp?"

"Yes, and your mom's constant struggle with him to not spoil Adelaide and you. The Weiss's were wonderful people.".

"Grandpa would come home, remove his coat, and say *vyazoy geyt es kinder Lach*, how is it going, children, and fish out two Godiva chocolate bars from his coat pocket, one for Adelaide and one for me," recalled Graham wistfully.

Linda took out a sheet of paper from her handbag, put on her customized rimless reading glasses that sat snuggly on her nose, and started to read the grocery list she had prepared for the Thanksgiving-cum-birthday dinner. She reemphasized that Cynthia need only worry about the birthday cake, setting the table, and drinks—she and David would do the rest.

"Sounds great," Cynthia said with a smile, then walked into the kitchen to turn off the whistling kettle and pour the boiling water into three cups, each containing an Earl Grey tea bag.

A few minutes later, while holding her teacup in her palms, Linda asked Cynthia if she`d look in her pantry to make sure that she had the spices and other ingredients needed for making some of the planned dishes.

The next morning, as Linda and Cynthia went shopping and picked up the previously ordered fourteen-pound fresh turkey, Graham and his father went to the airport to pick up Nigel, who was going to spend the next few days home. While driving to the airport, David asked Graham, who was leaning back in the passenger seat, how he was coping with the disease and the treatment.

"Right now, I have no symptoms and still have to undergo several more rounds of chemotherapy. Early in December, I`m scheduled for an MRI and will know if there`s any sign of another growth. You know, Dad, recurrence of the type of tumor is quite common. This fact overwhelms me, even when I'm physically feeling fit and performing my daily chores. I feel worse for Cynthia because she constantly worries about me and yet remains stoic. I catch her often sitting alone and brooding, something she never did before."

With great empathy, his father said, "I've read that some patients escape recurrence, so maybe the prognosis isn`t so grim. One reads of so much progress in cancer treatment. Perhaps newer treatments will soon emerge."

"I told you about CancerTech, which has gotten some

of the tumor tissue removed from my brain to do genomic studies. Maybe something will come of it."

Graham's father wistfully said, "I hope so. I really hope so."

The Thanksgiving traffic going north towards San Francisco was beginning to pile up just before the airport exit, though traffic going south was still moving. Graham was hoping that they would not have to wait long for Nigel when his mobile phone rang. It was his son saying that the flight was a bit early and he was waiting curbside at Terminal 1.

Grandpa David soon spotted Nigel waving his hand and carrying an oversized backpack, which he threw onto the back seat then hopped in as the car stopped. He gave a high-five to his father and thanked Grandpa for picking him up.

All during the drive back home, Nigel talked excitedly about his research work on how ordinary household pollutants getting into the ocean combined with global warming are beginning to wreak havoc on the pristine coral reefs.

Unable to control his excitement, he blurted, "Dad, I`ve been offered a chance to spend three months next year at a new research center on coral reefs that will open at James Cook University in Townsville on the Great Barrier Reef."

"That's great. Maybe Mom and I will come and spend some time snorkeling with you," said Graham halfheartedly.

* * *

The Thanksgiving dinner was elaborate, and the food

was delicious, with everyone having second servings of the turkey and yams. After dinner, instead of Linda's famous pecan pie, Grandpa David cut the chocolate birthday cake while everyone sang "Happy Birthday."

Graham gave his father a family album where he'd painstakingly put together a marvelous collage of pictures from his boyhood to recent years. He'd started this project way back in July when still recuperating from his surgery.

His father immediately started to look at the pictures and became teary-eyed and very emotional.

Linda, always tactful, handed him the next present from Nigel, a Golden State Warriors pullover hoodie signed by power forward Mike Dunleavy, Grandpa's favorite player on the roster.

He immediately put it on and gave Nigel a big thank you, high-five, and a hug.

The sisters gave their grandpa a framed poster of a grizzly bear with three cubs from Mangelsen's Nature Gallery.

Grandpa David put his arms around his three grandchildren and said, "Ah, my three cubs."

The evening ended around 9 p.m., and David gave his son Graham an extra-tight hug, subliminally conveying that this could be his last Thanksgiving.

He wondered how many more pages would be added to the album.

The next day, Graham started his fourth cycle of chemotherapy and had no adverse effects, except for the same feeling of needing to vomit and some nausea the first few days. Another blood test revealed low platelet counts, so Dr. Mehra asked Graham to reduce the dose to 300 mg, hoping to mitigate adverse effects to a minimum. Because it was a holiday weekend, he was able to take more rest. He also planned with Cynthia their upcoming Christmas holidays in England.

Nigel was staying home after Thanksgiving and said that he had already planned a trip to Mexico with two of his friends during the Christmas holidays, and Cynthia added, "Not sure if Jessica wants to spend her Christmas with her boyfriend's family in Colorado."

"Better to book airline tickets now before they get more expensive and scarcer," Graham said then added, "Let's check tomorrow with Amber to see if she wants to join us."

Cynthia spoke wistfully, "I was hoping that we could all be back home to celebrate the new year together."

Nigel said that he would be back on the 30th of December and could come home for New Year's Eve.

In the end, they settled on leaving for London on December 18th and returning on December 28th, and their daughter Amber would join them. Graham's mother also informed him that his sister and her husband would be in England during Christmas as well.

He finished taking his chemo pills on November 30th, and as planned, on the morning of Friday, December 10th, saw Dr. Mehra, who was generally satisfied with his progress. Graham asked if he could delay his fifth chemotherapy by a few days, as he would be in the UK, which Dr. Mehra approved. Graham was scheduled to go for his routine MRI later in the afternoon.

Chapter 12

RACE AGAINST THE CLOCK

ABOUT 5 P.M. ON DECEMBER 14TH, as Yacov was packing to go home early to celebrate Hanukkah with one of their neighbors, the phone rang. It was Rakesh.

"Graham's tumor is coming back…there is progression from the last MRI. He displays no symptoms of the disease, but it is just a matter of time."

Shaken, Yacov Kaufman exclaimed, "Oh shit…Are you sure that it is a tumor and not scar tissue left over after radiation therapy?"

"No," replied Rakesh. "But I have seen enough MRIs to hazard a diagnosis of recurrence. We`ll do another MRI at the end of Graham's fifth course of chemotherapy in late January to confirm the reemergence of cancer. Graham is currently asymptomatic, so I haven`t discouraged him from taking his upcoming trip to England to celebrate Christmas with his family," replied Rakesh Mehra.

"How long before he begins to show symptoms of the disease?" inquired Yacov.

"Hard to say because it varies from patient to patient and with location of the initial tumor."

"Rakesh, how much time do we have?" asked Yacov anxiously.

"Can't be sure. Maybe six to nine months. I'm just guessing," said Rakesh, feeling weary.

"Hopefully, if we can make a deal with this east coast company, Immune Bio, regarding their lead product similar to our 'killer' molecule, we may have a shot at treating our patient before it is too late," said Yacov.

The next day, as Yacov was leaving the weekly meeting of the senior management of the company, Sandy, the business development officer, stopped him and said, "Can you later come by my office? I have news from Immune Bio regarding their product."

"Sure. I'll follow you there now." Yacov was really hoping that Sandy's news would be positive.

As Yacov plunked down onto the brown leather chair, Sandy said, "Immune Bio has successfully completed their Phase 1 clinical trial with their compound called IB-617. It has a good safety profile, and early indications with the twelve patients show that it's efficacious."

Yacov leaned forward in his chair. "Go on."

"They're trying to raise funds for phase II a/b trials and have not yet succeeded in making a deal with any major Pharma company, so they've a cash crunch and are very willing to talk to us."

Yacov couldn't help but be pleased to hear this. "Did they indicate any rough numbers of what it may cost us if we're to use it for another disease totally unconnected to their primary focus?"

"No, no. We didn't get into details. I'd just wanted to know if they have any interest in talking to us," replied Sandy.

"Sandy, can you find out who the founders, board members, and scientific advisors of the company are?" "Maybe we can first try on an exploratory basis an earlier series of compounds than the one they have in the clinic to test if it works in killing the tumor cells obtained from our Patient X.

Yacov speculated, "I doubt they will give out the current molecule used for Phase 1 trials."

"The founders, board members, and the scientific advisory board are all listed on their website. Let me print it for you."

A few minutes later, Sandy handed two printed pages to Yacov.

While scanning the names, Yacov was excited to point out, "I know one of the founders from MIT very well. He's on their board and also chair of their scientific advisory board. Tim was also an advisor at my previous company and is really a very nice and helpful fellow. I'll contact him once I get to my office. Thanks, Sandy, for all your help. Great work."

Once back in his office, which was overflowing with scientific journals and dozens of handwritten notes affixed on his workspace, Yacov searched for an old email from Tim Griffin and found one from September where Tim had acknowledged Yacov's congratulatory note on receiving a prestigious award from The Biochemical Society. He sent an email to Tim asking for a mutually suitable time to chat.

Unfortunately, soon after sending the email, an automatic response came back that Dr. Griffin was away from Wednesday, December 15th to Tuesday, December 28th with only intermittent access to the internet.

Yacov was disappointed. Nevertheless, he sent an email to Dr. Tim Griffin explaining the urgency of his message.

Dear Tim:

It`s been a while since we last touched base, and I`m sorry to have missed your plenary lecture at the annual meeting of The Biochemical Society due to a scheduling mix-up.

About six months ago, we at CancerTech obtained tumor tissue from a patient with stage IV glioblastoma who had undergone surgical resection. We were able to grow the tumor cells and have generated immortal cell lines, which, upon injection into the mouse brain, form tumors similar to those observed in the patient.

As you may know, recurrence of GBM is quite common, and usually the life span of individuals with GBM is twelve to fourteen months from the initial diagnosis. Our working hypothesis is that every tumor cell has acquired the properties of a stem cell, which if not eliminated, will go on to become a tumor.

Despite the fact that the patient was treated with radiation and chemotherapy after surgery to eliminate any escaped tumor cells, the tumor appears to be coming back, and symptoms could start to manifest at any time.

Using a drug similar to IB-617, we were able to stop the growth of tumor cells in a petri dish and in experimental mouse models.

I understand that IB-617 performed well in safety trials and is now being taken forward for Phase IIa/b clinical trials for IBD. Our business development officer contacted her counterpart at Immune Bio regarding the possibility of extending the use of IB-617 for another medical indication, albeit brain tumors, and got a positive response. Of course, it is all very preliminary, and the devil is in the details…

Before entering into business negotiations, it will be important for us at CancerTech to show that IB-617 or an earlier derivative is able to kill our patient's tumor cells. Frankly, we do not have the time to manufacture and test our current compound for safety and toxicity because the patient's tumor is showing signs of recurrence.

I was wondering, if in your capacity as a board member and Chair of the SAB of Immune Bio, you could help us to contact the appropriate person(s) at the company to obtain an earlier derivative of IB-617 to test its efficacy in killing brain tumor cells.

If the results are positive, I will be able to make a strong case with our leadership to enter into serious negotiations with Immune Bio. Because we are in a time crunch and the holiday season is descending upon us, I was hoping to have my staff start some of the experiments with the drug before they take off for the Xmas holidays. But it appears that you are away and will not be back till late in the month, so we may have to postpone the experiments till early next year.

Looking forward to hearing from you, and a happy 2005.

Best,

Yacov

Not long after sending the email, Yacov received a response from Tim Griffin:

Nice to hear from you. I am intrigued by the results and am forwarding your note to Nate Young, CSO of Immune Bio, to see if he can be helpful. I know that IB-617 is ready for Phase IIa/b clinical trials and that the company is trying to raise capital, so they may be interested in a relationship.

I am sitting with my family in the United Red-Carpet Club at Logan Airport instead of being in Colorado heading towards the ski slopes. First, it was the weather, then a delayed in-bound craft, and now some mechanical problem with an estimated time of departure at 6:30 p.m.., so hopefully, we will at least make it to our hotel tonight. Have you ever travelled with two bored teenagers who are making you feel guilty every time there is announcement of further delay? Thank God for all the "munchies" in the club, which they are devouring, much to the consternation of the two helpers in the kitchen who have to constantly replenish them.

Good luck, Yacov, and let me know if I can be of further help.

All the best,

Tim

CC: Nate Young

Yacov did not waste any time replying to Tim's message.

Thanks, Tim, for a prompt response. Sorry about the delayed flight, but it worked in my favor of getting a lead to a connection at Immune Bio. Didn't Nate Young head the inflammation group at Novartis?

Re: traveling with teenagers, wait till they whistle past you at "Kamikaze speed" on the slopes to make you feel old…

Enjoy your vacation and again, many thanks.

Best,

Yacov

Within a few minutes of sending his note of thanks to Tim, he sent an email to Nate Young at Immune Bio. After a few back-and-forth messages, he arranged a conference call at 10 a.m. the next day. This meant that he might be late for the previously scheduled call with their Pharma partners to discuss the start of clinical trials for the breast cancer program, which would irritate the CEO. But Yacov saw this as more important and was willing to risk his displeasure.

Before the end of the day, Yacov talked to Erica and the other senior leaders of the GBM team, apprised them of the possibility of obtaining the IB-617-related compound, and discussed setting up experiments before the start of the holidays to make some headway before the end of the year.

"When do you think we can get materials from Immune Bio?" asked Erica.

"No idea if they're even willing to make a deal. I'm counting on the goodwill of a scientist to another scientist," said a hopeful Yacov. "I'm an eternal optimist."

The call with Nate Young, CSO of Immune Bio, was very pleasant and productive. As is often the case in the world of science, they had many common acquaintances, likes and dislikes of some individuals, almost always stories of injustice of reviewers and willingness to revile journal editors. The biotech and Pharma had a common beef against the academics for exaggerating the importance of their findings and lack of rigorous statistical evaluation to support their claims.

Nate agreed to talk to the CEO and business development officer at Immune Bio to send IB-556, which was very similar to IB-617, now in the clinic, except that it had poor retention in the plasma so needed higher doses, making it a bit more toxic. Otherwise, they were interchangeable in their efficacy.

"Is IB-556 brain penetrant?" asked Yacov.

"Unfortunately, yes because we would have preferred that the drug was not brain penetrant because of safety concerns. IB-617 also can be found in the brain for many hours after administration of the drug," replied

Nate.

With a smile, a cheerful Yacov opined, "Great, perfect for brain tumors, that's where we want all the action."

Nate, not surprisingly said, "I'll ask our legal department to send a Materials Transfer Agreement (MTA) to you so we can get the ball rolling."

Yacov thanked Nate and again emphasized the time crunch because of the likely recurrence of the disease in the patient.

At 10:45 a.m., some fifteen minutes late, Yacov joined the senior management group in their conference call and right away plunged into discussion of the need for additional preclinical data for toxicology studies for the lead compound for the breast cancer clinical trials. Apparently, there were some issues at the company doing toxicology studies that were leading to current delays in getting the final data. The leader of the toxicology group at the Pharma promised to have the results by the end of the first quarter in 2005. Eager to get away for the holidays, they agreed to reconvene right after the tox studies data was available.

As the management team was shuffling out of the conference room, Yacov quickly apprised Bill of his interactions with Immune Bio.

"If all goes well, we will have results by the beginning of February to make a decision."

While shutting off his computer, Bill was distracted but replied, "Great. Keep me informed and remember that we will need our partner's approval."

"You mean our owner's approval," chuckled Yacov.

"Do not forget who is paying our bills," replied the CEO with a disapproving shake of his head.

Yacov immediately forwarded the Materials Transfer Agreement sent by the attorney at Immune Bio to the newly hired leader of the technology transfer group at CancerTech.

The patent attorney of the outside legal firm employed by CancerTech raised the issue that their Pharma partner would need to approve the MTA request, which could take days, if not weeks. Since this clause in the agreement was ambiguous, Yacov pleaded with the business development officer to allow this one-time exemption before closing the loophole in the agreement.

Since Bill was already halfway out the door for his vacation in Hawaii, the business development officer, unable to consult him, reluctantly gave approval to sign the document, an act that could have jeopardized her job. Yacov commanded enormous respect from the scientists and senior staff at CancerTech to get his way.

In anticipation of receiving the materials from Immune Bio, Yacov sent notes to the team leaders to plan for the experiments that would show if the compound mimics the properties of the "killer" molecule in preventing the proliferation of tumor cells of Patient X.

When one of the team members asked why Immune Bio was sending IB-556 and not IB-617, currently being tested in the clinic, Yacov reminded him, "Companies are very reluctant to send the lead compound for fear that if anything went wrong, they would have to report it to the FDA, which could halt trials or lead to a recall. Not surprisingly, they prefer to give out a similar compound to have some wiggle room in case of any adverse results." Many of the team members were a bit unhappy to have to postpone or delay their holiday plans and anxiously awaited the arrival of materials from the company. Thanks to FedEx, a packet addressed to Yacov Kaufman arrived around 10a.m. the following day and was given to Erica to organize its distribution for different experiments.

By the evening of Wednesday, December 22nd, most of the planned experiments were underway, and just in time because the next day, CancerTech looked like a ghost town with only essential emergency staff left.

* * *

Graham, Cynthia, and their daughter Amber had flown to London on Saturday, December 18th, arriving on a chilly and wet Sunday morning at Heathrow Airport in London. They were driven to his family home in Elsworth in a taxi prearranged by his mother. Sister Adelaide had arrived two days earlier but first went up north to visit her husband's parents and would join them later in the week.

Cynthia and Amber had hoped for a white Christmas but instead had to cope with wet and chilly days. However, Grandma's house was warm, decorated in festive colors, and the heat from the wood-burning fireplace was most welcoming.

Scotty, bound to a wheelchair, stayed mostly in his bedroom or parked near the fireplace reading his book and made witty comments from time to time. Amber, always close to Grandma Karen, often engaged in conversation with Scotty about the American lifestyle compared to life in the UK and the continent. Like many compatriots, she vehemently defended American values, even though at home she would have found flaws with them.

Graham, though still jet-lagged, was very excited to be back at his childhood home and was surprised that the box with his insect collection was still left intact in the basement, as was his cricket bat and an old and rusted trophy.

The catered Christmas dinner was a grand affair that included the Bunkers, Adelaide, Roger, and an older lady who lived two houses away and was Scotty's distant relative.

No one could have noticed that Graham had a tumor in his brain that had started to sprout again. He was relaxed, jovial, and made many jokes at the idiosyncrasies of the English lifestyle in the countryside.

But Cynthia, outwardly happy, could not shake the fear that Graham's tumor would return and many times lapsed into long silences while everyone else was merrily chatting away.

Could it be Graham's last Christmas? He is barely fifty. Such a loving husband, father, and son. It all seemed so unfair. He had bravely weathered the surgery, radiation, chemotherapy, and days of discomfort without any complaints. What will I do without him? Tears welled in her eyes, but she had now become an expert in internalizing her feelings and maintaining a brave façade.

Graham, however, sensed Cynthia's worries but didn't know how to allay them, except by acting normal. He too feared that this may be his last Christmas.

A day before they had to leave, Cynthia, Adelaide, and Amber went to London for some post-Christmas sale shopping, while Graham spent the day with his mother, mostly talking about the old days, especially the times when he was first left alone with his father in Palo Alto.

"Strangely, what I missed most was Adelaide practicing the piano and the familiar scene of you sitting on the sofa with reams and reams of papers piled around you," reminisced Graham.

After lunch, his mother, sitting near the roaring fireplace, held his hand and said, "I`m so glad that all of you made the effort to spend Christmas holidays with us. I`m sorry that Jessica and Nigel couldn't be here. I`m so very fond of my grandchildren and wish I could spend more time with them." After a brief pause, she continued, "This`s a large house, and with Scotty's deteriorating health, I`m not sure how long we can manage to live here."

"Sell it mother, and move to a smaller apartment." "Maybe that is what Scotty says."

Holding his hand a bit more tightly, she turned towards him and asked, "How about you? Will you be ok with this decision?"

"Mother, you know my disease doesn`t have a good prognosis. I'm in remission now, but it can flare up any time. I`d love to be one of those 5% outliers who escape a recurrence, but I`ve to face reality. I know the children will be fine in the long run. It`s Cynthia I worry about the most. She acts brave, but she`s increasingly becoming emotionally fragile. I can't bear to leave her." And he broke down.

For once, the English reserve of his mother cracked, and she buried her grown-up son's head in her bosom and stroked his hair.

Early on December 28th, after hugs, a few tears, and goodbyes, Amber, Cynthia, and Graham flew back to San Francisco, and Jessica, back from Christmas vacation with her boyfriend's family, picked them up from the airport.

Cynthia and Graham, exhausted from the long trip, went to bed after hot showers, woke up very early in the morning, and after coffee, went through the mail and email messages. A message from the hospital that Graham needed to have another MRI at the end of January jolted him back to the reality that he had brain cancer. However, his concerns were somewhat mitigated because it was a previously scheduled MRI. Nevertheless, he became restless and spent many anxiety-filled hours. The worry of a recurrence weighed heavily on him, no matter how well he felt.

The next day, Graham started his fifth dose of chemotherapy and suffered minor side effects, including being tired, which could have also been due to his recovering from the recent long trip.

His son returned from his trip to Mexico the following day with a suitcase full of old laundry and small gifts for his parents and sisters. Cynthia immediately took the soiled laundry to the garage and loaded it into the washing machine.

As she had hoped, on New Year's Eve, the entire family was together, along with Jessica's boyfriend, Adam, who was slightly shorter and less gregarious than her but was very polite, respectful, and had a wicked sense of humor, a trait that quickly endeared him to the family.

Feeling no ill effects from the chemotherapy, Graham resumed his teaching responsibilities, keeping a light load but got more engaged in the long-term planning of the school's expansion program.

Cynthia, too, continued her part-time teaching obligations and other social activities but was always watching Graham for any tell-tale signs of the recurrence of his tumor. A slight shuffle in his gait, any hint of being tired, excessive yawning, occasional nodding while reading his book, lack of appetite, or increased irritability made Cynthia jittery and alarmed. Much as she tried to conceal it from Graham, anxiety and apprehension began to dominate her life. Inexplicably the more Graham looked normal, the more restless she grew.

After finishing his fifth cycle of chemotherapy in the last week of January, Graham went for his MRI on February 1st and afterwards stopped by the main cafeteria at the hospital to get a cup of coffee. He heard a familiar voice, turned back, and saw Dr. Mehra holding a cup of coffee, sitting on a chair at one of the twenty or so tables in the cafeteria and chatting animatedly with a slightly balding man in an oversized warm jacket, also holding a foam cup in both hands.

Dr. Mehra also saw Graham and beckoned him to join them.

"Hello, Graham," he said as he shook his hand. "Let me introduce you to Dr. Yacov Kaufman, Chief Scientific Officer of CancerTech and leading the team working on brain and breast cancer. Yacov is very familiar with your case since the tumor tissue you agreed to donate was sent to his team."

Yacov suddenly froze. Surprised to unexpectedly come into face-to-face contact with the person whose tumor, tumor cells, and drugs to prevent their growth had consumed him and his colleagues for the last half-year.

He instinctively stood up, shook Graham's hand, and heard him say, "What a privilege to meet you, Dr. Kaufman."

"Please, call me Yacov." He then motioned Graham to sit down in the chair next to him. "How are you doing?"

"Fine. I was here for my MRI and am looking forward to finishing my sixth and last cycle of chemotherapy. Then I'm done," said Graham with a sense of relief.

Dr. Mehra added, "We're just talking about the progress CancerTech has made in trying to find drugs to kill brain tumor cells."

Yacov said, "You're a pioneer because the cells from your brain tumor are the cells we're using to test drugs to not only kill but to block the recurrence of tumors."

Just then Cynthia came to the table to say hello, and Graham introduced Dr. Kaufman to her.

"How nice meeting you. I have heard so much about you. A few months ago, I met Erica Hagen, who gave us a tour of CancerTech and let Graham's sister, his mother, and me look under a microscope at the feverishly growing cancer cells obtained from Graham's tumor. We missed seeing you because you're out of town," said Cynthia to Yacov, who had stood up when being introduced to her.

"Ah, the story of my life.," said Yacov a bit sheepishly and with a sly smile. "My wife thinks I travel too much. My New Year's resolution is always to cut down on my travel, and by February, I'm back to my old routine."

They again thanked Dr. Kaufman and Dr. Mehra, and then Graham said, "We'll leave the two of you so you can continue to talk and plot ways to prevent the recurrence of my cancer."

After Cynthia got her parking ticket validated, they walked hand in hand to the parking lot and mused how nice and sympathetic both Dr. Mehra and Dr. Kaufman were.

Meeting the patient and his wife in person left a big impression on Yacov. It was no more just Patient X—instead it was a handsome, healthy man with a lovely wife, who looked and acted normal but was carrying a ticking bomb in his brain. Yacov, a veteran of the 1973 Yom Kippur War in Israel and normally very stoic, was shaken. During the drive back to CancerTech, was overwhelmed with sadness at the cruelty of cancer and its devastation on families.

He cheered up after returning to his office because Erica had stopped him in the corridor to tell him that the Immune Bio drug was still as effective in repeat experiments as the "killer" molecule in preventing the growth of tumor cells from Patient X...*the man he had just met in the flesh...*

Chapter 13

RECURRENCE

THREE DAYS LATER, ON FRIDAY AF-TERNOON, one of the scientists enthusiastically told Yacov that no tumors were observed in the animals treated with the Immune Bio compound. He added that he was repeating the experiments using lower doses of the compound.

Good news has this odd trait, or some may say curse, of being evanescent.

A few hours later, Yacov got a call from Dr. Mehra, who said, "My initial diagnosis that Graham's tumor was back has been confirmed by the new MRI scan. There is clearly a larger mass of the tumor as compared to the nearly imperceptible one observed in the MRI scan in mid-December before he left for the UK. He is still largely asymptomatic. My hunch is that by late April or May, when the tumor mass gets larger, the symptoms will manifest, starting with the usual headaches, irritability, loss of memory, inability to make decisions, and feeling of being chronically tired."

"Oh my God, he and his family will be devastated by the news," remarked Yacov, who went slightly ashen.

"Though I was prepared for the bad news from the MRI, nevertheless I`m both saddened and disappointed. Since Graham shows no signs of the disease, I`m reluctant at this point to inform him about the new growth, which still could be the extended scar tissue caused by radiation. The only way we'll know for certain is by taking a biopsy, which will be done at surgery, a course I'll most likely recommend once the symptoms begin to appear," explained Rakesh.

"I know the ethics of my medical training call for being honest with the patient, but I'm not sure if telling Graham about the recurrence until I'm fully sure will be helpful. It'll only cause the family extreme anxiety."

"Did the recurrence occur around the site from where the original tumor was removed?"

"In the type and location of Graham's tumor, nearly 90% of the time, new growth occurs within two to three centimeters of the site of the original tumor. But some tumor cells can infiltrate to other places in the brain, which are not even detectable by MRI, and can yet lead to symptoms of the disease," replied Rakesh.

"I see why you want to wait to inform Graham about recurrence based on the current MRI results," said Yacov in agreement.

"I've scheduled a few more MRIs in the coming months and will closely monitor the situation. Graham and his wife are a very intelligent and realistic couple who know the nature of this disease, odds of recurrence, and will take the news with equanimity. More than likely they`ll be more interested in knowing about the next set of treatments," responded Dr. Mehra.

"And what are Graham's options?" inquired Yacov.

"Most probably another surgical resection and a repeat of radiation and chemotherapy. This may buy him a few more months," replied Rakesh without much conviction in his voice.

After a long pause, Yacov divulged, "Rakesh, I wanted to be a doctor and was all set to join the Hadassah Medical School in Jerusalem in 1978 when I went to see my uncle in the hospital who was undergoing treatment for pancreatic cancer. The doctor's words to my aunt still ring in my ears. "I'm really sorry, Mrs. Karczak. We'll do our best, but I wish science had made more strides in understanding and treating cancer. More research is needed." "I also knew that I'd never have the courage to pronounce judgement on who lives and who dies. Instead of going to medical school, I enrolled as a graduate student to do research in cancer biology."

Rakesh responded, "Over the years, thanks to scientists like you, we now know that unless the immortal cancer stem cells are prevented from growing, the tumors will come back, invade other parts of the brain, and patients will succumb to the disease."

"Our initial experience with the drug from Immune Bio is encouraging because it does not allow the brain tumor stem cells to divide and grow, but we`re a long way from taking it to the clinic. If we could come to some understanding with Immune Bio, probably the best time would be to administer it to the patient right after surgery to prevent any remaining tumor cells from proliferating and growing uncontrollably," opined Yacov. Resigned and sounding dejected, Rakesh said, "We will need the approval of our Institution and that of the FDA to conduct any clinical trials, which could take weeks or months."

"The most important issue for us is to see if Immune Bio would be interested in allowing us to use their lead compound, IB-617, which is in the clinic, to treat Graham. I really need to have a serious talk with our CEO about initiating a discussion with the management of Immune Bio," surmised Yacov.

With lukewarm enthusiasm, Dr. Mehra said, "Good luck. I just hope it's not too late."

* * *

Yacov was apprehensive in meeting with Bill Hollander, who had to date been only a very reluctant supporter of Yacov's efforts to find cures for brain tumors. On every occasion, he'd reminded Yacov of their primary obligation to start the Phase 1 clinical trials for breast cancer with their proprietary molecule, now owned by their Pharma collaborator.

He secured a one-on-one meeting with Bill in mid-February and laid out all the data on the successful killing of brain tumor cells with the drug from Immune Bio, waiting for some congratulatory comment on this achievement in such a short period.

Instead, Bill's first reaction was an outburst. "How did you get the drug? Who authorized that we get the drug from Immune Bio? Our Pharma partners have the final authority to permit any business transactions with another company. Yacov, you are jeopardizing the lucrative deal we made with the Pharma partner with your insistence on treating patients with brain tumors. I can't believe you'd do this and undermine our contractual obligations."

"Relax, Bill," Yacov said as he held his hands up to try to calm him down. "We`ve made no deals, just tested if one of their compounds being used for IBD also works in brain tumors by inhibiting a key molecule perhaps common to both diseases. Since there's no overlap between the interests of the two companies, it's a win-win situation. Sandy has made preliminary inquiries, and Immune Bio is cash-strapped and willing to come to some arrangement."

"I'm not sure how our partner will react since we have essentially gone around their back. I need to call their CEO to explain why they weren't consulted before setting up this collaboration with Immune Bio," spoke Bill, raising his voice to express some anger and frustration.

"We've made no arrangements. The only thing we did was to test if one of the earlier versions of their approved drug was effective in killing brain tumor cells. It was a scientific collaboration, not a business deal," replied Yacov, explaining again.

Their conversation was interrupted when Bill's administrative assistant poked her head in to inform him that the chairman of the CancerTech board was on the line.

Clearly irritated, Bill raised his left hand and with his palm facing Yacov, said, "Let me talk to the folks at Pharma," as he reached toward the phone with his other hand.

A few days later, on February 17th, Bill walked into Yacov's office and said, "I`ve talked to the senior management leaders of our Pharma partners, and they`re quite irate and adamant that CancerTech abandon its work on brain cancer and focus on their primary mission of breast cancer. They are threatening legal action if we divert any resources to work on brain cancer."

"Incredible," Yacov responded. "I don't get it. Why are they so opposed to work on brain tumors when we have a drug that can make a difference to the outcome of a deadly disease? We haven't used any major resources. They only own 80% of our company, so we still have the ability to explore other areas not covered in the agreement."

"But our agreement does stipulate their approval if we want to diversify our portfolio," retorted Bill, now quite agitated by Yacov's insistence. "We'd already started some work on brain tumors before our agreement with the Pharma partners was finalized," said Yacov, trying to find a way to circumvent the agreement.

"Look, Yacov, our Pharma partners have their own active program in the area of brain cancer, and they do not want any competition from one of their own subsidiaries," admitted Bill.

"We can collaborate with them," replied Yacov.

"They`re using immunotherapy approaches and are not interested in the small molecules approach that you are taking," said a slightly defensive Bill.

Dispirited with Bill's response, in an overtly defiant tone, Yacov said, "I didn't realize that by making a deal with our Pharma partners we'd lose all our independence and ability to do innovative research."

"Don't get me wrong, Yacov. I admire your efforts to find cures for brain tumors, but as CEO, I've got to be mindful of our obligation to our partners and the stipulations of our agreement. It`ll of course depend on the resources you need to move forward with your brain tumor clinical trials. Perhaps I can ask Sandy to informally ask the management at Immune Bio what it would cost to repurpose their drug for brain tumors." Bill was trying to placate Yacov, one of the most important assets of CancerTech.

Yacov was in low spirits after Bill left his office and was contemplating the possibility of asking Bill to form a subsidiary of CancerTech devoted to brain cancer when one of the scientists working in the brain tumor group walked into his office and announced, "Tumor cells from four other patients with malignant gliomas also failed to grow in the presence of the drug."

This was exactly the kind of news that acted as a tonic to bring cheer and bounce back to an eternal optimist like Yacov. He was a scientist first, and data was the staple diet he thrived on. He often thought that perhaps he should have been in an academic institution, but then he reminded himself of the horror stories of his academic colleagues—writing ten grants to get one and always chasing resources, tenures, recognition, and election to professional societies.

He began to dwell on what kind of resources Immune Bio would require. Would it be cash or stock? *Will the results obtained from the additional four patients make the case much stronger with Bill?*

Time is of the essence. *I must convince Bill and do it soon.*

In the meantime, Graham was outwardly doing fine, in good health, and looking forward to life without radiation or chemotherapy. There were days when he forgot all about his disease and felt no different than any of his other colleagues at the school. Cynthia and he visited friends for dinner, entertained, and even indulged in long-term planning to redo the kitchen. Their daughter Jessica was thinking of moving in with her boyfriend,

Adam, and there was even talk about possible grandchildren in the not-too-distant future. Graham's father suggested that Cynthia and he spend part of their spring break at Vancouver Island.

Nothing could be more normal.

But cancer patients have that sixth sense, perhaps the fear that something evil was lurking under the calm. Bad news was never far away, and the cruel fate that led to the cancer could again exert its perverse influence. Some patients and survivors sought solace in their faith, and others hoped for miracles. Graham's strength came from family and friends, and he was mindful not to make his disease the center of his relationships. Still, he sensed a distance and a certain labored softness around him from his intimate friends and family.

During spring break, both Cynthia and Graham had a very relaxing and fun-filled few days on Vancouver Island, where Linda and Graham's father have a beautiful house in a wooded area just 100 yards from the ocean.

Upon return, they resumed their routine, and Graham started to run longer distances, even hoping to get in shape for a marathon.

* * *

Negotiations between the business teams of Immune Bio and CancerTech began in earnest in mid-March, and a term sheet was agreed upon and presented to the management of both companies. The basic proposal was that CancerTech would provide $7.5 million up front to secure the rights to use the Immune Bio drug exclusively for the treatment of malignant gliomas. Bill Hollander managed to expand the drug usage to include brain metastasis of breast and lung cancers. If the drug became successful in treating deadly brain tumors, Immune Bio would receive a very handsome royalty.

The Pharma partners of CancerTech had made it abundantly clear that they had no interest in supporting the brain tumor trials with the Immune Bio drug and were opposed to the formation of another subsidiary by CancerTech. Bill Hollander was also explicit that CancerTech was not in a position to provide the funds, but he would not oppose it if Yacov raised the funds by private philanthropy.

Where and how could he raise the $7.5 million, which represented a year's worth of expenses for CancerTech? To soften the blow, Bill promised to make a small contribution to start such a fund.

Yacov Kaufman was at a loss where to even begin finding the resources required to acquire the drug from Immune Bio. He had been exclusively focused on the science and the drug that might provide relief to patients with brain tumors. He called Rakesh to strategize not only for raising the required funds but also initiating dialogue with the regulatory bodies for permission to use the drug compassionately to treat Graham, since standard clinical trial protocols would take months.

"Great. At least we now know the terms under which Immune Bio would be willing to provide IB-617 to treat Graham," said Rakesh.

"Right," said an anguished Yacov. "But how do we raise the $7.25 million, considering that Bill has indicated his willingness to contribute $250K.

"We can start by reaching out to some brain cancer foundations, maybe private philanthropy," suggested Rakesh.

"Even if we raise the funds required by Immune Bio, we`ll still need FDA approval for compassionate use on the basis that there are no comparable or satisfactory alternative treatment options for this deadly disease. IB-617 is an investigational new drug that has never been used for brain tumors, and there just isn't enough time to undertake standard clinical trials to treat patients with this drug. Requests for drug access must be made by a licensed doctor," explained Yacov, who had experience with this process at the previous biotech company where he had been a group leader dealing with hematological malignancies.

Rakesh said, "As the attending neuro-oncologist, I can request the use of the investigational new drug from FDA."

"You will also require approval from the Institutional Review Board (IRB). I'll set up an appointment with our Chief Medical Officer to go over the details and ask him to start the process to save time when we are ready to administer the drug. Immune Bio will need to approve the use of IB- 617 for brain tumors before the FDA will give approval. So, we need to get them on board as soon as possible, and for that, we still need to raise the big bucks," said Yacov with grave urgency.

Before ending their conversation, Rakesh reminded Yacov that he will be taking a few days off since the baby was due any time.

"Of course, and my very best. I hope that all goes well. Let Nurit and me know if you need any help," replied Yacov.

"Thanks, and let me know when to move forward with IRB approval," said Rakesh before hanging up.

Lakshmi gave birth to a healthy seven-pound baby boy in the wee hours of March 27th, 2005. Two days later, they brought him home and named him Sudhir, meaning 'very wise and considerate' in Sanskrit, the holy and ancient language of India. The next few weeks went by in a blurry haze, mostly due to lack of a full night's sleep. Both felt the absence of close family and remained hopeful that the arrival of the baby might eventually change the attitude of their families, stuck in false pride and prejudices.

* * *

Cynthia and Graham quietly celebrated his fifty-first birthday on May 6th with their daughters and a few close friends, a low-key affair. But neither Cynthia nor Graham had forgotten the fiftieth birthday when it all started. Their attitude now was to take one *day at a time*.

In late May, Graham woke up alone in the middle of the night, drenched in sweat, feeling very nauseous, and had a splitting headache. Cynthia was away helping Nigel pack up before his departure to Australia for a three-month internship at James Cook University in Townsville on the Great Barrier Reef.

Instead of going back to bed, he sat down in the dark on the living room sofa, and started to relive the unbearable headaches, restlessness, and fear of walking lest he fall—terrible experiences he had gone through a year ago. Had the tumor come back in enough force to overwhelm his future with misery and hopelessness? Did he want to go through the surgery, radiation, and chemotherapy again? Did he want to put his family through another round of agony and uncertainty? Should he just give up and make peace with his maker? In this darkening despair, he quietly recited a stanza from Tennyson's poem, "All Things Will Die."

The stream will cease to flow;
The wind will cease to blow;
The clouds will cease to fleet;
The heart will cease to beat;
For all things must die.
All things must die.

He was relieved that Cynthia was away and not witnessing his broken spirit, gloomy thoughts, and utter sense of helplessness. Yet, he missed her reassuring presence, a certain calmness and closeness that needed no spoken words.

He did not inform Cynthia of this episode upon her return, nor did he tell his neuro-oncologist, Dr. Mehra.

However, Cynthia, ever alert to the slightest of nuances in Graham's behavior, moods, and actions since last year, quickly sensed that something was awry. She was grateful that the school activities were significantly reduced during summer holidays, leaving them more time together. She made sure to buy his favorite food, rented old movies they enjoyed as young lovers, extended hand-holding, loving caresses, and kisses. She did not want to alarm him by being overly protective but wanted to allow him to maintain his dignity, while also desiring to spend every minute she could with him. Outwardly they remained stoic, but their time together was punctuated by long silences, furtive glances, and silent tears.

Chapter 14

THE MONSTER RETURNS

GRAHAM AND CYNTHIA MET Dr. Mehra in his office at 11 A.M. on Wednesday, June 1st, 2005 to review his latest MRI. Since they hadn't had an in-person appointment with Dr. Mehra for some time, Cynthia engaged in small talk with him, inquiring about his family and his baby boy.

"He must be ten weeks old now."

"That's right, and thanks for asking. Mom and son are doing well. Finally, we can sleep uninterrupted for at least four to five hours. His main activities remain eating, sleeping, and excreting…" replied Dr. Mehra.

"Hope we'll someday get to meet your lovely wife and your little boy."

Graham was quietly listening, but his eyes were transfixed on the screen of the computer facing sideways on Dr. Mehra's desk. There he saw the familiar picture of an MRI scan of his brain with the big, white, fuzzy structure he had seen a year ago on the same computer screen, affirming what he already knew in his heart.

Perceiving Graham's anxiety, Dr. Mehra swiveled his chair to face him and, in a grave, voice said, "I`m sorry, Graham, but the tumor that was excised from your brain nearly a year ago has reemerged and is growing fast." Pointing with his pen, he then showed on the screen the region of the brain where the tumor had been removed. It was clear that there was new growth in the same region, as well as in some additional surrounding tissue.

"I know that this is most disappointing news, considering that the surgery had been successful, and the subsequent radio and chemotherapy treatment kept the tumor at bay. Most importantly, you`re leading a nearly normal life, and now the tumor has returned. Have you had some of the symptoms that you had experienced before surgery?" inquired Dr. Mehra with great sadness in his voice.

Holding tears back, Graham slowly volunteered, "Yes, I had bad episodes of vomiting and severe headaches when Cynthia was away a few weeks ago. The intensity of my headaches and restlessness have also increased. I`ve been hoping against hope that these symptoms were not due to a recurrence of the tumor, but I knew better."

Cynthia's heart had nearly stopped when she'd heard the words, "Tumor…has reemerged," and she took Graham's head in her embrace for what appeared to be an eternity.

Neither could contain their emotions now and wept openly.

Collecting himself, a defeated Graham asked in a choking voice, "What's next?"

"The tumor is still largely localized and can be excised

again. We'll follow it with radiation and chemotherapy. In the last year, newer protocols have been approved that recommend the two treatments be undertaken at the same time. Your physical condition is good, and I'm sure surgery will alleviate many of your current symptoms and give you additional quality time with family and friends," said Dr. Mehra with decreasing confidence in his voice.

"Is it really worth having my family go through the agony and uncertainty again when the outcome is certain?" implored Graham. "The tumor is recalcitrant and will not retreat."

Cynthia, holding her tears back, put her arm around Graham and said, "Darling, don't worry about the family. It's you who has to go through the treatment. You know we'll always be there. Please don't give up if there is even a small hope of having you with us longer."

Dr. Mehra, waiting for the right opportunity, addressed Graham, "Remember you allowed CancerTech to have a small sample of the tumor we excised from your brain for research purposes. They've made great progress in devising new strategies to kill your brain tumor cells. I have arranged a meeting this afternoon with Dr. Yacov Kaufman, who you met some months ago, to tell you about the progress they've made and the possibility of novel therapy. He'll be here around 2:30 p.m. with another member of his team. Can you stay that long and come back after lunch? I'll ask my admin to open the conference room where we will meet so you can use it to rest prior to the meeting."

Cynthia volunteered, "We'll be back for the conference with Dr. Kaufman." She then stood up along with Graham, thanked Dr. Mehra, and escorted themselves out of his office.

Dr. Mehra was left standing for a while, engulfed with enormous sadness. Once again, he could not help but think of his newborn son, whose life was ahead of him, and Graham, whose life may soon be behind him.

* * *

During lunch at a small café near the hospital, Cynthia tried to lift Graham's spirits by sharing some family news. Nigel had arrived in Sydney and was going to take a few days to sightsee before flying to Townsville to start his internship. Adelaide was planning to come next week from Singapore with Roger, who was attending a conference in San Francisco. Jessica was moving in with Adam at the end of June, and Amber was not sure if she wanted to keep the duplex or rent a smaller apartment in the same complex.

Graham nodded but was not listening. He was lost in thought about his dismal future, the futility of fighting the disease, and was terrified of what lay ahead. He had hardly touched his ahi salad when the waiter came around to pick up the plates and asked if they wanted some dessert, coffee, or tea. Before Cynthia could say anything, Graham pushed away his salad and asked for a cup of black coffee.

The waiter offered to pack the leftovers, which she politely declined.

Uncharacteristically, Cynthia ordered dessert, hoping that Graham would share it. She knew that lack of any appetite would only accentuate his irritability. She held onto hope that the scientists at CancerTech could come up with a new therapy that would get rid of Graham's cancer once and for all.

Dr. Kaufman, wearing a yellow Polo T-shirt that barely contained his belly, and trailed by a rod-thin Erica Hagen with a fashionable bag hanging from her shoulder, made an odd couple as they walked into the conference room. They reintroduced themselves to Cynthia and Graham, who had been in the room for the last twenty minutes, looking through some professional journals strewn over the central table. Although Yacov had briefly met them before, he wanted to make sure that they remembered him.

Cynthia reminded Erica, "We have met you before when I visited CancerTech with my husband's mother and sister."

Erica nodded, sat down near the projector, and connected it to Yacov's laptop.

After a brief hesitation, the haphazard and disorganized contents of his computer screen were displayed on the large screen of the conference room. Yacov then opened the file labeled '*Patient X May 28th, 2004.*'

Soon Dr. Mehra walked in and said, "Hello, everyone. I guess you had time to get acquainted. Yacov and Erica will update you on their efforts at CancerTech to find drugs that have the potential to kill the cancer cells now lodged in Graham's brain.

"Yacov, can you please lead the Bunkers through some of the highlights of research that has led to the development of IB-556 as a possible therapeutic drug to treat patients with glioblastoma?"

A chill went down Cynthia's spine, and she immediately put her hand in Graham's slightly sweaty palm.

Graham also felt that a shockwave had just jolted him.

"Rakesh, can we dim the lights please?" Yacov asked.

Using a laser pointer aimed at the screen, he began, "*Patient X* is Graham Bunker, whose tumor tissue was brought to CancerTech on May 28th of 2004. With Erica's help"—Yacov pointed to her, and she demurred on being recognized— "we were able to grow tumor cells in petri dishes that produced tumors when introduced into the brains of mice, which we use as experimental animal model systems. We then identified the drugs that killed the cancer cells and also eliminated the tumors in the mice brains. Recently, we had samples from five additional patients, and the drug was able to kill tumor cells from four of the five patients with brain tumors similar to Patient X's, I mean yours, Graham." Yacov turned to face him with a nod.

Erica added, "We`re working hard to figure out why the cancer cells from one of the patients did not respond to the drug."

Yacov then advanced to slide #9 and said with a slightly dramatic flair, "And here we hit the jackpot! The drug that we`re working on had been used by another company working on a different disease, and they had done quite extensive toxicity studies. The regulatory authorities had allowed them to proceed to what we scientists call, in our jargon, 'Phase 1 clinical trials.'"

Graham, who was now quite energized, asked, "You mean it's already been tested in patients and found to be safe? What were they using it for?"

"A completely different disease called Inflammatory Bowel Disease (IBD) that affects the digestive system. a very nasty disease also sometimes called Ulcerative Colitis," responded Yacov.

"Honey, Christine, our chemistry teacher, suffers from

this disease," added Cynthia.

"What got us interested in this drug was that it had the potential to stop the growth of immortal stem cells, which is what malignant brain tumors are—cancer stem cells growing uncontrollably," said Yacov. He then changed slides and pointed to a petri dish with thriving and menacing tumor cells and then another, under the influence of the drug, where the tumor cells were shriveled, dying, and bereft of the threatening stance.

Dr. Mehra chimed in, "These are spectacular results."

"Can this drug be used to prevent the growth of my brain tumor?" asked a startled Graham, barely able to conceal his excitement.

Yacov looked directly into Graham's eyes and slowly nodded his head, saying, *"Ken* (Yes in Hebrew), I mean yes, definitely!"

Cynthia's eyes were brimming with tears, and in a choked voice, she pleaded, "Dr. Kaufman, are you sure?"

"Yes, but there is always the uncertainty of whether the data obtained in experimental systems can be replicated in humans. We will only know for certain after clinical trials in patients."

"What will I have to do to be part of the clinical trials?" asked Graham.

Yacov then carefully but candidly explained to them some of the unresolved bureaucratic and financial hurdles for obtaining the drug.

Before he could finish, Graham interrupted, "Even if the drug were available, it would be several months of clinical trials before I could be enrolled. My tumor is growing so fast. I may not be around to benefit from it."

Dr. Mehra responded, carefully choosing his words, "The Federal Drug Agency (FDA), responsible for approving the use of investigational drugs like the one Yacov mentioned, has a program that allows 'compassionate use' for seriously ill patients for whom there are no other approved therapies. There just isn't time for proper clinical trials, so we've started the process for approval to use the drug without waiting for the outcome of phase 1 clinical trials."

Yacov turned off the projector, asked Dr. Mehra to turn on the lights, looked directly at the couple, and said, "There are monetary issues that may hinder the immediate use of this drug for Graham's treatment. The company, Immune Bio, which developed the drug, wants a $7.5 million prepayment as the cost of supplying the drug. My company, which is now largely owned by a Pharma company, is not willing to foot the bill for the drug since their primary focus is breast, not brain cancer."

There was dead silence in the room, and then Dr. Mehra spoke, "Yacov and I have not yet fully explored the ways to raise the required amount through support from brain tumor foundations and private philanthropy. We have even considered the possibility of forming a new business entity for the treatment of brain cancer."

Looking directly at Graham, he continued, "We still have a few weeks' window to find ways to raise the required capital for obtaining the drug. I've agreed to be the physician in charge of conducting the clinical trial and have submitted a request to the Institutional Review Board at Morton Hospital for approval."

Cynthia, seizing the moment, immediately volunteered to help raise the required amount, while Graham, appearing defeated, said in a subdued tone, "This is a lot of money, and there's no guarantee that the drug will work."

After some additional discussion and clarifications, Dr. Mehra thanked Yacov and Erica for coming over to explain the results of the new drug and its implications for Graham's disease.

After Yacov and Erica left, Dr. Mehra asked Cynthia and Graham if they could come by the following week for a consultation and to plan a course of treatment of the recurrent disease.

"Graham, I know recurrence of your cancer is a setback, but the longer we can keep your disease in check, the greater are the chances to use the experimental therapeutic drug from CancerTech that looks so promising."

"Thanks, Dr. Mehra. I will do my part."

Before escorting them from the conference room, Dr. Mehra said, "I'll see if Dr. Jabbar can also join us for a brief period when you come for consultation in the coming week."

* * *

Cynthia, clinging to any ray of hope for a cure of Graham's cancer, was very encouraged after the meeting with Erica and Yacov and felt that her body would explode with excitement. Graham, though hopeful, felt that it might be too late for him, especially because his symptoms were getting more pronounced and he would probably have to go through another cycle of surgery, radiation, and chemotherapy.

It was a beautiful day with warm but not hot temperatures and a cloudless blue sky. While driving back home,

Cynthia suggested a diversion to take a short walk at Half Moon Bay coast-side trail.

Graham would have liked to go if for nothing else than to please Cynthia but felt exhausted after listening intensely to Yacov Kaufman, and the familiar headache was intensifying to the point of making him nauseous. He demurred hesitantly, and Cynthia, by now an expert in reading Graham's mind, did not persist and instead continued to drive straight back home to Palo Alto. They spent the rest of the week at home and decided to skip the engagement party of one of their colleagues at the school.

* * *

On the following Tuesday, June 21st, when they arrived at Dr. Mehra's office, Dr. Jabbar was looking at the MRI scan on the computer screen. She was in her operating attire and looked back to greet them with her broad smile.

Shaking her head, she said, "I thought that I had excised the last of the tumor tissue, and here the monster is clawing back," pointing with her forefinger to the computer screen. "It is still contained, maybe two to three centimeters farther than the original tumor and can be excised quite cleanly. If the surgery can be arranged before July 16th, I can operate, otherwise, we may have to wait till mid-August when I am back from my annual mission to Africa."

Dr. Mehra reminded Cynthia and Graham that Dr. Jabbar was part of a charitable foundation of surgeons who, on their own time and dime, performed operations on patients, mostly children, in West Africa. After a little more talk about the work of the foundation, Dr. Jabbar got up, waved at Graham and Cynthia, and walked out of the office towards the surgery ward.

In what felt like completely familiar territory, Dr. Mehra led Graham through the protocol: taking Decadron pills before surgery, the craniotomy, rest for two to three weeks followed by radiation and chemotherapy, which according to new protocols could be administered simultaneously rather than sequentially as was done the last time.

Graham asked, "Are surgery, radiation, and chemotherapy necessary if I can be treated with the drug that Dr. Kaufman had mentioned a few days ago?"

"Yes, both for ethical and medical reasons. The tumor is growing, and we know that its removal will reduce the symptoms, and a radiation- chemotherapy regimen will slow the progression. The treatment with the experimental drug still needs to cross the bureaucratic and financial hurdles, which could take months. Yacov and I are still working on various possibilities to raise the funds required to obtain the drug from the company. Ethically, in the absence of any alternative treatments, we're obligated to undertake conventional treatments, which in your case would be surgery, radiation, and chemotherapy," explained Dr. Mehra.

"Do I really have to undergo another round of treatment when we'll know that this's a terminal cancer?" urged Graham.

Before Dr. Mehra could respond, Cynthia interjected, "Graham, you're not in it alone. We're all here for you. The new drug seems very promising, so please, darling, don't give up. There's hope on the horizon."

Dr. Mehra supported Cynthia's contention and re-emphasized that surgery, radiation, and chemotherapy would buy him time to try the new drug. As an afterthought, he added, "Of course, it is your decision, but remember that a lot of us are pulling for you."

Graham was torn, especially now that he was currently experiencing one of those intolerable episodes of headache that made him want to crawl into a dark space, close his eyes, and not think or talk.

He cupped his face into his palms and groaned, "I`m so tired…I just want it to be over…"

Cynthia hugged him and sat quietly while Dr. Mehra again felt his helplessness in being unable to provide greater reassurance to Graham. After some time and feeling defeated, Graham said, "I should have the surgery before Dr. Jabbar leaves for her philanthropic mission in Africa." On the drive back home, Graham seemed more at peace, so Cynthia raised the issue of either getting a second mortgage or selling their Palo Alto home to help raise part of the $7.5 million needed to get the therapeutic drug.

Graham, who was slouching in the passenger seat, sat up and said, "No way. I'm not going to squander my children's and your future inheritance. There's absolutely no guarantee that the drug will work nor for how long. Cynthia, we must come to the realization that my days are numbered, and all I want is a pain-free, peaceful death."

Since last year when Graham was first diagnosed, Cynthia had learned to control her emotions and not succumb to crying in Graham's presence, but this was the first time he'd used the word *death*, and it completely unhinged her.

She took the next exit, pulled into the parking lot of a

fast-food restaurant, and stopped the car. Bursting into tears, she buried her head in Graham's lap, and between her sobs, cried out, "I don't want to be left alone without you. For your children's and my sake, you have to, you must fight hard to survive. We'll put every resource we have into finding the best treatment or drug for you. We love you and don't plan to lose you."

Graham, overwhelmed with Cynthia's mournful plea, now also burst into tears and, stroking her hair, said repeatedly, "I want to live and not die. I'm, for God's sake, only fifty-one and have much to live for. I`ll try to muster more courage to fight this horrible disease. Sometimes I feel that I'm being pulled into a dark tunnel where there is no end and no going back."

They stayed in the car, intertwined with each other, saying nothing more and yet silently communicating their fear of the future.

* * *

Back home, there was a message from Adelaide asking if she and Roger could come by on Friday evening to go out for dinner. The second message was from Amber, informing them that she could move to a one-bedroom apartment in the same complex without breaking the lease, so there would be no penalties. There was also a solicitation for donations by a Nature Preservation Society.

Utterly shaken by the life-altering news received in the last few hours, Cynthia sat down on the sofa and for a long time looked out of the window into the front yard. After a while, she collected herself, picked up the phone, and left a note for Adelaide at her hotel, asking if she and Roger would come around 5 p.m. for drinks before dinner. She decided to call Amber later after dinner when she was more likely to be at home and Cynthia herself would be more composed.

After a light supper and some TV, Graham said, "It was a long day," and then added, "Of course, it's June 21st, the longest day of the year."

"Yes, a day which brought news of a miracle drug that can lengthen your life."

After Graham went to bed, Cynthia first called Amber and then Jessica, both of whom were away, but she did not leave a message. She didn't try to call Nigel because it was the middle of the day in Townsville and he was probably busy. She will talk to them tomorrow. Unable to concentrate, she went to the living room to halfheartedly read a book, but soon decided to go to bed and curled up next to Graham's warm body.

How many more nights do I have left to lie next to him-my husband, my love, my friend, my confidante, and father of my children? I will do anything to raise the funds needed to get the drug. So long as there is hope, I will cling to it…

* * *

Though Graham woke up late, he felt tired and unwilling to get out of bed. After some gentle prodding from Cynthia, he joined her for breakfast and glanced at the newspaper with its blaring headline, "Klansman Convicted for 1964 Civil Rights Killings," then put it aside. He had switched from his beloved morning coffee to tea because coffee made him nauseous.

Cynthia said, "Instead of going out for dinner, I will

cook for Adelaide and Roger. This way we can stay home, and if you are tired or not feeling well, you can rest."

"Good idea. Adelaide used to like Cornish game hen, but I do not know what Roger's favorite foods are," advised Graham.

"Okay. I'll see if the Schaub's have game hens, and I can buy some bell peppers, apples, celery, and onions for stuffing. We can serve them with long-grain brown rice and cranberry sauce. As an appetizer, maybe I will make a caprese salad and buy strawberries with vanilla bean ice cream for dessert." Cynthia mulled over the menu with Graham.

How good it feels to talk about simple things like planning a dinner menu and to temporarily block the impending reality of life and death.

On Thursday evening, she again called Amber, who excitedly told her all about new apartment and how tomorrow evening Jessica and Adam would come to help her move.

Amber said, "Mom, why don't Dad and you come Saturday afternoon to see my new place?"

"Sure," Cynthia replied, adding that Aunt Adelaide and Roger were coming for dinner tomorrow.

"I know. Jessica, Adam, and I are having breakfast at their fancy hotel on Sunday morning," replied Amber.

"Good, darling. Goodnight, we'll see you Saturday afternoon." She realized that it was the first time that the girls were moving and their dad was not helping them carry their boxes, and this realization made her very sad. Choking back tears, she sat down on a chair in the dining room and started to think about the day the twins moved out of the house to their apartment in San Francisco with all their possessions in a U-Haul truck that Graham drove. How she followed them in her car, loaded with groceries and two lovely orchids, one for each of her daughters. How sad Graham was to return to a home without his daughters and wandered around their half-empty rooms.

* * *

Graham had a short nap in the afternoon and was well-rested when Roger and Adelaide arrived a few minutes before 5 p.m. After hugs and hellos, Roger sat down on the sofa next to the chair Graham was occupying, while Adelaide wandered toward the kitchen with Cynthia, who was looking for an appropriate vase for the beautiful yellow and pink tulips they had brought.

"How's my little brother doing? He looks thinner, gaunter, and like Dad, seems to be thinning at the top," surmised Adelaide in almost a muted voice.

Trying to be calm but unable to keep her composure, Cynthia, with tears brimming in her eyes, said, "Oh, it's been up and down, a roller coaster of emotions. Outwardly Graham looks normal, but two days ago, his neuro-oncologist informed us that his tumor is back. Your brother is struggling. It's been tough all around, but we're coping as best as we can."

"Oh, no! I thought that the tumor was in regression, and Dad said that during the time you both spent in Vancouver Island a few months ago, Graham was doing fine and seemed happy," said Adelaide, shaken by Cynthia's news. She immediately hugged Cynthia, and with choked emotions, said, "I'm so sorry. It's so unfair. Graham is a wonderful person, a great husband and dad. We have not always kept up, but he is one of the dearest people in the world. I hope there are newer treatments that can help him."

They remained holding each other for a while, then separated, found kitchen paper towels to wipe their tears, and composed themselves.

Soon Cynthia carried a large plate of hors d'oeuvres, some black olives, cashews, and four small ceramic plates, and placed them on the glass table in the living room. Adelaide helped her to carry the napkins and small forks.

Cynthia asked if they preferred Chardonnay or Pinot. Roger opted for a glass of Chardonnay, and Cynthia joined him, while Adelaide and Graham chose to have sparkling water.

Adelaide, now fully composed, sat next to Graham, put her hand on his wrist, and said, "Linda and Dad are thinking of coming over to spend a few days in Singapore on their way to Bali in December. Little do they realize that exotic Bali is now swamped with foreigners and unruly tourists."

Graham asked if she had recently talked to Mum, and Adelaide replied, "Yes, but Scotty is now pretty much bed-ridden, so Mum stays mostly in Elsworth, which is closer to hospitals than their country manor in Essex. Mum also has to watch her diet and weight because the doctors have told her that her blood sugar levels are borderline for diabetes."

To add a bit of lightness to the conversation, Cynthia told them that Jessica was moving in with her boyfriend and was talking of a possible fall wedding. She also mentioned that Nigel was in Australia and suggested he stop by in Singapore before returning home.

Adelaide quickly added, "Great. Maybe Roger can take him sailing on his new boat."

Graham asked Roger if he was enjoying the quiet and predictable life of organized Singapore compared to the chaos of Africa.

Swirling his wine, Roger thoughtfully replied, "I'm soon going to hit sixty, so I like routine, security, and a bit of the good life. Africa is wonderful, but there is increasing violence and corruption. Of course, I do miss the daily hustle and bustle and chaos compared to the calm and peace of Singapore."

Graham, holding a nearly empty glass of water in his hand, glanced at Cynthia as if asking for her consent, and during a pause in the conversation said, "I'm sorry to tell you, but my tumor is back, and I've started to experience the same horrible symptoms I had before my surgery nearly a year ago."

Adelaide put her arm around her brother and said, "Cynthia just told me. I`m sorry, Graham."

Roger, slouching on the big leather chair, straightened up and said with great empathy, "I`m so sorry to hear this dreadful news. I was under the impression that your tumor was completely excised and the disease was under control. What do the doctors say are your options?"

"My doctors recommend that I go through the same ritual of surgery, radiation, and chemotherapy as before. I remain of two minds—go through it again or just give up because ultimately, it's an untreatable cancer," replied Graham in a broken voice.

Cynthia, putting her glass down, added, "But, Graham, you haven`t yet told Roger and Adelaide about the discoveries at CancerTech and the new drug they want to try to treat your cancer. I'm excited and very hopeful."

Adelaide and Roger put their plates down and looked towards Graham for more explanation.

Graham recapped the meeting with Dr. Kaufman and Dr. Mehra and the possibility of using the drug developed for another disease to kill his brain tumor cells. He added, "Tumor cells from four other patients with a similar disease as mine were also killed by this drug. However, there's a catch. The company that developed the drug is asking for an upfront payment of $7.5 million to release the drug and accompanying safety and clinical data. CancerTech is not willing to foot the bill because its mandate is to find cures for breast cancer, not the cancer growing in my brain."

A slightly incredulous Roger said, "You mean that there's a possibility of treatment, but it couldn`t be executed because the company wants an upfront payment of $7.5 million? That's a crying shame. If such a drug exists, why shouldn't it be tried on terminally ill patients?"

He immediately regretted using the word *terminally*, as he saw Cynthia flinch at the word.

"From what I could gather between the lines, the Pharma company that owns 80% of CancerTech also has some of their own programs for treatment of brain cancers in the pipeline and are reluctant to support a competing drug," said Graham with great disappointment and anger in his voice.

Cynthia added, "Dr. Mehra, the neuro-oncologist, has raised the possibility of reaching out to some foundations and private philanthropy to raise the capital required to get the experimental drug. Graham is totally opposed to the idea of taking a second mortgage on our house, which has considerably increased in value since your father first bought it in the sixties. I bet it is now probably well over $2.5 to $3 million, so we could probably get at least a $1.5 million second mortgage or home equity loan."

Graham vehemently and a bit agitatedly said, "No. Cynthia, no! As I said earlier, this option isn't on the table. I don't want to compromise my children's and your future, especially for an unproven treatment."

A look passed between Adelaide and Roger.

Cynthia knew better than to dwell on this topic any further, so she let it go and asked everyone to come to the dining table for dinner.

Adelaide followed her into the kitchen, put her hands on Cynthia's shoulders, and said, "I feel bad putting you through this trouble to prepare dinner when you've so much on your mind, but I guess it's better for Graham to stay home."

"Yes, that's why we wanted to have dinner here, so that Graham could rest if needed. I also couldn't bear the prospect of being surrounded by strangers joking and laughing," replied Cynthia with a tone betraying slight bitterness.

After the first course, as Cynthia was clearing the empty salad plates, Graham pushed back his chair, said that he wasn't feeling well, apologized, and went to his bedroom. He asked Adelaide and Roger not to leave before saying goodbye.

"Sometimes the headaches subside. I'll then come out to join you all."

After he left, Adelaide, with tears in her eyes said, "This isn't my brother—the fast and fearless leader I always looked up to, even though I'm two years older. He's my rock. I'd hide in his room when Mum and Dad had those acrimonious quarrels before their divorce."

"Wiping off her tears, she continued, "He`s diminishing and fading. We need to do all we can for him to get this miracle drug that the company has. Have you talked to Mum and Dad?"

"No. We haven't even told the children about the recurrence of the cancer, but they'll soon find out. I'm trying to spare them, especially since they have gone through it once already."

"Cynthia, you must be going through an impossibly difficult period. I can't imagine your sorrow and fear of what lies ahead," lamented Graham's distraught sister.

"I'm still in shock, an emotional wreck, trying to conceal my sadness, but Graham is too smart and sensitive not to notice. Some days we walk like zombies, avoiding eye contact. Other days we talk about utterly mundane things to avoid talking about the future. I want to hold him all night in my arms, but his sleep is restless, and he wakes up dazed and sweaty. I`m so scared of what lies ahead," Cynthia confessed, trying to wipe her tears.

Adelaide put her hand on Cynthia's arm and said, "Graham is stronger than you think. He`ll come through. Roger and I will also try to find ways to get that drug to treat my brother."

Roger immediately echoed his wife's sentiment and said, "Yes, we must find ways to raise the funds...it is appalling that a lifesaving treatment is hostage to availability of funds."

Cynthia thanked them, got up to go to the kitchen. Adelaide followed and returned to the table, carrying the pots containing rice and cranberry sauce. After washing her hands, Cynthia, donned her quilted gloves to take out the glass pan containing the game hens and put it on the counter. She expertly transferred the four game hens onto a large ceramic serving plate and made her way back to the dining table. As she set the plate in the center, she announced proudly, "Graham reminded me that his sister loves stuffed Cornish game hens, so Adelaide, that's what we're having."

"Oh, they look divine, smell delicious, and are definitely one of my favorites!" Adelaide exclaimed.

Though Graham's disease lurked in the background, the conversation moved on to Jessica's boyfriend, how Amber was too busy to find one, and how Nigel was likely to bring back with him some Aussie blonde intent on surfing and playing beach volleyball.

"I think Nigel has many girlfriends," said Cynthia with a twinkle in her eyes.

Graham didn't return, and when Cynthia checked in on him to see if he wanted Adelaide and Roger to say goodnight before leaving, he appeared to be in deep slumber.

"Can I go in and give a hug to my brother, even if he is sleeping? I don't know if I'll have a chance to see him before we leave on Sunday," said Adelaide.

"Sure. You've known him a lot longer than I have. Besides, your brother adores you and wishes that Roger and you had chosen San Francisco instead of Singapore," said Cynthia, trying to lighten the atmosphere.

After they left, Cynthia, feeling totally alone, sat down at the dining table with a glass of wine, reliving her life from the time she'd met Graham to the present. After a while, she realized it was approaching the hour of 10 p.m. She got up to clean the kitchen and load up the dishwasher.

When she went to bed, Graham was still asleep, and

she gently slipped under the sheets and lay next to him.

The next morning, Graham was already up and browsing the paper when she walked into the kitchen and heard him say, "I`m really sorry for leaving the dinner early, but I was in no shape to carry on the conversation. Hope they enjoyed the rest of the dinner."

"I think so, and Adelaide really liked her Cornish game hen. I've kept one for you if you feel like having it later for lunch. Roger is more reserved, but I think he enjoyed himself. Adelaide went to the bedroom to give you a hug, even though you were asleep," said Cynthia, pouring a cup of coffee for herself.

Graham put the newspaper down and said, "Have I ever told you that she often came to hide in my room when Mom and Dad's quarrels became shouting matches?"

"Knowing your mom and Dad, I still find it hard to imagine that they had bitter quarrels. Both are such nice, decent, and loving people," said Cynthia while pouring a cup of coffee and settling with her bowl of cereal.

Graham looked up and opined, "I think Dad was jealous of Mom`s success and rapid career advancement, "and went back to reading the paper.

"By the way, I`m going to San Francisco in the afternoon to see Amber`s new apartment. Do you want to come?"

"No, I will stay home and do some research on the process of clinical trials, brain tumor foundations, and the company that has the drug. Maybe we should soon have Amber, Jessica, and Adam for lunch to tell them what lies ahead for me," said Graham, looking up from his newspaper.

"I think that's a good idea, but I am not sure that I can hide the news of recurrence from Amber since she will most likely figure out that something is amiss from my grim tone. But I won't bring it up on my own."

Chapter 15

HOPE AGAINST HOPE

AROUND 6 P.M. ON SUNDAY, JUNE 26TH, Graham received an email from his sister Adelaide, who was on her way to London to visit Roger's family before getting back to Singapore. The email would change Graham's life:

My Dearest Brother:

I am sorry that Roger and I were not able to say goodbye after the dinner, though I did sneak into your bedroom to give you a hug and a peck on your cheek.

We have been continuously thinking of you since our dinner last Friday. Distressing as it was to learn about the recurrence of your cancer, but we were most encouraged by the news of the possibility of trying new therapies that could change the predicted outcome of your disease. The drug you mentioned, which kills your tumor cells in petri dishes and mice, sounded extremely promising. The catch seems to be the price tag demanded by the company pro-

ducing the drug.

As you know, Roger is an only child with no siblings, and we were unable to have children. You are my only brother, and your family are our closest relatives. A large part of our wealth will eventually go to Amber, Jessica, and Nigel. But what good is this wealth if it cannot be used to give a chance of life to my brother and their father?

Remember when we were little, we used to make forts from the furniture in the living room. You always had a little chair in the middle where I sat, and you'd take out your sword made of cardboard wrapped with tin foil and loudly proclaim, "I will protect you from all the invaders." Now it is my turn, and I want to protect you from the evil invader—your cancer.

Roger and I would be glad to make the donation of $7.5 million that is required to get the drug to treat you.

I know your first reaction will be to say no, but please think of Cynthia, your three lovely kids, Mum, Dad, Linda, Roger, and me…We want you to be with us as long as possible.

Graham, please think about it. Please!

Much Love,

Roger and Adelaide

When Cynthia walked into Graham's study to ask if he was ready for dinner, she saw him staring at the computer screen with tears rolling down his face. Alarmed, she rushed to his chair, put her hands on his shoulders, and asked, "What happened?"

Graham pointed to the letter on the screen, and after reading it, Cynthia too, had tears streaming down her face. She tightened her embrace and stayed in that position for a while with her chin on his head.

"I can't really accept this most generous gift because there's no certainty that the drug will work or for how long. It would be very selfish of me. This large sum can be used for many other worthwhile causes," said Graham.

Cynthia, loosening her grip around Graham's shoulders, said, "Let's think about it before you respond. Anyway, Roger and Adelaide are on the plane for the next twelve hours."

They did not discuss the email from Adelaide and Roger during dinner, and Graham, visibly tired and stifling yawns, went to bed early. For several days now, Graham felt exhausted by early evening, despite multiple naps in the day, and had been going to bed earlier and earlier.

Around 9 p.m. there was a call from Graham's father, who had spoken to Adelaide before she boarded the plane for London.

"Cynthia, I'm so sorry and sad to hear that Graham's cancer is back. During your spring visit, he appeared healthy and free of disease. Linda and I thought the worst was over.

"Yes, we thought the same. We're devastated to hear that the cancer was clawing back. I couldn't summon the courage to inform you and the rest of the family. Just this afternoon, we told the girls, and of course, they're disconsolate but were very mature in their response and saw a ray of hope in the possibility of new treatments. I was planning to call you tonight. Tomorrow I'll call Karen, and Nigel is in a boat on the sea and unreachable."

Graham's father excitedly said, "I, too, am very encouraged to know that Graham can be enrolled for treatment with a new therapeutic drug."

"We learned of this treatment early in the week and are also very excited about its potential to treat Graham's cancer. However, his doctor has advised that before starting treatment with the new drug, he still recommends a second round of surgery followed by radiation and chemotherapy, what you once referred to as 'cut, burn, and poison treatment.'"

"But why? Why don't they treat him with this new drug?"

"His neuro-oncologist explained to us, for ethical reasons they have to undertake the recommended protocols. The new treatment has not been previously used in humans for the treatment of cancer. It's an experimental drug."

"Besides," Cynthia added, "There are some issues regarding the procurement of the drug."

"Yes, Adelaide mentioned that and also the need to raise $7.5 million to get the drug from the company that owns it. Linda and I have some investments that we can easily divest and use the proceeds toward the amount required for the drug," said Graham's father.

"Thanks, Grandpa David, but I know Graham will be very resistant to the idea of Linda and you selling your assets to help him. He is afraid that the treatment may not work and the money would be wasted. I'm sure he would resist any moves that could lead to the depletion of your retirement funds," replied Cynthia.

"But we have enough. Neither Linda nor Adelaide has any children, so all that we have will go to your children. Why not use some of it now and give Graham a chance to remain part of our lives? We'd do everything to help my boy to fight his disease," said a very emotional David Bunker in a choked voice.

"I raised the idea of a second mortgage on the house, but Graham vehemently refused to consider this option. A few hours earlier, Adelaide and Roger sent an email to Graham, offering to pay the entire $7.5 million required to get the drug. Graham was very moved by this enormously generous offer, but I'm not sure that he'll accept it. He feels it's too much to ask." She sighed heavily, and David could hear the weariness in her voice.

"He gets tired easily, sleeps a lot, and his headaches are back. I think he will soon undergo surgery again to remove the tumor and gain relief from some of the symptoms of this disease. Dr. Mehra, his neuro-oncologist, is adamant that ethically and medically it's the right choice, even if Graham is treated with the new drug," said Cynthia, who was by now physically and emotionally drained.

After a short pause, Graham's father said, "Roger has amassed a fortune from his businesses in South Africa and is capable of providing the amount required to buy the drug required for the treatment. I, too, am deeply touched by Adelaide's love for her brother and your family. Though the two did not spend much time together, they have this silent and tight bond established decades ago. Would it help if I talk to Graham?"

"Let us see how he reacts tomorrow after a night's rest," replied Cynthia.

"Darling Cynthia, you hang on. Graham relies on you, as does the rest of the family. Please call Linda or me anytime. We can come on a moment's notice and stay as long as you need," implored Grandpa David.

"I do appreciate that. I should get some rest myself. Say hi to Linda, and goodnight, David." After hearing his reply, she placed the phone down and went to bed.

When she entered the bedroom, Graham was awake

and asked who she had been talking to.

"Your father. He called to see how we're all doing and if Roger and Adelaide had a nice visit," said Cynthia, trying to avoid any discussion of raising funds for the drug.

Graham did not pursue the conversation, just rolled onto his side with his back towards Cynthia.

A few hours later, he gently slipped out of his bed, feeling nauseous, very hot, and totally restless, and went to the bathroom. There he stayed for a while, first sitting on the closed toilet seat and then leaning on to the wash basin, looking into the mirror and pondering his fate.

Instead of going back to bed, he went to the kitchen, turned on the light, and decided to make some tea. With slightly shaky hands, he filled up the tea kettle, and after a while, with his teacup ensconced in his palms, walked to the living room and sat in his beloved chair.

He started to think about Roger and Adelaide's generous offer and the possibility that the drug could actually give him a few more months of life. What did he have to lose by trying an experimental drug, considering the bleak and predictable outcome of his disease? Was he willing to be the guinea pig for this drug? Could others with the same disease benefit from the knowledge gained from his treatment?

He again thought of his sister's email, put his nearly empty cup of tea onto the side table, got up with some effort, and picked up the family album from the wooden shelf below the center glass table. He leafed through his early childhood pictures, many in black and white, taken during visits to their grandparents. He nearly choked up seeing the picture of his sister on a pony being led by a lead rope held by him. Then there was the picture of his mum sitting cross-legged on the grass with Adelaide and him sitting next to her, squinting and looking straight into the camera. Tears welled up in his eyes as he went through these early pictures of his childhood.

At some point, he must have fallen asleep because Cynthia found him sleeping in his chair with the open album on his lap. Instead of coaxing him back to bed, she turned off the light and slowly walked back to the bedroom.

The following day, Graham talked to both his father and mother about Roger and Adelaide's very generous offer. Both parents knew that Roger and Adelaide were very well off and could afford to contribute $7.5 million without making any significant dent in their wealth. Persuaded by the arguments made by both Cynthia and his parents, Graham wrote to his sister and her husband:

My Dear Adelaide & Roger:

What a wonderful gift of life you are offering me. You know that there is no certainty that the proposed drug will give me a better quality of life or extend it. It holds promise and hope, something patients with brain tumors like mine seldom have. I will take your proposal to Dr. Yacov Kaufman, Chief Scientific Officer at CancerTech, and Dr. Mehra, who will be the lead clinician carrying out the clinical trial. I will soon undergo surgery to remove the recurrent mass and find out if the tumor is still localized or if it has invaded other parts of my brain.

Needless to say, I am overwhelmed by your offer. My first reaction was that I could not accept this very generous offer, but I do want to live longer to be with my loved ones, and your offer gives me that chance. Thanks again from Cynthia and me for this most generous offer of helping to obtain the drug for my treatment.

I will get back to you as soon as I hear from Drs. Kaufman and Mehra.

With all my love,

Graham

* * *

The surgery was performed on the morning of Wednesday, July 7th, and following recovery in the Neurology ward, Graham was allowed to go home a week later. Dr. Jabbar reported that everything went normally and she excised the maximum amount of the tumor mass, including some scar tissue. Unfortunately, the margins of the tumor tissue were irregular, and she was not able to fully excise them for fear of damaging the normal brain functions. Some cancer cells had migrated to other parts of the brain that she was not able to access, but hoped radiation and chemotherapy would eliminate them.

A small sample of the tumor tissue was again taken to CancerTech and given to Erica to grow in petri dishes to test if the drug could prevent the tumor cells from growing and withering. Some cells were to be injected into mice to form tumors in the animals and later test for the drug's ability to stop their rampant growth. One change that Erica would be making was to also use IB-617, the drugs approved to treat patients with IBD and was available orally as 5,10, 20, and 50 mg tablets.

Unlike the first surgery, Graham felt much weaker—even walking a few steps was an exhausting exertion, and he needed to sit down and rest. At times he was very disoriented and searched for the right words. Cynthia discouraged visitors, and only Amber and Jessica came by and kept company with their father, allowing Cynthia to do shopping and other household chores.

This time, Graham's disease, treatment, and recovery were taking an emotional toll on all of them, but they tried to be cheerful and engaged around him.

Occasionally, he would surprise them by asking questions like, "Amber, does your new apartment have one or two bathrooms?" Another time, after waking up from one of his frequent naps, he asked Jessica, "Are you happy with Adam? Are you planning to get married?"

The family persuaded Nigel to continue to stay in Townsville and finish his three-month assignment. They promised to keep him fully informed of Dad's health, a kind of daily bulletin sister Amber agreed to manage.

Both Cynthia and David kept Graham's mother fully informed since she was housebound due to Scott's extreme infirmity. She had seen Adelaide and Roger and was also very grateful to them for promising financial support to buy the drug. Cynthia made sure to call Graham's mother as often as possible.

About three weeks after coming home, Graham felt much better, regained a lot of his strength, and looked forward to going for short walks and seeing colleagues from the school. But compared to last time, he felt much weaker and exhausted. This time, there would be no going back to teaching, even for a few hours a day. He was now formally put on medical leave.

In another three weeks, he would begin his radiation and chemotherapy.

Graham had a sense of déjà vu.

* * *

In the meantime, Dr. Mehra diligently filed all the paperwork required for his institution's approval to treat Graham with the new experimental drug.

Upon being informed of Adelaide and Roger's offer to put up the $7.5 million required to obtain the drug from Immune Bio, Yacov approached Bill Hollander for guidance, as it was quite an unusual circumstance.

Bill suggested that the two of them talk to the legal counsel, and before that, Yacov should directly talk to the couple in Singapore to confirm the offer.

All along, Yacov emphasized the urgency of moving fast because he knew from his conversations with Dr. Mehra that despite surgery, the remnants of tumor would spread rapidly and that they had a narrow window for treatment. Additionally, the neurosurgeon had advised that it had been difficult to remove all the tumor tissue, and she had observed microscopic lesions in other parts of the brain. Clearly, the drug would be more effective if the tumors were small, localized, rather than when they had spread throughout the brain.

Bill Hollander was trying to keep the Pharma partners happy by not overtly diverting resources away from the breast cancer program to support the treatment of a patient with a brain tumor. He was, however, impressed by Yacov's enthusiasm and strong scientific data to treat a patient with a terminal disease, so he looked the other way when some crucial resources of CancerTech were being used by Yacov's team.

The legal counsel offered three possible solutions: 1) convince the Pharma partners to allow CancerTech to provide the $7.5 million to buy the drug and allow the treatment of the patient under expanded access (compassionate use of investigational new drugs. 2) have CancerTech form a subsidiary that would get the $7.5 million as a charitable gift to buy the drug and undertake treatment of the patient, which would still require approval by Pharma partners because part of the data required to undertake the patient's treatment was collected at CancerTech, 3) form a new joint company with the Pharma partner and use the $7.5 million not as a gift but as an investment.

After some intense discussions where Yacov passionately advocated for the fate of the patient whose tumor was growing unabated and the promise of extending his life with the drug, option three was implemented by forming a new virtual company with Roger and Adelaide as the initial investors.

While the exact details still needed to be hashed out, it allowed Yacov to obtain the drug and apply to Federal Drug Authorities for compassionate use IND (Investigational New Drug), now that Rakesh, as physician in charge, had approval from Immune Bio to obtain the clinical-grade drug.

By the beginning of August, all the technical hurdles to treat Graham with the experimental drug were overcome. Further, a good piece of news was the preliminary results from Genechip that the molecular signatures of the first and recently resected tumors were largely similar, indicating that recurrence likely involved the cancer stem cells that had escaped the previous treatments and were not from new tumors. There were some changes which the scientists at CancerTech attributed to be the result of chemotherapy following initial surgery. Erica Hagen had also started to grow tumor cells from the recently resected tumor tissue to test the clinical-grade drug that would be used for Graham's treatment.

* * *

Five weeks post-surgery, Graham's latest MRI further indicated a recurrence around the primary location, and there were several areas of the brain with spots indicative of likely tumor invasion, as the surgeon had indicated following the latest surgery. The treatment could be started with the new drug, but there was another ethical dilemma. Should Graham first receive the standard radiation and chemotherapeutic treatment, which could delay the treatment with the drug for six weeks, during which time the tumors may grow back? Since the pre-clinical work had not been done in combination with radiation and chemotherapy, there was no way to know if simultaneous treatment with the drug would be effective. It could even interfere with the efficacy of the drug.

Dr. Mehra explained to Graham and Cynthia these options and the possible complications, "We`re in uncharted territory, and my recommendations aren`t going to be based on prior data but on my scientific instincts, which in this case is to start the drug treatment right away."

Graham said, "From all that I can glean from the literature on brain tumors on the internet, my tumor will be back, and maybe I will have another four to six months of miserable life before death. I have also read that patients who don't receive any radiation or chemotherapy after a second surgery live three to four months past surgery."

Dr. Mehra nodded, and Graham continued, "Dr. Kaufman and you have said before, chances of success are greater when the tumors are small. So, my preference would be to start the treatment with the experimental drug now and not wait a day longer."

"Yacov and I agree that it would be better to start the treatment with the drug now than to wait. The tumor is growing, invading other parts of the brain, and will soon start to compromise the quality of your life. But again, you know that the treatment we are offering is still experimental and may not work," said Dr. Mehra a bit defensively.

"When can you start?" asked Cynthia.

"We require my institution's permission to treat Graham with the drug and bypass the standard radiation and chemotherapy. I needed your agreement before requesting the exemption. Once we have that permission, we can start the treatment right away. Graham, do you want a second opinion regarding the wisdom of not undergoing radiation and chemotherapy before you sign the release papers?" suggested Dr. Mehra.

"You know, Cynthia and I fully trust your recommendation, and I've done some homework of my own and am comfortable and ready to start treatment with the investigational drug. It's important to start now while the tumors are still small, so time is of the essence," reaffirmed Graham.

Dr. Mehra asked Graham to sign a consent form and added, "Though the drug will be given orally, we would like to have you stay in the hospital to monitor your vital functions for at least a week."

"Ok with me," replied Graham, looking at Cynthia, who nodded in agreement." Looking forward to my Jell-O desserts."

They all chuckled to break the tension.

"Good, I'll let Yacov know and have my staff make preparations for your hospital stay. We'll call you with the details," said Dr. Mehra.

Before bidding goodbye to the Bunkers, Dr. Mehra put his hands on Graham's shoulder and told him,

"You're a very brave man." Then he left the conference room.

Brave, no, I am not brave, just gasping at the last shreds of any hope.

* * *

The clinical trials team at CancerTech, with some input from Yacov Kaufman, devised the protocols, dosage, and methods for monitoring any anticipated and unintended side effects based on the information provided by Immune Bio. The biggest challenge would be some toxicity in the liver and possibly an increased risk of infections.

Chapter 16

THE TREATMENT

O N MONDAY, AUGUST 15TH, Cynthia drove Graham to the Hospital and went to the neurology ward, where Dr. Mehra greeted them and took them to a room to sign some additional papers. Graham was transferred to a private room, where he changed into the regulation hospital gown and lay in the bed while Cynthia putting away his street clothes, watch, wallet, socks, and shoes in a bag to take home later.

At 10 a.m., Dr. Mehra, Dr. Kaufman, a clinician from CancerTech, and the senior nurse in charge arrived in Graham's room and exchanged greetings.

Dr. Mehra explained that the dose of the drug they were going to try was a 20 mg capsule, given twice a day. If there were no discernable side effects, the dosage may be increased.

Graham took the brown-colored tablet with water

from a small paper cup and became the first patient to receive the novel experimental drug for one of the deadliest cancers.

For Cynthia, it was the culmination of a strange climax. After months of anticipation—a tablet swallowed with water in an indistinct paper cup—it did not inspire confidence, but it was all she had. She remembered part of Emily Bronte's poem on hope:

> *Hope, whose whisper would have given*
> *Balm to all my frenzied pain,*
> *Stretched her wings, and soared to heaven,*
> *Went, and ne'er returned again!*

She sat in a chair next to Graham's bed, held his hand, and prayed and hoped that he would be spared of any serious side effects.

Just as she was about to leave, Dr. Mehra popped in to see if all was well and tried to reassure her that the staff was very vigilant and would keep him informed of any adverse events.

Cynthia slowly drove back home, filled with a bundle of emotions, seesawing between hope and despair, life and death, a world with and without Graham, a feeling of defeat, even though the chance given to Graham with the new drug should have lifted her spirits. In the last eighteen months, she had seen her hopes cruelly dashed by the reality of this terrible disease. Try as she might, the word "terminal" began to haunt her and follow her like her shadow.

Upon returning home, Cynthia sent an email to Graham's father, mother, Roger, Adelaide, Amber, and Jessica, and decided to call Nigel around 4 p.m., which would be 9 a.m. the next day in Townsville.

Dear All:

Today Graham started treatment with the experimental drug that Roger and Adelaide made possible to procure. It was a single brown tablet. A second one will be given before he goes to sleep. Though Graham was feeling well, except for the chronic fatigue, the doctors wanted him to stay for a week in the hospital to monitor any adverse effects since this pill is being tested for the first time for this disease. Graham is happy to be the guinea pig if it helps others. Everyone was very nice and hopeful. I will go back later this evening and keep you posted.

Graham has his mobile phone with him, but he takes many naps and may also take a walk around the corridor from time to time.

Lots of Love,

Cynthia

She then called a few close friends and delivered the same message. Nearly everyone asked if they could be of any help, but Cynthia politely said that for the time being she was fine.

Around 4 p.m., she called Nigel, who was getting ready to go to the campus and was happy to hear his mom's voice. His first question was, "How did Dad do with the new treatment?"

She excitedly told him, "Honey, Dad took his first pill of the experimental drug this morning at 10 a.m., and we're all feeling very hopeful." "That's great news, Mom. I wish I was there to record this historic event.

The first person with a brain tumor to be treated with this novel drug. I hope someone took a picture," said Nigel. "My stay is coming to an end, and if Dad is doing well, I may stop in Singapore on the way back home."

"They`d love it. Uncle Roger can take you sailing in his new boat," said Cynthia.

After sharing some more news of Amber and Jessica, they said goodbye, and Cynthia promised to keep Nigel informed of his dad's health.

When she later arrived at Graham's room, he was having tea with Dr. Kaufman, who had come by to ensure that all was ok. Dr. Kaufman stood up when Cynthia entered and offered his chair to her, which she declined, opting instead to sit on Graham's bed.

"Cynthia, Dr. Kaufman and I were born in the same year, just a few days apart. Only difference is that I am a patient, and he is trying to save me," said Graham with a twinkle in his eye.

With a smile, he said, "Oh, please call me Yacov to avoid confusion with the real doctors in their white coats."

"Where were you born?" asked Cynthia.

"In a small town, not far from Tel Aviv."

"It's one of the countries on my bucket list," Graham said wishfully.

"Great country to visit," Yacov said and promised to come by again to continue their discussions to solve the problems of the Middle East.

Dr. Mehra also popped in to check on Graham before leaving for home and was obliged to give an update about the welfare of his six-month-old baby boy. The mood in Graham's hospital room was cherry, rife with hope.

***

The first signs of concern came on day four of the treatment when blood tests showed substantially elevated levels of certain enzymes, indicative of liver toxicity.

Dr. Mehra explained to Graham that many drugs, including off-the-shelf drugs like Advil or Aspirin, can lead to some liver toxicity. "We will carefully monitor you and discontinue the drug for a period if toxicity persists."

All of Graham's other vital functions were in the normal range, though he remained lethargic and restless when not sleeping or taking naps.

Cynthia had brought his laptop and some books to keep him engaged and informed. Because the drug had the potential to suppress the immune system, visitors were discouraged, and the only people Graham came in contact with were Cynthia, the nursing staff, and the doctors. Amber and Jessica were disappointed but understood the reason for keeping them out of close proximity to Dad.

On Sunday, August 21st, witnessing no major adverse events and no further increase in the enzyme levels due to liver toxicity, Dr. Mehra agreed to let Graham go home and continue taking the 20 mg capsules twice daily.

Five days after Graham swallowed the first "Magic" pill to kill his cancer cells in his hospital room, Cynthia drove him to their home in Palo Alto, where their daughters and Mylar balloons awaited him.

Graham again felt an eerie sense of déjà vu but was happy to be home, away from the hospital and the continuous monitoring by a bevy of hospital staff, nurses, and doctors.

A few days after returning home, Graham woke up in the middle of the night sweating profusely and very warm. He was incoherent, very agitated, and had trouble breathing. Cynthia's first impulse was to dial 9-1-1, but Graham persuaded her to drive him to the hospital herself to avoid alarming the neighbors.

The emergency ward staff immediately notified Dr. Mehra, and the attending physician ordered blood tests and administered sedatives to calm Graham's agitation and Ibuprofen to reduce his fever. Soon after, Dr. Mehra arrived and after consulting with the attending physician, suggested that Graham stay in the hospital for observation and discontinue taking the experimental pill.

Two days later, Dr. Mehra explained to Cynthia and Graham that the high temperature had likely been due to a viral infection and that the blood tests showed a reduced number of disease-fighting white blood cells. There were no signs of increased liver toxicity, which had been one of the primary concerns of the drug-induced side effects.

Graham was disappointed with this setback but was happy to be back home after a three-day stint in the hospital, the first two days of which shared a room with another patient and was poked multiple times to take blood samples for a variety of tests.

Graham restarted taking the 20 mg pills twice a day without any further serious adverse events. He felt less lethargic, took walks around the block, was free of the headaches, and generally in very good spirits when Dr. Mehra scheduled an MRI to see if the drug had effectively stopped the tumor growth.

Suddenly, fear gripped Graham because the MRI might show no effect on the killing of tumor cells, and the tumor could instead still be growing, dashing hopes of any recovery. But he was feeling better.

Could that simply be a placebo effect, improvement due to the patient's belief in their treatment?

Reluctantly, he subjected himself to the familiar MRI ritual some six weeks after starting treatment with the experimental drug. The images of the dark tunnel in his recurrent dreams that constantly pulled him away from light to further darkness, came hauntingly back. He was weakening in his resolve to fight the disease, and the time he spent at home was now filled with hours of quiet, silence, and fear of the inevitable end. Most do not survive this deadly cancer, and he was reaching the end of the average survival time following his first surgery.

Is the grace period coming to an end?

* * *

It was Thursday, September 29th when he heard Cynthia returning from her morning exercise at the school gym and simultaneously, the phone in the kitchen started ringing.

Before he could get up and grab the phone, Cynthia picked up the receiver and in a very friendly tone said, "Hello? ... Oh, Dr. Mehra, how are you? Yes, we`re free this afternoon… At CancerTech in Dr. Kaufman's office at 2:30 p.m.? Sure, we can come over at that time… It's on Lakeside Drive in Foster City… Yes, we`ve been there before… Ok, see you then."

Cynthia noticed fear in Graham's eyes and that he was shaking a bit despite the warm day.

She walked over to him to ask if she could brew some coffee when he said, "I think it's all over. They're going to tell me that despite their best efforts, the tumors are back. Why are they asking us to meet at the company rather than the hospital?"

Cynthia, with optimism in her voice said, "Maybe they want to share good news with members of the team who made it possible for you to use the drug."

Graham remained unconvinced, and Cynthia had to literally drag him to join her.

* * *

As soon as Graham and Cynthia entered the conference room, they knew that the news was good. On the screen was the MRI of Graham's brain dated 8-11-05, before the treatment with the drug, and one taken a few days prior on 9-23-05. There was no change in the region excised by surgery and a near absence of any white spots, likely the sites of tumor invasion.

It appeared that the brown pills that Graham had started to swallow twice a day for the last six weeks had potentially blocked the march of his tumor cells, stopped them in their tracks, and some seemed to have withered, leaving small scars, perhaps pools of dead cells. Could it be that this drug, IB-617, really stopped the proliferation of the brain cancer stem cells as predicted from CancerTech's research in petri dishes and mice?

Yacov Kaufman, surrounded by his team, was beaming and was opening the champagne bottles placed in an ice bucket when he saw Dr. Mehra and Bill Hollander walk in. He beckoned them to join him.

After the cork had been popped and plastic champagne glasses filled, Yacov thanked everyone on the team: Bill for his help in obtaining the drug, Rakesh Mehra for introducing him to the idea of working on the tumor excised from the real hero, Graham, who along with his most remarkable wife, Cynthia, had not once flinched from their complete cooperation and involvement with grace and dignity.

"I realize," Yacov added, "it's only one case, not statistically meaningful, but as they say, the journey of a thousand miles starts with a single step…" He raised his glass and offered a toast to Graham, Cynthia, his team, Rakesh Mehra, and Bill. "I hope that Graham is the pioneer, opening the doors for the treatment of others with this terrible disease."

Cynthia was choked with emotion and held onto Graham.

Graham thanked everyone for their efforts and help in giving him the chance, a gift he could never repay. He also thanked Adelaide and Roger for making this possible for him. This may be the beginning of a treatment for many facing this wretched disease.

There were few dry eyes, and many hugs and kisses, high fives, a sense of great relief and accomplishment.

On the drive back, Graham asked Cynthia if she was

willing to take a detour so they could walk on the Half
Moon Bay coastal trail.

Epilogue

GRAHAM CONTINUED TO TAKE THE 20 mg pill twice daily until it was reduced to one pill daily in mid-November. Dr. Mehra, based on the recommendation of the clinicians at CancerTech, had told Graham that he would need to take the pill every day, at least for the foreseeable future. He could resume his daily life, including his long-distance running, if he felt physically fit.

Cynthia invited Dr. Mehra, Dr. Kaufman, and their families for Thanksgiving dinner on November 24th, along with Amber, Jessica, and Adam. Nigel, who was now back home with his parents and planning to apply to graduate schools in Environmental Sciences, helped his mother set the table for the festive dinner.

Rakesh and his wife Lakshmi not only brought their little boy, Sudhir, but also several mouth-watering Indian appetizers, while Yacov's family brought a large, luscious cheesecake sprinkled with saffron and pistachio. Adam oversaw the drinks, especially the expensive wines that he had brought from his wine cellar.

Nigel spent all his time trying to impress and please Tali, the nineteen-year-old, green-eyed beautiful daughter of the Kaufman's. Both fathers couldn't help noticing it and just shrugged their shoulders. It was a very happy celebration that no one, especially the Bunkers, would have dared to imagine just a few months ago.

In mid-December, GlioTech was formally launched with investments from CancerTech, Immune Bio, Adelaide and Roger's donation, and a few venture capitalists to provide a cure for patients with advanced brain tumors. It was located adjacent to CancerTech, and Yacov Kaufman accepted the offer to be the interim CEO.

By mid-March 2006, the other five patients whose cancer cells succumbed to the drug IB-617 would be treated with it as part of the compassionate use, but a formal Phase 1 clinical trial would also be initiated at different centers with the enrollment of twenty patients. As an investor, Adelaide would agree to join the board, giving her the opportunity to visit her brother and Cynthia more often.

* * *

At the family Christmas dinner, Jessica announced that Adam and she were planning to get married in the spring of 2006, which thrilled the family. All eyes shifted to Amber, who defensively said, "I'm not looking for a mate!"

Nigel then said, "I am having dinner tomorrow night

with the Kaufman's for the beginning of Hanukkah." All eyes now turned on him, and he got flustered and said, "We are just friends."

* * *

It was New Year's Day, and Graham, sitting in his living room next to the fireplace on a very cold, wintry morning, looked wistfully at Cynthia and said, "Here I am in 2006, alive, kicking, and even daring to think of celebrating my fifty-second birthday in a few months." He sighed contentedly. "Next week I may even start to teach again, and am looking forward to the ordinary life of a middle-aged school teacher with a loving and devoted wife…"

"I love you, Mr. Graham Bunker," Cynthia said as she sat in his lap.

Cynthia, too, now began to plan to go back to work, no longer haunted by the image of that fuzzy white shadow in Graham's brain. They also started a support group to help and provide guidance and comfort to other patients undergoing similar drug treatment.

* * *

Graham, Yacov, and Rakesh became good friends and often met for drinks to talk about their lives and families. In mid-August, they met for dinner in a newly opened Vietnamese restaurant to celebrate the first anniversary of the use of the drug to combat the growth of deadly cancer in Graham's brain.

Yacov said, "Here we are, three Americans, all born abroad, yet fate has brought us together."

Rakesh added, "Only in America, where opportunity abounds if you are willing to learn and work hard."

"I`m lucky that your tireless efforts have given me a new lease on life. Our three independent paths intersected to find a cure for a deadly disease. I'm, however, even more excited at the thought of how many others with this deadly disease may benefit from our interactions. I used to make long-term plans, but now I just want to live day by day and count my blessings."

With a chuckle, he added, "You know the best news? I am going to be a grandfather in early 2007. Make sure that the medicine keeps working till I can hold my first grandchild in my arms…"

Cancer 2021

NEARLY ONE HUNDRED YEARS AGO, Senator Matthew Neely of West Virginia exhorted his colleagues on the Senate floor in support of the first effort to pass a bill for cancer research with the words, "I propose to speak of a monster that is more insatiable than the guillotine; more destructive to life and health than the magnificent army that ever marched to battle; more terrifying than any scourge that ever threatened the existence of a human race…the name of this loathsome, deadly, and insatiable monster is cancer…"

Despite the fact that four out of ten human beings will be diagnosed with cancer during their lifetime, treatment still largely depends on the decades-old practice of surgery, radiation, and chemotherapy, described by some as, "cut, burn, and poison." For many cancer victims, these treatments worked, but for an equal number, they didn't work, and patients were left without effective alternatives.

Since the 1990s, science has made tremendous progress in understanding the basic mechanisms of how cancers originate, grow, evade our immune defenses, feed their voracious appetites, metastasize from one organ to another, and escape normal cellular processes designed to eliminate damaged cells. This remarkable body of scientific knowledge, generated by thousands of scientists working worldwide has produced a road map to design treatment for individual cancers, ranging from inactivating key enzymes needed for their uncontrolled growth, starving the cancers of blood supply carrying the nourishments, or forcing elimination of a cell with damaged genome capable of limitless growth.

But the most remarkable progress in the last decade has been learning ways to prevent cancer cells from evading our usual defense marshalled by the immune system designed to get rid of any foreign invaders, like viruses, parasites, and the bugs. It turns out the devious cancer cell, in its single-minded focus on its expansion, takes advantage of tricks that shut off the immune system and slips by it. Scientists have now uncovered this trickery of the cancer cell and have devised treatments that reveal it to be an invader and hence face the fury of the newly unleashed immune attack.

These drugs, also called checkpoint inhibitors, now advertised extensively on TV, newspapers as Keytruda, Yervoy, Nivolumab, Tecentriq, and Infinzi, are providing cures to patients with incurable cancers, and often without compromising the quality of their lives. This is truly a breakthrough, as one scientist called it, our eureka moment…like the discovery of Penicillin!

Newer technologies, like the chimeric T-Cell therapy (CAR-T), which reengineers patients' own killer T-Cells, are powerful new agents eliminating certain forms of deadly cancers, perhaps forever.

Unfortunately, many of the newer forms of immuno-therapy do not provide relief to all patients. Perhaps the lucky one in three or four will respond and become cancer-free. What about the rest? We are still in the process of learning, but currently, several thousand clinical trials with hundreds of novel immuno-therapeutic drugs are underway.

With new approaches, the reduction of smoking, and advances in early detection, the number of deaths caused by cancer have declined by twenty-seven percent in the United States in the last twenty-five years, which will translate into 2.6 million fewer deaths from cancer. The death rate for lung, prostate, and colorectal cancer has dropped by half, while mortality for female breast cancer has diminished by forty percent. These are undeniably success stories in the assault on cancer, but at the same time, little progress has been made in finding any cures for the near fatal pancreatic and malignant brain cancers.

Looking forward, cancer treatment in years to come will be a combination of conventional therapies, like surgery, radiation, chemotherapy, with immunotherapies, and defined molecular targets. Cancer will become a chronic disease, not unlike rheumatoid arthritis or psoriasis, treatable, if not curable.

* * *

In 1978, Susan Sontag described cancer as, "overlaid with mystification…a triumphant mutation…charged with fantasy of inescapable fatality…a scandalous subject for poetry," in Illness as a Metaphor.

"The mystification is not a black box: the triumphant mutation has been exposed, and cancer is in retreat. We see new ways by which to confront that inescapable fatality. And there is every reason for poetry for millions of cancer survivors..."

- J. Michael Bishop,

Nobel Prize in Physiology and Medicine, 1989

Acknowledgments

I HAVE ALWAYS WANTED TO WRITE, write a story, tell a tale, make it interesting enough so others may want to read and share with their friends and family. I have written over 400 scientific papers, edited journals, written numerous editorials, even edited books, but never attempted to write fiction, a daunting task. Instead, I chose to write a hybrid. The disease is real, the patient is fictional. The science involved in the diagnosis and conventional treatment of the disease adheres closely to reality. The novel medical treatment that gives hope to the patient is not a fantasy but has scientific basis, for which I thank many of my former students, collaborators, and colleagues.

I am extremely grateful to Wendi Baker, who edited the first version of the book and struggled to fix the grammar, syntax, spellings, and timelines of the story. All along she maintained her composure, never failed to compliment on a well-structured sentence, and proffered sustained encouragement to keep writing. Wendi also propelled me to trim the original version by half without compromising the story. I am also very grateful to Laurie Chittenden for offering her editorial advice and further restructuring of this book. She never intruded on the content of the book yet managed to tweak the sentences to convey more precisely what I had in mind. As a novice writer, I couldn't have asked for better editors to guide me in telling my tale.

I am extremely grateful to Sharona Ben-Haim, a neurosurgeon, for her patience to respond to myriad queries about surgery and post-op rehabilitation. I am further thankful to her and her husband, Eiman Azim, a neuroscientist, for their unstinting encouragement to write this book. Special thanks to Annamaria Calabro for help in choosing the title of the book. I am also very grateful to my friends Anton Berns, Vishva Dixit, Karen Vousden, Lalita Ramakrishnan, Shankar Subramaniam, Smita Panda, Sudhir Verma, and Mark Groudine who read earlier versions of the book and provided their comments. My friend Jacqui Beckmann and my brother Surinder Verma have been constant sources of encouragement and enthusiasm.

I am also very grateful to my long-term friend and artist Jamie Simon for help and advice in designing the cover of the book.

Finally, the love and support of my family kept me going, as they eagerly awaited to read the next chapter of the book!